Sherlock in Shanghai

Sherlock

Stories
by

in Shanghai
of Crime and Detection
Cheng Xiaoqing

TRANSLATED BY
TIMOTHY C. WONG

University of Hawai'i Press
Honolulu

Published with the support of the
School of Hawaiian, Asian, and Pacific Studies,
University of Hawai'i

Library of Congress Cataloging-in-Publication Data
Cheng, Xiaoqing.
  [Short stories. English. Selections]
  Sherlock in Shanghai : stories of crime and detection / by Cheng Xiaoqing ;
translated by Timothy C. Wong.
      p.   cm.
  Includes bibliographical references.
  ISBN-13: 978-0-8248-3034-2 (hbk. : alk. paper)
  ISBN-10: 0-8248-3034-2 (hbk. : alk. paper)
  ISBN-13: 978-0-8248-3099-1 (pbk. : alk. paper)
  ISBN-10: 0-8248-3099-7 (pbk. : alk. paper)
1. Cheng, Xiaoqing—Translations into English.   I. Wong, Timothy C.   II. Title.
  PL2841.H75A29 2007
  895.1'351—dc22
                          2006015043

Designed by University of Hawai'i Press production staff

Printed by the Maple-Vail Book Manufacturing Group

Contents

Preface

ANYONE ACQUAINTED with modern detective fiction will instantly find familiar elements in most of the stories collected and translated here. Unlike the so-called crime-case fiction popular in dynastic China, the majority of these stories feature a detective fully intended to be a Chinese version of Sir Arthur Conan Doyle's Sherlock Holmes—complete with a fondness for tobacco, well-kept bachelor quarters in the middle of a bustling city, and a partner-narrator the equivalent of Dr. Watson. In contrast to the traditional wise and righteous judge solving cases as an authority figure presiding over a host of underlings, and alternately manipulating and intimidating those brought before him, here we encounter Huo Sang, a crime solver whose superior intellect and attitude, rather than any ascribed authority, are what enable him to solve his cases. As someone functioning in the social milieu of a large modern metropolis, he is a nearly exact counterpart of Holmes, even though he and his partner, Bao Lang, live on Aiwen Road in Shanghai rather than on Baker Street in London. Like Holmes, Huo Sang cuts through superstition or preconceptions by employing incisive reasoning based on factual evidence obtained through meticulous investigation, quite in keeping with the early-twentieth-century drive to instill in Chinese readers a more scientific approach to solving problems. Using detective fiction to do so makes the lesson effortless, even enjoyable.

Indeed, Cheng Xiaoqing, whose skill in producing these accounts of Huo Sang's adventures far eclipsed that of all other Chinese writers of popular detective fiction in his time, has said in retrospect that he considers his stories "textbooks in disguise," devised to awaken readers to the advantages of careful observation and rigorous reasoning. Why, then, would he need to disguise them? The answer has everything to do with the character of native Chinese fiction, from China's dynastic past through most of the first quarter of the twentieth century, when Cheng Xiaoqing developed from a translator of the Conan Doyle stories into a writer who was obviously stimulated by what he had read in English and subsequently rendered into Chinese. In the first decade of the twentieth century, as David Pollard tells us, "there occurred in Chinese language publications the rare phenomenon of translated works of fiction exceeding in number original works of fiction."[1] In the case of Cheng, his translations, having undergone a certain adaptation, became essentially undistinguishable from contemporary native creations. In the cosmopolitan Shanghai of the time, this would have been easier to do than in any other part of China.

The rare phenomenon to which Pollard refers has much to do with China's efforts to modernize from the late-Qing dynasty in the first decades of the Republican period, which began in 1912. After over a half-century of trying to resist the West and their cultural incursions, the Chinese were finally compelled to try to learn what the West was all about culturally. Fiction— translated directly from Western languages and secondarily from Japanese— was a natural means to do so. Detective fiction, which provided an escape expected from traditional fiction as well as the "renovation" so ardently called for by China's reformers of the time, became the perfect medium to introduce what was then considered Western thinking to the Chinese. Adaptation from traditional fiction, however, did nothing to address the problem of the readers' attitudes; for traditional fiction in China, despite all its achievements, had never earned the general respect commensurate with its popularity. Detective fiction, which Cheng Xiaoqing clearly stated was "made up," was never admitted into the company of those socially critical "modern" works of fiction designed to say directly *what* was wrong with the nation, in contrast to Cheng's stories, which were written in part to show *how* his readers could improve their country by improving themselves.

---

1. *Translation and Creation: Readings of Western Literature in Early Modern China, 1840–1918* (Amsterdam/Philadelphia: John Benjamins Publishing Company, 1998), p. 5.

The fact that Cheng, who achieved a popularity in Shanghai reminiscent of Conan Doyle's in London, could be relegated to the status of a peripheral writer can be attributed to the continuation of traditional attitudes, which considered all invented narratives to be minor, and hence easily forgettable. Never mind that Cheng was "shanghaiing" Sherlock, turning a foreign icon into a completely natural inhabitant of China's most modern metropolis and easily acceptable as a native hero, even though the institution of private investigators was unknown there. He was still categorized with purveyors of escape narratives known pejoratively as "Mandarin Ducks and Butterflies" or "Saturday" fictional narratives considered decidedly inferior to those of such writers as Lu Xun (1881–1936) or Mao Dun (1896–1981), who wrote for political ends, and who denigrated the motive to entertain as subversive of the nation's efforts to modernize. Lu Xun took up writing in order to "change the spirit" of his countrymen; and Mao Dun once declared that what China needed was "a fiction of blood and tears."

As at least one modern scholar has pointed out, "the impetus for fiction translation in the late Qing [shortly before and after the turn of the twentieth century] was non-literary. Translation was needed in this mass education movement to carry out the necessary knowledge transfer and cultural transfer; that the instrument happened to be literary was initially coincidental."[2] What Cheng was attempting in his stories about Huo Sang and Bao Lang in order to achieve this knowledge and cultural transfer was really another kind of translation. By affirming rather than negating the translations of Western detective fiction done by many others since the 1890s, however, his stories further advanced the more natural use of entertainment as an educational tool than his "serious" contemporaries ever realized. For what he ultimately contributed, both to Chinese fiction in the modern world and to reshaping the understanding and acceptance of "scientific" thought, Cheng deserves far more credit—and attention—than has been given him. With the exception of "The Ghost in the Villa," a very short story he pub-

---

2. Eva Hung, "Giving Texts a Context: Chinese Translations of Classical English Detective Stories 1896–1916," in David Pollard, ed., *Translation and Creation*, p. 154.

lished in 1947, the stories collected here represent the first translations of his writings available to readers of English, or of any other non-Chinese language.[3]

These stories, on the other hand, show that Cheng Xiaoqing was a writer who did not simply ignore his native traditions, including those traditions connected with storytelling. While the opening three, "The Shoe," "The Other Photograph," and "The Odd Tenant," can be taken as fairly direct transfers of Sherlock Holmes stories from a Victorian English to a Republican Chinese setting, the next selection, "The Examination Paper," tries to account for the deep friendship between Huo Sang and Bao Lang, showing that it was not exactly identical to the Sherlock Holmes–John Watson relationship. "On the Huang-pu" introduces the shadowy character known as the South-China Swallow, a rather romanticized individual who operates as much outside the law as Huo Sang and Bao Lang do within it, in order to achieve identical social goals. The South-China Swallow, who appears without Huo and Bao in "At the Ball," is reminiscent of Robin Hood in the West and of traditional Chinese heroes from such works of fiction as the *Three Gallants and Five Altruists (Sanxia wuyi)* or the *Water Margin (Shuihu zhuan)*, even though he fights with his mind rather than with a sword. In "Cat's-Eye," he becomes much more Huo Sang's collaborator than his nemesis.

Thus, it would be neither fair nor accurate to classify Cheng Xiaoqing, who never left Chinese soil, as a simple westernizer. Rather, these stories have been selected to demonstrate that, like so many modern Chinese intellectual patriots, Cheng did not, like his better-known contemporaries, essentially reject his nation's past, even though he clearly wished to adapt it to modern realities. This is abundantly evident in "One Summer Night," placed last because it contains none of the characters for which he is known. Even with its traditionalist references—such as a gall bladder bursting from fright—the story makes it clear that, here too, Cheng is enjoining his countrymen to look behind assumptions and appearances in order to discover the truth. In choosing to do so through the medium of crime fiction, he,

---

3. See my *Stories for Saturday: Twentieth-Century Chinese Popular Fiction* (Honolulu: University of Hawai'i Press, 2003), pp. 175–189.

perhaps more than all others assigned to obscurity because what they wrote mostly entertained, deserves to be noted in any history of twentieth-century Chinese fiction. I hope further that the stories gathered here will help to break down the misleading and artificial barrier between the fiction of traditional and modern China that has been such an obstacle to understanding China's native tradition of fiction making as a whole.

T.C.W.

Acknowledgments

THE BULK OF these translations were made in the spring and summer of 2004, while I was on sabbatical leave at Arizona State University. I wish to thank Y. F. Wu, a resident in Shanghai in the early 1930s, for sharing his knowledge of the urban scene there with me. In addition, I wish to express my appreciation both to the Center for Asian Studies at Arizona State University, and to the East Asian librarians at the University of California, Berkeley.

An undertaking of this sort cannot come to fruition without the support of many individuals over a span of time. I would like to express my appreciation to John Berninghausen, Ju-hsi Chou, Kirk A. Denton, Bryna Goodman, Theodore Huters, Jeffrey C. Kinkley, Thomas E. Moran, and Stephen H. West for their help and friendship that, in some cases, date back a good number of years. My special thanks go to Pamela Kelley, who provided the encouragement and assistance so necessary to the completion of the project, and to Barbara Folsom, who saved me from so many pitfalls. I also want to bow to the memory of the late Sharon Yamamoto, who was responsible for turning me into a late-career translator of fictional narratives, and of the late William A. Lyell, who helped me retain my interest in modern Chinese fiction since I began my teaching career over three decades ago.

Finally, I want to acknowledge with gratitude the enormous contribution my wife, Lib, made to this undertaking. Without her sharp critiques and editorial skills, the book would have been far less than what it has become. Whatever imperfections remain are of course my own responsibility.

①The Shoe

I. The Crime Scene

This rather troubling little case occurred in 1921. Although that was quite some time ago, the moment I opened up my notebook, the facts that had given rise to such finger-pointing, as well as the mist and gloom that seemed to have hovered over everything, reappeared starkly before my eyes. In the context of the waves of disturbances washing over Shanghai society at the time, the case should be considered as no more than a minor ripple. Nonetheless, recalling it now brings back to me the disgust and sorrow that so colored my feelings then.

On a blustery and nippy mid-October morning, Detective Ni Jinshou of the Shanghai police phoned our residence on Aiwen Road to ask for help from my old friend Huo Sang. A mysterious murder had occurred at 12 Nanchang Road. He had already looked around the place and felt that, while a number of things appeared suspicious, he could make neither head nor tail of what he had found, so he was asking Huo Sang to help him by going over to take a look for himself. Huo Sang immediately assented and asked me to go along. For one thing, the word "mysterious" was full of magnetic attraction and quickly piqued Huo Sang's curiosity. Also, since Ni Jinshou had always been a pretty good friend of ours, we of course felt we should respond to such a direct call for help.

When we arrived at the address, the tall, slim figure of Ni Jinshou had been waiting at the door for some time. After greeting us with warm handshakes, he wasted no time in familiarizing us with the facts of the case.

The family's name was Gao, headed by Gao Youzhi, manager of the Bank of Hangzhou; the victim was his wife, Ding Fangzhu. At 7:30 that morning, the family's servant Wang Four had gone to South Station to report that his mistress had been murdered by an unknown assailant. Since the station chief, Fan Tong, did not spend nights there, there was no one in charge, so the officer on duty had to call the Main Station. When the head detective, Ni Jinshou, was alerted, he went first to South Station, then, after asking a few quick questions, hurried to the house on Nanchang Road. On examining the crime scene there, however, he grew more and more mystified. It was at that point that he decided to contact us.

"Mr. Huo, Mr. Bao, I'm so sorry to have to trouble you again." Jinshou kept his eyes on us; his expression quite resembled that of an elementary school student facing his teacher after giving a wrong answer in arithmetic.

I reassured him with a quick smile. "Hey, we're old friends. You needn't be so formal with us."

"Far as I'm concerned, unraveling mysteries is rather enjoyable." Huo Sang smiled at him as well. "You said that the more you thought about it, the more puzzling the case's become. What's been going on, really?"

"Everything's so bizarre! The timing of the crime seems to have been deliberately arranged. This house normally has four people in it. Last night, though, aside from the victim, only the twelve- or thirteen-year-old maid was home. As for material evidence, all we have is this one shoe. We're really in a quandary!" Ni Jinshou slowly knitted his eyebrows, clearly quite disheartened. "Frankly, I can't figure how to make sense of what's happened, and Lieutenant Fan is not pleased with what I've done."

"What's Lieutenant Fan upset about? Tell us frankly, please," I said.

"He also got here at 8:30 or so. When he heard that I'd called you two for help, he was obviously irritated. 'A simple little matter like this, and you're worried that we can't handle it ourselves?' he said to me. 'Why go looking for help all over the place?' It appears he's most concerned about someone else taking the credit he expects to be his. What an annoying person he is!"

I remembered having met this Lieutenant Fan once before. He was a half-cocked functionary with a narrow mind, and prone to jealousy—in other words, a run-of-the-mill government bureaucrat. Having to work with him now would not mean smooth sailing for us. We could expect problems ahead.

Huo Sang did not betray his feelings. "Where is Lieutenant Fan now?" he asked quite matter-of-factly.

"He's gone upstairs again. Let's go up and have a look," Ni Jinshou replied.

Huo Sang gave him a nod as Ni Jinshou went ahead.

The building was Western-style, constructed with dark bricks set in pale mortar. It faced north–south and was on Gao Youzhi's personal estate. Another structure, an exact duplicate, was attached to it. Gao Youzhi himself resided in No. 12. No.14 was rented out to the Du family. Each residence had two entrances, one of them at street level. The upper entrances were accessed from stairways inside the buildings. A divided balcony with a metal balustrade jutted out above.

The entrance we went up to led us to a large bedroom, in which all the furniture was of rosewood in Western style. The thick, soft carpeting on the floor made everything look extremely rich and luxurious. Directly opposite was a pair of long windows, flanked on either side by shorter ones. The panes were of blue glass, screening out the bright sunlight from the interior. Outside the long windows overlooking the street was the balcony, furnished with rattan chairs and tea tables. The tall, corpulent Lieutenant Fan was in the room when we entered. Seeing us, he turned his head and greeted us perfunctorily before returning his gaze to a shoe he was turning over and over in his hands, evidently engrossed in examinating it. Huo Sang walked straight over to the big carved rosewood bed without a word. I was right behind him.

The body of a woman of about thirty lay upon the bed. Although her face was still contorted with fear, she had clearly been attractive in life, with delicate eyebrows and a straight nose on a comely face. She had on a thinly padded vest of light-gray brocade that was somewhat worn, dark silk-lined trousers, gray silken socks, and cloth shoes embroidered with purple flowers. On her pale neck were dark purple slashes of coagulated blood, presumably the fatal wounds.

"So she was killed with a knife?" I asked under my breath.

"Yes. I've already examined her carefully. Her throat was cut with a sharp blade," Jinshou answered.

"Do you have the murder weapon?" Huo Sang asked.

"No, we don't. But we have a man's shoe."

"There's only one? Have you looked around carefully?"

"Yes, there's only the one. It's most peculiar, most baffling!"

"I assume that's what Lieutenant Fan is holding?" He glanced at the fat man standing by the window.

"Yes." Ni Jinshou nodded his head as he reached out to receive the shoe from the Lieutenant.

"Wait." Huo Sang stopped him with a gesture. "Have you moved the body?"

"No, we haven't. It was laid out on the bed like this all along. But when I got here, the white mosquito netting was over it. The neatly folded brown crepe quilt, though, has been left as it was."

Huo Sang stroked his chin. "From what I can see, it would appear that the victim was not in bed when she was killed. The bed covers aren't disturbed, and she had not removed her clothing or her shoes. She seems to have been placed on the bed after the fact," he added, still pondering.

"Right!" Ni Jinshou could not help clapping his hands together. "Your thinking accords with mine exactly. The greater amount of blood on the floor is another clear indication."

Huo Sang nodded as he looked at the carpeting next to the dressing table, where the bloodstains had already darkened. Then he bent over to study the neck of the dead woman with a magnifying glass.

"There are two cuts, relatively short but both very deep. Evidently each slash was applied with great force," said Huo Sang, giving voice to his thoughts.

"Just so," Ni Jinshou nodded his agreement. "The murderer was not only strong, he was also calculating. He was even cool-headed enough to take the murder weapon away."

Huo Sang's gaze remained on the dead body. "From the appearance of the wound, the blade entered from behind the right shoulder and continued across the front. The person was apparently standing behind her and struck at her suddenly as she sat unaware in front of her dressing table. She was not only unable to defend herself, she didn't even have a chance to cry out." A thought then occurred to him. "Is anything missing?"

"Nothing. The lock on the trunk was left untouched. Apparently nothing was taken."

"You can't rely on outward appearances alone. Even when things inside a trunk have been removed, the lock on the outside can be put back on as before."

"Oh," Jinshou mumbled uncomfortably. "When the old aunt comes back in a while, I'll open it up and take a look in her presence."

"That shoe, where did you first see it?"

Ni Jinshou pointed at the place. "Right there, on the carpet near the bed."

Huo Sang stood up and turned around. He smiled as he walked toward the window, nodding his head in the direction of Lieutenant Fan.

"Well, what do you think about the shoe, Lieutenant? Discover anything?"

Now Lieutenant Fan was a tall person with broad shoulders and a prominently protruding midsection. With a dark robe on, he looked especially hulking. He turned his large head around to hand the shoe over to Huo Sang.

"I think this shoe is very much tied to the crime," he answered. "It's probably the key to solving the case."

"Oh?" Huo Sang responded distractedly. He examined every part of the shoe, flipping it over in his hands. "Hey, are those liquid stains on it?" He sniffed at it and murmured, "How odd!" Then he casually passed it to me for my inspection.

The shoe was a man's, in the latest "woven-rush" style; it was for the right foot. The vamp was of a light violet-blue satin embroidered with tiny cherry-apple blossoms, the sole of yellow ox hide. The color was as eye-catching as the style was fashionable. I noticed that, aside from the stains on the top, the bottom area was spattered with dark mud.

Huo Sang inclined his head toward me. "Bao Lang," he said smiling, "don't you appreciate the pretty color and gorgeous styling?"

"If a westerner saw it, he'd think for sure the shoe belonged to some stylish woman," I answered.

At the time, the young nouveaux riches in Shanghai had lots of leisure, with little to do aside from filling their bellies. So they spent their time and effort dandifying themselves. All of them seemed to be fond of putting on brightly colored footwear, and the abominable practice had spread even to other youths whose fathers were not at all commercial tycoons. My skin crawled at the sight of so many young men wearing women's shoes, and Huo Sang undoubtedly felt the same way. His use of the adjectives "pretty" and "gorgeous" was clearly meant to be sarcastic.

Huo Sang looked up. "Lieutenant Fan," he asked, "since you said the shoe was an important link to the murder, am I right in concluding that you have already found out something about it?"

"In my opinion," Fan said, "the owner must be one of those 'pretty' young men."

Huo Sang drawled his response. "Hmm. Your use of the word 'pretty' is perhaps a bit too nasty. It would have been better for you to label him directly as a 'frivolous' young man; or perhaps 'no-good' would be more fitting still."

"I would say that this young person's even smaller than I am," Ni Jinshou managed to interject quickly.

"Are you assuming this from the size of the shoe?" Fatty Fan immediately took over. "Hmm. Not bad. I've also come to the same conclusion."

Huo Sang nodded his approval. "Both of you have outstanding eyesight, but how did the shoe get here? What is the connection between it and this crime? Does either one of you have any answers?"

"Hmm. The answers to your first two questions are the key to this case, aren't they? Mr. Huo, tell us what you think." Fan Tong was looking directly at Huo Sang as he spoke.

Standing in front of the rosewood dressing table, Huo Sang inclined his head. "As for the origin of the shoe, I would say that it's not the property of Gao Youzhi, the master of the house." He placed the shoe on the dressing table as he was speaking. On the table were some cosmetics as well as a copy of the novel *Dream of the Red Chamber*.[1]

"No, it's not," Ni Jinshou broke in to confirm. "I've already asked the manservant, Wang Four, and the young maid, Xiangling. They've testified that Gao Youzhi is over forty years old and that they've never seen him wear anything like that."

Huo Sang nodded as he pointed to a photograph on the wall. "Right. This is presumably a picture of the couple. Hmm. I can see that the man has

1. Known now in English as either *The Story of the Stone* or *A Dream of Red Mansions*, this narrative of love and decline in a Qing dynasty aristocratic family (first published in 1792) is widely regarded as the best piece of fiction produced in traditional China. See the translations by David Hawkes and John Minford, in five volumes (Hammondsworth: Penguin, 1973–1986).

got to be about forty-five or forty-six; he's even going bald. No doubt he would not wear women's shoes. The woman seems to be in her early twenties. With her oval face and slim, high-bridged nose, she's quite a charmer! There's perhaps too much of a difference in their ages, though."

The photograph was a head-and-shoulders portrait of the couple. The man had a square face with a broad chin and thick eyebrows; he looked rather animated. The woman had beautiful eyes and a small mouth in a round face. In terms of age, the difference between them was at least fifteen or sixteen years.

"I've already asked," Lieutenant Fan said. "The victim is Youzhi's second wife."

"Now, that fits." Huo Sang gave another nod. "What's been going on? What questions should we be asking here?"

"There are five in the household—three family members and a couple of servants," said Ni Jinshou. "Gao Youzhi's official residence, however, has always been in Hangzhou.[2] He has yet to be notified about what happened. He has an old maiden aunt who was living with the victim. On the evening of the thirteenth, however, this aunt had gone to the home of her other nephew Gao Youhui. I've already sent someone there to tell her what happened, but she hasn't yet gotten back. So there's nobody to interrogate right now."

"Is Gao Youhui the younger brother of Gao Youzhi?"

"He is."

"Where does he live?"

"Number 9 Jing'an Street, in the Hongkou district, according to Wang Four. Right now, Wang's downstairs in the kitchen."

"What else has Wang told you?"

"He's the watchman and valet, and has been here for a year and a half. He said that last night he was in his own house. When he came to work this morning, he was surprised to find the front door unlocked. He called out as he came in, but no one answered. When he went upstairs after that, he saw that the door to the back room was locked, and the key left in the keyhole. The room is where the old aunt and the maid Xiangling live. Though the aunt was

2. The capital of Zhejiang Province, Hangzhou is a prosperous industrial and agricultural center on the Qiantang River at the southern end of the Grand Canal. It is about a two-hour train ride from Shanghai.

away and Xiangling nowhere in sight, soft whimpering sounds were nevertheless emerging from within. Astounded, Wang Four turned the key and opened the door. Xiangling rushed out, saying she didn't know who had locked her in. After she had awakened that morning, she had found she couldn't open the door. But not daring to raise any fuss, she had just sat down and waited. Wang Four was even more flabbergasted. He called out to his young mistress but got no response. Only then did he enter her bedroom, to discover the body on the bed. As no family members were around at the time, Wang Four and Xiangling were frightened and at an utter loss. They remained in shocked silence for some time before Wang Four ran off to the district police station to report the crime.

"That maidservant, does she know anything?"

"Xiangling's only thirteen. She ordinarily does odd jobs like sweeping the floor or washing the dishes or dusting. She was sound asleep last night and was unable to tell us anything, not even when the whole thing started."

Huo Sang hesitated. "Hmm. That's really rather strange." His expression seemed to show that he was taken aback. "Isn't Wang Four downstairs? Please ask him to come up here. I have a few questions for him."

II. A Premature Conclusion

Ni Jinshou was on his way downstairs at the instant of Huo Sung's request. Meanwhile Huo Sang walked over to the window to look out at the balcony that extended to the edge of the sidewalk. I followed suit. Unexpectedly, Fan Tong also came over and tugged at Huo Sang's sleeve.

"Mr. Huo," he whispered, "what in your view is the principal motive for this crime?"

"What do *you* think it is?" Aware that this officious little functionary was invading his territory, Huo Sung was moved to counterattack.

"Me? Hmm. I think it all comes down to a single word." He was pushing out his potbelly, seemingly delighted with himself.

Huo sang turned to face him. "What word?"

Lieutenant Fan assumed an unnecessarily serious expression as he inclined his head close to Huo Sang's ear. "The word can be rendered in nine letters, just three times three. Don't you agree?"

"Three times three will do it?" Huo Sang countered with mock surprise. Then he pursed his lips and opened his eyes as wide as he could, as if he truly had no idea what the word could be. "Lieutenant Fan, please. Share your valuable insight with us. Why invent a riddle for us to puzzle over?"

The sound of heavy footsteps interrupted Fan's answer. Ni Jinshou had reentered the room, Wang Four in tow.

Wang was a man of about forty. He was big and tall, with a powerful upper body, a darkish complexion, shiny jet-black hair, and anxious dark eyes. He was neatly dressed in shoes of dark fabric, white socks, and a yellow flannel robe with a willow pattern that was still seventy or eighty percent new. Huo Sang greeted him with a smile before asking him to relate clearly all that he had seen and heard that morning. Wang Four's account was identical to what Ni Jinshou had just told us.

"If you're employed here, why do you return to your own house at night?" Huo Sang asked him.

"I have a wife and mother at home," Wang replied. Then he added, hesitantly, "I don't get home every night, only once a month. That's what the master agreed to."

"Oh, so it was according to a set schedule? That's really remarkable. Last night, then, was the night you were to be away?"

Wang Four gave no answer but inadvertently stuck out his tongue.

"Say something," Huo Sang urged him. "Is the fourteenth of each month when you are off?"

The dark-faced manservant stammered out his answer. "No . . . no. It's supposed to be the twentieth. I went home last night on the young mistress's orders. It wasn't my own idea."

"Oh? What did she say to you?"

"The young mistress told me she planned to be away from home in a couple of days, and that I would have to be here to keep watch. So she said to go home a few days early to make up for the time off I would be missing this month. Who could have guessed that this kind of calamity would occur at the very time I was not around?"

The manservant's tongue appeared again as he lowered his head. Huo Sang was standing next to the dressing table, focusing his gaze on him. The two officials, seated directly across from them on the couch with the yellow brocade cushions, were also training their eyes on Wang Four. I was next to the rosewood desk by the window, detachedly observing the whole scene.

"Wang Four," Huo Sang continued his questioning, "did your mistress really give you such orders?"

"Yes, sir." He kept his head lowered.

"You should realize that this is a homicide case, and it's very complicated. If you make even one false statement about it, you'll wind up hurting yourself. You have to be clear on this point."

"Don't get it into your head that the dead can never contradict your testimony, that you can just say whatever you want. Anything you tell us we'll have the means to verify," Ni Jinshou jumped in to add.

Wang Four looked up, his eyes wide open. "Everything I've said, sir, is the truth," he protested, obviously overwrought. "I wouldn't dare utter one false word!"

"That's fine, then," Huo Sang nodded. "But let me ask you, exactly when was it that your mistress told you you could go home ahead of schedule?"

"Toward evening, yesterday."

"When did you leave here for home?"

"I ate dinner and washed the dishes before I left. It was about half past six at the time."

"Half past six and you were done with dinner? Do you finish eating that early every day?"

"Ordinarily we don't have dinner until six-thirty. Yesterday, because the old mistress went to the second master's place, the young mistress did the cooking, and so we ate earlier."

"Where is your own house?"

"24 Fangbin Road. It's very near here."

"At the time you were leaving here, how was your mistress?"

"She was fine."

"Were there other people in the house?"

"No. Other than Xiangling, there was no one else."

The answers came smoothly, with no hesitation whatsoever. Ni Jinshou listened in rapt attention. Fan Tong, however, had his right leg crossed over his left and was waggling it all the while, making it obvious that he had long since come to a conclusion and could hardly bear to sit through Huo Sang's detailed questioning.

"Yesterday, did anyone come to the house during the day?" Huo Sang continued after a slight pause.

Wang Four shook his head.

"And ordinarily? Are there friends or relatives who usually come over?"

"That's also rare. The young mistress's relatives are from Ningbo,[3] and they don't usually get here to see her. There are even fewer visits from friends. The master lives in Hangzhou, and the mistress is not fond of social gatherings. So people don't come around here often."

"By 'rare,' then, you mean of course that no one at all comes calling. Is that correct?"

"Yes, that's generally correct. But young Mrs. Du next door occasionally comes over to chat. Mr. Du has also been here, but that's rather unusual."

"Was either of the Dus here yesterday?"

"No."

"Anyone else?"

"Um. Sometimes the second master comes to visit."

"The second master. Would that be Gao Youhui, who lives in the Hongkou district?"

"Yes. He was here the day before yesterday, to take the old mistress over to his place."

Now, Huo Sang quickly shifted gears. "Surely there's got to be mail and other kinds of written communication with outsiders. I can see that your mistress is an educated woman," he said, glancing over at the book on the dressing table.

"Yes, sir. The young mistress is an educated person. She wrote letters often. I remember her getting a letter in the morning the day before yesterday. I was the one who brought it to her to stamp with her chop."[4] "Ah, so she needed to certify receipt? Where was the letter from?"

3. Ningbo is an ancient port city in the eastern part of Zhejiang Province. It is seventy nautical miles south of Shanghai.

4. A personal seal or stamp that functions as a signature.

"I don't know. I can't read."

"Then you would have no idea where any of the letters she regularly received came from."

"That's right. I wouldn't have any idea."

As he stroked his chin with his right hand, Huo Sang held onto his right elbow with his left. He glanced quickly over at the two people seated on the couch and saw that Ni Jinshou, head up, was listening raptly to Wang Four's answers. Fan Tong, though, was puffing on a cigarette, his legs still crossed and his eyelids drooping. It was obvious his mind was elsewhere.

"Jinshou, have you looked over the letter?" Huo Sang asked.

"Er—I haven't gotten around to that." Detective Ni seemed just a little embarrassed. He stood up immediately after responding. "I'll see to it right away."

But almost before Ni Jinshou had a chance to straighten up, Fan Tong suddenly developed an interest in examining the letter and seized the initiative for himself, moving quickly over to the rosewood desk behind me. Jinshou was right behind him, and both began their examination. As before, I concentrated my attention on Huo Sang, who slowly moved from the dressing table to where Wang Four was standing.

"I still have a few important questions, Wang Four," he said in a quiet voice. "What is the usual time span between your master's visits here?"

Wang looked up at Huo Sang with a quizzical expression. "The master does not visit on a set schedule," he said hesitantly. "In a month, he comes around maybe one or two times."

"Your mistress, what's her normal behavior?"

"Huh? What do you mean by that, sir?" Biting his lip, Wang didn't let on whether or not he understood the implication of Huo Sang's question.

"I mean, for example, was she a proper lady?"

"Oh, *that*—the mistress was a very proper person. She didn't go out for entertainment, and there were no men to speak of who came around. Only—only—"

"Go on, man. Why are you hesitating?" Huo Sang's eyes were flashing.

Wang Four licked his lips again. "There were times," he said, "when young rowdies would kick up a fuss outside when they saw the mistress reading or sewing on the balcony."

"What kind of fuss?"

"Sometimes they would gather outside the door and not leave. They would be making all sorts of outlandish remarks, or laughing out loud, or sometimes letting out weird-sounding calls."

"During those occasions, what would your mistress do?"

"She always went back into her room and shut the windows. I've seen that a number of times. She never had anything to do with them."

At this point Fan Tong rushed over with his protruding belly, clutching a couple of envelopes. "Mr. Huo," he said. "There are two letters here, both kept inside the locked drawer in the desk. We had to pick the lock to get at them. But they are ordinary family communications. Nothing suspicious in them."

Huo Sang took the letters to see for himself: I also sidled over for a look. One of them was from Ningbo in the handwriting of the victim's father, Ding Xiaotian; the other was from her husband in Hangzhou. Sure enough, the contents consisted of nothing other than family matters. Her father was telling her that her older brother had just had another child. Gao Youzhi informed her that he'd made fifty thousand in the current stock market and was extremely delighted. There was a fairly large time gap between the two letters. The one from Ningbo had been sent two months previously, where as Gao Youzhi's was from three weeks ago.

"No other letters besides these?" Huo Sang asked.

"None. We've looked carefully," said Ni Jinshou.

"What about the letter from the day before yesterday, then?" Huo Sang was thinking out loud. "If its receipt had to be acknowledged, then it was sent either special delivery or registered mail—definitely important in either case. Where could it be now?"

He scanned every part of the bedroom with his sharp eyes. I helped him examine every nook and cranny, when suddenly I noticed some ashes near the corner of the wardrobe.

"Look, Huo Sang," I said, pointing. "What's that over there?"

Following my finger, Huo Sang directed his eyes to the corner. He hurried over and bent down for a closer examination.

"You've got sharp eyes, Bao Lang," Huo Sang said in happy surprise. "These are certainly ashes, but there's still a bit left of the paper that was burned. Look, this little piece is clearly from a manila envelope!" Carefully, he picked up the charred remnant. "Too bad I can't make out what's written on it."

"Could this be the letter that came the day before yesterday?" I asked.

Huo Sang threw down the unburned edge. "Very probably."

Having exerted himself without result, Lieutenant Fan once again sat down on the couch. But Ni Jinshou didn't join him. Instead, he went to the tall window over the balcony to look out at the rattan chair there, with its finely constructed circular patterns. Huo Sang returned to the dressing table to continue questioning Wang Four.

"The rowdies you were telling me about, Wang Four," he said, "how many were there altogether?"

Wang licked his lips once again. "Um, there were two or three of them."

"Could you identify them?"

"No—uh, there was this runty, sissyish looking one, maybe twenty years old. He was always making weird noises. I've seen him quite a few times."

"Please be more specific. Why was he especially noticeable to you?"

"He was the one who was here most often. One evening last month, I heard strange sounds outside the door. They were like the calls of a thrush— *xuya xuya xuya*. I went out for a look and saw the short fellow, in a light-gray gown, looking up to the balcony. I noticed his black hair was slicked back, and he had a pale, chubby face. He looked like a real pretty-boy."

"Was the young mistress on the balcony at the time?"

"Yes. I was there just as she was walking back into the bedroom and closing the windows."

"And after that?"

"The fellow saw me open the door to go outside, and so he went away."

Huo Sang broke off briefly to turn his body around to face the dressing table. He picked up that shoe with the violet-blue satin vamp.

"Had you seen this shoe before this morning?"

Wang Four shook his head. "No, I hadn't."

"How did you come upon it?"

"I called and called the mistress and got no answer. So then I came into the room—and found the shoe on the carpet."

"Where on the carpet was it?" Huo Sang pressed him.

"In front of the bed." Wang Four pointed to the spot.

"There's no need to go into such detail. All we need to know is that the shoe was in the room." Having grown quite impatient with all this questioning, Fan Tong jumped in to complain. "No doubt the shoe belongs to that pretty-boy with the bird calls. All we have to do now is to get hold of him and the case will be over."

"How can you be so darn sure of yourself, Lieutenant Fan?" I couldn't help voicing my own protest.

"I've known from the start," Fan Tong said as he wagged his head and blew out more cigarette smoke. "I took one look and saw through to the basic motive of the crime. As I said to all of you earlier on, it can be written out in a single word of nine letters." He cast a quick glance at Huo Sang. "To involve you in a minor matter like this, Mr. Huo, is truly unnecessary." Then he turned his head around. "Wang Four, do you know where this pretty-boy lives?"

"No, I don't."

"Should you see the little dandy again, would you be able to recognize him?" Fatty Fan was forging ahead doggedly, refusing to let go of his preconceived conclusion.

Wang Four shook his head once more. "No, I wouldn't," he answered. "I never got a good enough look at him."

Fan Tong glared at Wang angrily as he pursed his lips in disappointment. In front of us, however, he couldn't very well browbeat the man.

"In a while, I'll order everyone in the police station to look for him," he muttered unhappily. "We've got to find him."

"Lieutenant Fan, I don't see how it would be much of a problem to find that little fellow. To mobilize everyone you've got to do it—I would call *that* unnecessary." Huo Sang was grinning as he spoke. "Your conclusion about the motive of the crime—could it be a tad premature? Or, indeed, overly simplistic?"

Once again, before the fat man could reply, he was interrupted. Ni Jinshou came back in from outside the window with something tiny in his left hand; with his right, he pointed to the high-backed rattan chair with the circular patterns.

"Mr. Huo," he said, "I've found a bit of fabric; it seems to indicate that the woman did usually spend her days sitting out there on the balcony."

"That's right," Wang Four suddenly offered without prompting. "When the weather got warm, the young mistress would be out on the balcony sewing or reading day after day."

"Yes. Because the panes on the windows are tinted blue, there wasn't quite enough light in the bedroom. So she had to go out onto the balcony whenever she wanted to do any sewing."

Huo Sang said this rather perfunctorily as he lifted the shoe he was holding up to his nose for another sniff. After some further thought, he suddenly came up with an unexpected question.

"Wang Four, did any family in the neighborhood have a celebration yesterday? Anything like a birthday party, or a dinner party to mark a new birth?"

Wang Four seemed taken aback before screwing up his face in an effort to recall. Then he nodded. "Oh yes, there was. A family on Grass Sandal Cove up ahead had a wedding. It wasn't yesterday, though, but the day before."

"That's fine. Now please go downstairs and bring Xiangling up here."

III. The Point of Dispute

With the break in the questioning, Huo Sang seemed to relax a little as he sat himself down on a padded chair. I, too, settled into the swivel chair behind the desk, while Ni Jinshou took this opportunity to probe into what Huo Sang was thinking.

"Mr. Huo," he asked, "what in your opinion is the motive for this crime?"

"I've said all along that the motive is contained in a single word, a word that can be rendered in three times three letters. You still don't believe me?" Fatty Fan interrupted.

"I've heard that more than once," Ni Jinshou retorted as he shot a quick glance at his superior. "But to listen to Mr. Huo's opinion is to profit from another point of view. What he thinks can perhaps lend support to your views."

"That's fine. Yes. Good. Good." The fat man kept nodding his head. "Mr. Huo, let's see what you have to say. What is there about my conclusion that you would dispute?"

"I only suggest that your conclusion may be a bit premature, since we haven't as yet clearly taken everything into consideration," said Huo Sang mildly. "Up to the present, I feel that there are still areas of uncertainty—"

"Uh . . . uh, the areas of uncertainty you're concerned with—don't they all point to the shoe?" Fan cut in to ask.

"Of course. The shoe is one factor." Huo Sang remained calm. "But there are others. The ashes over in the corner of the room, for instance. It's obvious that some sort of letter was burned. And then Wang Four going home last night ahead of schedule seems somewhat more than just coincidental. Furthermore, the young maid Xiangling was locked in her room from the outside. Who do you think could have done that? And what could have been the reason?"

"Right. I've paid attention to all that. But what's most important is this pretty little shoe we have," Fan Tong said.

"What does this shoe show you? Please, Lieutenant. It would be better if you would tell us right off rather than engage us in a needless guessing game." There was a trace of scorn in Detective Ni's voice.

"So you insist that I get right to the point? Fine. Just think. An attractive shoe, obviously not her husband's but belonging to a man, turns up in the bedroom of a young woman. Now do I need to spell out for you what that means?" Fan Tong waxed increasingly enthusiastic as he spoke. He uncrossed his legs as he continued, evidently well pleased with himself. "What's more, those areas of uncertainty Mr. Huo was touching upon just now can, exactly as you indicated, be seen to support my conclusion."

"How do they support your conclusion?" Jinshou wanted to know.

"Every one of the areas of uncertainty points to the same thing: This woman sent her two servants off last night to clear the house. Her purpose was to receive her—well, her lover! To put it indelicately, she was getting ready to engage in that nine-letter word, in—in 'cuckoldry!' "

"You seem to be so sure, Lieutenant Fan. Don't you see that there are problems with what you say?" Huo Sang asked him dryly.

"Problems? Huh?"

"Wang Four has told us clearly that his young mistress almost never went out and that she had always been proper in her behavior. Doesn't this contradict your conclusion?"

"How can you rely just on the word of Wang Four?"

Huo Sang nodded his agreement. "Now, *that's* a proper question. Precisely because I can't, I've planned to consider the case from other angles, and the more caution I exercise as I do so the better. What I can't go along with are snap conclusions."

Xiangling was already coming into the room. She was still a child, with rounded cheeks and large eyes. Her face was somewhat sallow, framed by braids secured at the ends with red yarn. She had on a long-sleeved overblouse in light gray, with matching trousers. Walking in very hesitantly, she went over to stand near one end of the rosewood bed and, not daring to look at what was on it, kept her head down. Huo Sang stood up and went over to her. Stretching out his hand to pat her on her head, he asked her in a warm, soothing voice whether she had heard anything the night before. The young maidservant told him that she had slept very soundly from the time she went to bed at seven thirty until the next morning, and that she had heard nothing at all.

"What time did you get up this morning?" Huo Sang asked her.

"I was up very early, but because my room was locked from the outside, I . . . I couldn't get out!"

"Did you try calling for anyone?"

"I did call for the mistress a few times, but there was no answer. I got scared and didn't dare call out anymore. After that, I heard someone knocking at the front door. Then Uncle Wang Four came upstairs, opened the lock, and let me out."

"Is your door ordinarily locked during the night?"

"No, it isn't."

"What about the key, then? Is it regularly kept in the keyhole?"

"No. It's usually kept in that drawer." She pointed toward the dressing table.

"Who do you think locked you in last night?"

Her eyes grew even larger. "I don't know."

Huo Sang shot a quick glance over at Ni Jinshou and Lieutenant Fan. Ni was sitting straight up, listening, wide-eyed, with full attention. Fan Tong, however, was looking out the window, another cigarette in his mouth. He looked very much as if he would prefer to be elsewhere.

"Did you know that Wang Four did not sleep here last night?" Huo Sang went on.

"I didn't know at first," Xiangling answered. "He didn't tell me until he was letting me out."

"What did you do when you got out of your room?"

"I followed Uncle Wang Four in here to look for our mistress. We saw her like this as soon as we came in. *Aiya!* I'm so scared!" Her sallow complexion was turning pale; her voice trembled.

"And after that?"

"Uncle Wang Four went to call the police. I was so scared I didn't dare stay here any longer."

"You usually sleep in the back room with the old aunt, don't you?" Huo Sang asked after a slight pause.

"Yes. Old Aunty and I live in the room behind this one. Uncle Wang Four sleeps downstairs."

"If there's any noise in this bedroom, can you hear it from where you sleep?"

"Yes, if the noise is loud enough. It's just that . . . just that—" Xiangling's head sank even lower. "I sleep soundly every night, and last night I really didn't hear anything."

Huo Sang grabbed the shoe again to ask her about it. She, too, said she had never seen it before. He then wanted to know whether her young mistress ever had any dealings with those ruffians who came around. Xiangling's answer was the same as Wang Four's—that the young mistress never had anything to do with them. Huo Sang had no more questions. He put the shoe down once again and, after sending Xiangling back downstairs, turned to speak with Ni Jinshou: "Jinshou, my man, though I still can't determine what the motive in this case may be, from everything we've seen up to now, I am ready to say that the murderer is in all likelihood someone well known to the victim."

"That's right. It was someone she knew well. I totally agree." The annoying, pedestrian bureaucrat was sticking his nose in again.

Jinshou shot the man a look of disgust. "From all that we've seen, what are you basing your thinking on?" he asked.

"Xiangling didn't hear anything," Huo Sang said. "There are no traces of a struggle in the room; the victim's clothing remained tidy, so she was not putting up any kind of fight. The fatal wounds, especially, show that the man struck her suddenly and powerfully. All of these things demonstrate that the victim was aware the killer had entered her room, but that she never considered herself to be in danger."

"You're right. Your analysis is based on solid fact," Detective Ni took the opportunity to add. "How, then, should we proceed?"

Huo Sang pondered his reply. "We have yet to complete the investigation of all relevant facts. We should cooperate and divide up the tasks. When the old aunt gets back, for example, she must be carefully questioned. What would she say about the victim's normal behavior? With whom did the victim regularly associate?"

"Wang Four tells me that Gao Youhui also comes to visit."

"Good. You should go and see him." Then he looked around for me. "Bao Lang, why don't you pay a visit to the Du family next door? Both the husband and the wife come here every so often. As for me, I want to go out to Grass Sandal Cove."

"That's fine. Have your fun. All I want to do is to look for that pretty-boy." Thus did Fan Tong stake out his own territory.

"Very good. But there's a basic question we have to keep in mind as we go about our separate tasks," Huo Sang said.

"What basic question?" asked Fan Tong.

"Was this woman actually a faithful wife? We still don't have enough evidence about this and ought to pay special attention to the answer."

Lieutenant Fan curled his lip while remaining silent. It was evident that he had long since made up his mind on this point and saw no reason to follow the directive.

Ni Jinshou, however, was much more amenable. "Right," he said. "We only have the testimonies of Wang Four and Xiangling on this, and I think Wang Four's word might not be entirely reliable. I'm also planning to go out to his home on Fangbin Road to ask around." He then picked up the shoe from the dressing table.

With the tasks thus allocated, Huo Sang proceeded down the stairway and took his leave. The two officers and I gathered briefly in the living room downstairs. We agreed to go our separate ways and to return to the house when we were done. Ni Jinshou headed to Wang Four's on Fangbin Road. On his way, he stopped to tell a patrolman to keep an eye on Wang's movements. I wanted to visit the Du household at No. 14 right away, to probe into the question of the victim's behavior, but Fan Tong openly objected to the idea.

"What's the use of going to all that trouble?" he said. "You might as well come with me to find that little dandy. It's so clear that this is a case of illicit love and death. I've said that over and over."

"I'm still reluctant to come to that conclusion," I told him bluntly. "Wang Four and Xiangling have both testified that this woman appeared to be a completely proper lady."

"You trust them? The shoe alone is all the proof I need."

"The shoe is of course suspicious. But to consider it indisputable evidence against the murderer—I'm afraid that's a bit of a stretch."

"You're too trusting, Mr. Bao. I've already told you: To discover a man's footwear as pretty as this in a young woman's room and to know that the owner is not her husband—what more need be said? Do you think we ought to waste our time ascertaining whether the woman was a proper lady?"

If we were to consider the shoe alone, his argument was not without merit. But I was still unconvinced.

"That's not necessarily so," I said. "Someone could have killed her for another reason and deliberately left the shoe as a smokescreen to make us think it's a case of adultery to prevent us from finding out what's really behind the crime."

"Oh, so you're saying there could be other motives? What would they be? Robbery? Revenge? What's your reasoning? Where's your evidence?"

The biting tone of his string of challenging questions indicated the invincibility of his ignorance; he was someone who could never entertain another's point of view. I couldn't help growing quite annoyed. Strong-willed people like him often have a tendency to hang on tightly to biases and be enormously pleased with themselves for doing so. Even if some other opinion was well founded, they would never accept it. The man's attitude was so indicative of a closed and unreasonable mind that I could not help being thoroughly exasperated. It was indeed difficult to have to work with this Lieutenant Fan, typical government functionary that he was.

I proceeded to give him an icy reply. "Of course my speculations can't as yet be backed up with sufficient evidence. But, then, your theory of adultery and murder hasn't necessarily been substantiated either. That shoe indeed raises questions, but how did it get into the victim's room in the first place? There's got to be some explanation, don't you think?"

"That's easy," said Fan Tong. "After doing the deed, the murderer must have been in a dither to get away, and so left the shoe there in haste."

"But Huo Sang has observed that the killer took the time to move the dead woman's body onto the bed. Therefore apparently he remained cool-headed and in control. I agree with this thinking. Moreover, the room shows no signs of struggle. How, then, could the killer have been as flustered as you surmise?"

"Situations don't always remain completely constant. Even though he might have been unperturbed at the start, unexpected noises or disturbances could have occurred at any time, and his coolness then have changed quickly to anxiety."

Even though clever retorts like this were no more than attempts to seize the rhetorical high ground, his ability to argue was truly formidable: He actually sounded reasonable. At any rate, I controlled my emotions as I carried on the debate.

"Even so," I said, "why would the person leave behind just one shoe? Don't you think it's hard to explain why there's only one?"

"Not at all. It's probably because the shoe was a bit too wide for his foot." He let out a little chuckle. "I do think the fact that he left just one shoe behind rather than both shows he *was* in haste. You've got to believe that someone in such a situation would not only run for his life with one shoe off, but would do so stark naked!"

He was not yielding any ground, and I was finding it difficult to maintain my self-control.

"What you said in the beginning surely doesn't mesh with what you're saying now." I noticed that my voice was rising to a higher pitch than it ought. "You began by saying that the shoe belonged to the victim's lover. Now you say that the one who left the shoe behind is the murderer. What are you really getting at?"

"What do you mean they don't mesh? Aren't the lover and the murderer one and the same?" Fatty Fan's voice was not much lower than mine, but it was tinged with a triumphant tone.

"Oh, so it's the same person, is it? Then why did her lover want to kill her?"

"That's not a big problem. Even though I can't immediately put my finger on the motive, I'm sure I could make a very good guess."

"You're so sure? Then I'd like to share your insight."

"Any woman who would take one lover would have no scruples about taking another. If she did indeed have a second lover, wouldn't that be enough to provoke the kind of jealousy that could result in murder?"

"One lover, two lovers! How can you say that?" My words were clearly reproachful. "From the fact that she was not wearing any makeup and was plainly dressed, she doesn't appear at all to have been the strumpet you've concluded she was."

"Not a strumpet? Why then did she send her manservant away last night? Why did she lock her maid in? Let me say it again, Mr. Bao: You're really rather naive. *Heh, heh, heh!*" He had to laugh, apparently finding me amusing. "This is really like looking at an overripe pear: soft and luscious on the outside, rotten at the core. You can't simply rely on outward appearances, you know." He turned up the cuffs of his dark woolen gown and let out a cough. "To put it all in a single sentence, we only have to find that short little pale-faced fellow in the light-gray gown with the slick black hair and our knotty problems will instantly unravel. So, fine. Since you don't want to go with me to look for him, I'm sorry to have to leave you now." He gave me a nod, turned his corpulent self around, and ambled off, his potbelly leading the way.

At his departure I let out a sigh of relief and stretched, feeling as if I had suddenly been released from a suffocating enclosure. To allow this kind of self-important and muddleheaded person to handle a homicide case not only showed no concern for human life; it could also result in harm to the innocent. But the man was well established in police circles. Apparently, he had the support of some higher-up or other, which was too bad!

IV. The Bird Calls

No. 14 was connected to No. 12 next door. There was only a wrought-iron divider consisting of a line of pointed spears separating the two halves of the balcony on the second floor. The Du family rented No. 14. The male head of the household was Du Qinzhi, a literature professor at Donghua University who was already sixty-one years old. His wife was surnamed Yang. Only about forty, she was Du Qinzhi's second wife. When I went over to the residence to investigate, he was teaching class at the school and she had been hospitalized for some kind of illness. Only Qinzhi's octogenarian mother was at home, a paraplegic confined to her bed upstairs. I found their old woman servant from Yangzhou[5] on the lower level. Not wanting to disturb the old lady upstairs, I started a conversation with the servant in the living room. I told her that Ding Fangzhu, the mistress next door, had been murdered by someone during the night, and that the circumstances were baffling. I was hoping she could help me with some information about Ding Fangzhu's daily routines as well as those who usually came to see her. The woman might have been over fifty in age, but she spoke with great clarity and directness.

"*Aiyo!* The Gaos' young mistress was murdered?" She was clearly shocked. "That's incredible!" Her wide-open eyes seemed to glisten with horror. Then she volunteered the answer to the question I was about to ask her. "Mrs. Gao was absolutely the most proper and gentlest person you'd ever meet. She was always sewing one thing or another, morning and night. She made all her own clothes by hand, as well as those of the old aunt. My own young mistress once said, 'Mrs. Gao is truly wonderful. With her around, you'd never have to pay a tailor.' Ordinarily, she never left her house. It was rare for her even to come over to see us. This whole thing's just so outlandish. How in the world could she . . . could she have been murdered like that?" There was a tremor in her voice.

5. Yangzhou (perhaps better known as Yangchow) is a town at the juncture of the Yangtze and Hua Rivers in Jiangsu Province. The center of the salt trade in the Qing dynasty (1644–1911), it enjoyed great prosperity and dynamic growth in late imperial China and has been regarded as the precursor of modern-day Shanghai.

"It's precisely because it's so unexpected that we have to find out what happened," I said soothingly. "When you said she was 'absolutely the most proper,' what were you getting at?"

"I was thinking of those young rowdies!" She leaned closer to me to speak in a whisper. "Quite a few times I've seen those punks standing on the side of the road, lifting their heads to make weird noises toward the balcony. Mrs. Gao always ignored them, usually by going back inside her room. There were times when I heard her slam her window shut."

"What kinds of weird noises?"

"Oh, they would talk loudly about one thing or another, or mumble aimlessly, or sometimes let out howls."

"Could you recognize any of them?"

"Who would care to look them straight in the eye? They're just spoiled brats with nothing better to do after filling their bellies with food their fathers provide."

I saw Du Qinzhi's portrait on the wall. He was the picture of dignity, with a beard extending to his chest. I also heard that it was only during holidays that he would occasionally accompany his wife when she dropped in next door, and then mostly when Gao Youzhi was also there. So Du Qinzhi himself could be dismissed as a suspect. I then shifted the conversation to an even more immediate time frame.

"Last night, did you hear any noises from next door?" I asked her.

The woman's jaw dropped. She looked at me as if in a daze, and gave no answer.

"If anyone were to shout out from there, for example, you could hear it over here, couldn't you?" I pressed her.

"No, there was nothing." Her eyes kept blinking. "If someone shouts, I can of course hear it. But last night I didn't hear anything." She stopped here, then opened her eyes very wide. "Ah, I remember now. Eerie calls! There were those eerie calls!"

"Eerie calls." I echoed her, delighted at the information. "You've got to tell me more specifically. What kind of eerie calls?"

"It was after midnight when the young mistress's stomach acted up again. The young master came downstairs to wake me. He said the hot-water bottle was empty and wanted me to heat up some water so that the mistress could use it to warm herself. So I got up and lit some firewood, boiled the water, and brought it upstairs. It was then that I suddenly heard the calls coming from the road outside the window—*xuya xuya,* kind of like the sounds of a thrush, but really eerie!"

"Was it some nocturnal bird?"

"No. It was a person imitating a bird."

"Were the calls the same as what you heard from those rowdies?"

"Umm. More or less. But I'd never heard them after dark. When I did last night, I felt a chill go up my spine."

"How long did the calls go on?"

"I don't know. I sleep near the kitchen downstairs. Once I got back to my room, I didn't hear anything anymore."

This was a newly discovered fact. The pretty-boy upon whom Lieutenant Fan placed so much importance—could he after all turn out to be the perpetrator of this bloody crime? At midnight last night, this little dandy had actually been outside the door, making bird calls. Did he then go upstairs? Had that violet-blue satin shoe with the cherry-apple blossoms really been left there by him? I thought of Xiangling locked up in her own room, and of Wang Four being sent away. If the pretty-boy had indeed gone upstairs, the victim, Ding Shufang, had to have been the one to let him in. On the other hand, three people had now testified that she was not that kind of woman. The more I thought about it, the more puzzled I really became.

After I said goodbye to the Yangzhou woman, I went across the street to a little dry-goods store to see if I could glean any additional information. On the question of the victim's behavior, the answers I received accorded essentially with what the woman had told me. But the proprietress there had not heard any bird calls.

When I got back to the Gao residence, Ni Jinshou had also just come in, since Fangbin Road was close by. He said that Wang Four's movements the night before had been corroborated. According to his wife, Wang had played mahjongg all night with his neighbors and did not get to bed until after two in the morning. When Jinshou asked about Wang's character, what he was told was completely consistent with what had been said about him before.

For this reason, Wang's testimony about the mistress telling him to take his day off early was also entirely credible. I related to Ni what I had found out, as well as what the Yangzhou woman servant had told me.

Jinshou, too, was befuddled. "So we have now established that the victim did send the manservant away ahead of schedule and that there were those strange noises outside in the middle of the night. It does appear, then, that some kind of tryst was planned. But the woman's moral integrity has been established as unquestionable. This is indeed perplexing."

It was at this point that the old aunt and her younger nephew, Gao Youhui, rushed to the scene by automobile on receiving the news. Youhui, a manager in a rice mill, was a middle-aged man with an unshaven face. He was plainly dressed in a cotton gown and cloth shoes. We accompanied him upstairs, where he took a cursory glance at the body before engaging in conversation with Ni Jinshou. He said that his sister-in-law had been a very upright person who had had a fairly good relationship with his brother, and that what had happened was truly beyond comprehension. After that, he said he was going to the telegraph office to notify his brother by telegram. The aunt was a hunched-over woman over sixty. As soon as she saw the body on the bed, she started to wail. It was only after Youhui left that Ni Jinshou was able to calm her down somewhat and ask her questions. From the way she spoke, I gathered that she had had a loving relationship with this wife of her nephew. She told us that the victim had been a person of character and self-control, without any of the bad habits of those fashionable women in Shanghai. She also said that the victim had been a homebody who usually did not run around; she was certain she had never met up with any strangers. When the old lady saw the shoe, she could not help clicking her tongue in surprise. She then told us that Youhui had come to fetch her two days before because the victim had urged her to go and stay in Hongkou for a while. How could anyone have predicted that this kind of calamity would happen once she left? When the subject switched later to the problem of motive, the old lady was suddenly struck by a thought.

"What about the jewelry box?" she said in alarm. "Have you looked through it yet?"

"We haven't," answered Ni Jinshou. "We were waiting until you came back before opening anything."

"It's only a small red lacquer box decorated with gold leaf. It's on top of that big chest." She pointed to the tall chest of drawers next to the rosewood wardrobe with the mirror in front. "There are two or three diamond rings in it, and the jewelry is worth tens of thousands. Can I trouble you, sirs, to get it down?"

Ni Jinshou grew anxious. He went over there quickly, climbed up on a chair, and stretched to lift down the little box. The old woman opened it with the key from one of the drawers of the dressing table. She was starting to go through the contents when she let out a little yelp of surprise. All the diamond rings and precious gems had vanished, leaving only gold-plated ornaments and other cheap trinkets.

Ni Jinshou kept shaking his head as his eyes turned in my direction. He was clearly signaling me. It seemed that this case of adultery and murder now had an added robbery factor and had clearly become more complex.

A patrolman arrived clutching a note, which he handed to Detective Ni. "This was delivered to us by a colleague in Branch Office No. 2. I've been instructed to pass it along to you," he said.

I saw that Ni Jinshou's name was on the outside and the handwriting was Huo Sang's. The note read:

> The shoe's owner cannot as yet be clearly determined, but he is probably on the attached list. Please investigate, and if any listed person appears suspicious, report him immediately to your supervisors so that he can be detained. If you need to contact me, please call my residence on Aiwen Road.
> Jin Baosheng. 56 Fangbin Road
> Lin Xiaofang. In the dry-goods store on the corner of Nanchang Road
> Wang Yusheng. 260 East Haichao Temple
> Shen Yitian. 107 on the street behind Minsheng High School
> —Huo Sang

V. The Shoe's Owner

I knew that Huo Sang had already gone back to our house by then. The investigation here, moreover, could be considered complete for the moment, and there was no need for me to remain. So I shook Ni Jinshou's hand and took my leave.

When I got back to 77 Aiwen Road, Huo Sang was in his office playing his violin. Did his doing so at a time like this mean that he had reached a tentative conclusion about this case, with its multitude of confusing leads? Or was it because the puzzles and complexities were frustrating him, and he was using the violin to calm his nerves? I wanted to stop and listen, to see if I could discern his state of mind from the ebb and flow of the music. But as soon as I entered the room, he stopped abruptly.

"Bao Lang, have you completed your part of the job?" he asked as he put down the instrument to look at me.

"You mean ascertaining the character of the victim?" I responded.

"That's right. I can't believe this woman was any sort of profligate." He sat himself down. "What's the result of your investigation?"

"According to all the people I questioned, the victim truly stuck to the straight and narrow." I took a seat myself and recounted to him the testimonies of the woman servant from Yangzhou, the proprietress of the dry-goods store, the old aunt, and Gao Youhui. "But puzzles still remain," I said to him. "Aside from the shoe, last night the woman servant next door heard bird calls." Then I told him what she had said.

Huo Sang thought it all over, then suddenly clapped his hands together. "Ah, that's terrific! That's really outstanding! Another confirmation of what I think happened!"

"What do you think happened?" I asked.

"It does, after all, have to do with that mysterious shoe."

"Say, could you be a little clearer? What exactly are you getting at?"

"You already know the general idea. The owner of the shoe is most likely one of the four I listed in my note." He took a Golden Dragon cigarette from his shirt pocket.

"That's right. I was just going to ask you how you settled on those four names."

"I went over to Grass Sandal Cove to look around. The Zhu family in No. 39 had had a marriage celebration the day before yesterday. And last night the groom's friends gathered again for a post-wedding dinner. I learned everything from visiting the Zhu family home to investigate." Huo Sang handed me a cigarette as he started to light up his own.

"How did you proceed?" I also lit up.

"That was simple. I found an old woman servant who's been with the family for a long time and asked her who among the younger male guests from the neighborhood were most fond of dressing up in fancy clothes and carousing. She was the one who gave me the four names."

"I don't quite understand how you could have thought of asking around at a family's wedding party."

"It was Wang Four who gave me the idea."

"Oh, that's right. I, too, heard what he said. But what made you think of questioning people at a family celebration? I'm still hazy about that."

"You still don't see? I wasn't grasping at straws. I had good reason."

"What good reason?"

"It was that shoe." He slowly let out a puff of smoke.

"The shoe led you to do this?"

Huo Sang straightened up and nodded. "Didn't you notice that the right side showed dark stains? The stains looked very much like the mud found in gutters. They suggest that someone unsteady on his feet had slipped into a gutter along the road. There were also some liquid stains on the shoe. You surely must have seen them too. I sniffed at them a couple of times. The smell of alcohol was strong, indicating that the stains were actually from spilled liquor. From this we can surmise that the shoe's owner had been unsteady on his feet because he was inebriated. But there are no restaurants nearby, and the scent of liquor on the shoe was fresh. I therefore reasoned that there might have been some sort of private dinner celebration in a neighborhood home. That's why I asked Wang Four about it."

At the time Huo Sang was talking to Wang, I had felt that asking about a nearby party was odd and out of the blue. But after his explanation, I could see that it was perfectly logical. This was yet another example of the meticulousness of Huo Sang's investigative procedures.

I puffed on my cigarette for a while. "You said the late-night bird calls I told you about corroborate what you think happened and that they are also related to the shoe. What is your theory? I'm still in a fog."

"Very elementary," said Huo Sang gravely. "I always thought that the shoe's owner had been there last night. When you mentioned that the Du's servant woman had heard the sounds of a thrush, it proved I was right."

"Oh? Then you think that little punk had gone upstairs?"

"As for *that*—," Huo Sang hesitated. "Good thing Ni Jinshou will find him soon. It'll be best to let him explain himself."

"So then you think Ni Jinshou is up to the task?"

"The man's a pretty careful operator, not like Fan Tong, who's so sure of himself. Unless I've been overestimating him, he'll surely be able to find the person."

"Then we'll probably be able to wrap up the case right away," I said happily.

"Yes. When we find the owner, at least all the questions surrounding the shoe will be resolved."

"What? Once we settle the matter of the shoe, won't the rest of the case be settled as well?" I was a bit surprised.

Huo Sang looked down. "No, it definitely cannot be as simple as Fan Tong thinks . . . no, definitely not," he mumbled. Then he waved his hand at me. "Don't ask me about that for now, Bao Lang. But, let me ask *you*, has Ni Jinshou found out where Wang Four went last night?"

"He has determined that Wang was telling the truth," I answered. "His wife said that he did go home last night, although his family was not expecting him."

"Hmm. I, too, thought he wasn't lying about that."

"Not only that. The victim did indeed urge the old aunt to go to Hongkou the day before yesterday."

"Right. This, too, is not surprising to me."

I was startled. How could he have anticipated every bit of new information I was relaying to him? On what was he basing his conjectures?

Huo Sang looked at me. "Bao Lang," he smiled, "you're still lost, aren't you? Fine. Let me do some explaining. Think about it. After the victim received the registered letter, she burned it. It's clear that there must have been some secret in it that she couldn't reveal. Don't you think so? That's why I realized right off that the reason she sent away all the people in the house and locked in the maidservant was to have a secret rendezvous there. That has now turned out to be true."

"You're saying that it was only after she received the letter that she began setting up the hush-hush get-together?"

"That's right. The letter is the key to the whole case."

"So then the person she was meeting was not that dandy who makes bird calls. I can see the little punk making a racket, but I can't imagine him sitting down to write a proper letter."

"Of course it's not him," Huo Sang said, shaking his head. He sat up to put his cigarette butt into the ashtray on the desk. "But if it were him, Fan Tong would be some kind of psychic."

"Right. For sure it's someone else." I thought a while, then said, "Judging from the victim's proper behavior in the past, the meeting must have had nothing to do with an illicit love affair, right?"

"That's absolutely correct, Bao Lang."

"Who was the visitor, then? Do you have an idea at this point?" I was anxious to unravel the mystery.

"It's hard to say." Huo Sang's eyebrows suddenly knitted together. "I only have a vague notion, something I can't as yet talk about."

So my effort was for naught. Past experience has taught me that I can never force Huo Sang to reveal anything until he thinks it is the right time to do so.

"Go ahead. Keep me in suspense. I can't help letting you in on a piece of important news, though." Having just thought of it, I hurriedly added the last sentence.

Taken aback, Huo Sang looked steadily at me. "What news? Has there been some new discovery?"

"Yes, yes. A most important discovery."

"Oh?"

"All of the victim's expensive gems and jewelry are gone. They are worth tens of thousands."

Huo Sang blinked. A look of puzzlement crossed his face. "How did you find out about this? Did Ni Jinshou look inside the box?"

"Yes he did, right in front of the old aunt. And even though the jewels were missing, the box was properly locked, and the key was in the dressing table drawer."

Huo Sang looked down for an instant before standing up quickly to stretch. Putting his hands behind his back, he took a few strides around the room when, all of a sudden, his face took on a look of happy surprise.

Then he started mumbling to himself once more. "Hmm. That's right. It is an important piece of news. Because of it what I conjectured has now been seventy or eighty percent confirmed. It probably won't be difficult to solve the case now." He quickly went back to the desk, picked up that day's newspaper, and ran his eyes over it. "Bao Lang, I've got to run. After your lunch, can you stay here for me and take any telegraph message that may come? I'll see you later."

"Oh? Where are you going?" I asked as he hurriedly put on his dark-gray tweed overcoat.

"I've got a lot to do right now," he answered. "I'm going over to the Gao residence, and then to the photography studio. Sorry. We'll talk later." Then he rushed out.

Because his words were so mysterious, and his actions so abrupt, I had no idea at the time just what was going on. Even though I had worked hard on the case myself, I was still in the dark as to the murderer or the motive. From Huo Sang's expression as he left, he seemed to be getting near to the answers but remained unwilling to express his thoughts. He's always had this odd trait of not wanting to reveal any part of a solution until he has the case completely settled. Even though he is characteristically cautious and unwilling to jump to conclusions, those who work with him cannot help feeling frustrated over being left uninformed.

At noontime, as I was eating by myself in the dining room, the phone rang. I put my lunch aside to answer it. The caller was Ni Jinshou, who, in great excitement, asked to speak with Huo Sang. I told him that Huo Sang had gone out but that I could take a message for him.

"I want to report to Mr. Huo that I have found the owner of the shoe," Ni told me. "I've also told Lieutenant Fan. The lieutenant sent out a large number of police officers to search here and there, with no results. Now, however, with the name and address I provided, he has picked up the little dandy and taken him to the South Station."

"Oh! Who's this person? How did you locate him?" I was delighted.

"He's indeed one of the four on the list. His name is Shen Yitian and he's the young chief at the Dahua Customs Brokerage, only twenty-one years old. His residence is Number 107 on the street behind Minsheng Middle School. He's a rather short fellow and, with his head of shiny, pomaded hair, looks every bit the dandy. When I found him, he was wearing a brand new pair of light-green embroidered satin shoes, so I knew he was probably the one. I got him to come out and engaged him in conversation while I sent someone inside his house to try to find that other shoe, which he might have kept around. It was just as I'd thought. We did find a left shoe with a light violet-blue satin vamp."

"Excellent! What did he have to say?"

"He wasn't forthcoming at first. But he's young, still not all that confident, and can therefore be intimidated. When he saw that we meant business and that we had the other shoe, he stopped trying to dance around the truth. He admitted having been at the Zhu residence for last night's post-wedding dinner party, playing drinking games, and generally raising a ruckus until after midnight. He drank too much, grew wobbly, and fell down as he was going out the door. His friends were concerned that he might fall again, so they called him a yellow cab and helped him inside. When the cab passed the front door of the Gao residence, he took off his right shoe without thinking and threw it onto the balcony. He said he did it because he was drunk, and that he didn't mean anything by it."

So that was it! The shoe got up there because it was tossed there by a drunk. What had seemed like a mind-boggling mystery was finally cleared up. Who could have guessed beforehand that it would turn out like this?

"Does he admit to any kind of relationship with the victim?" I asked further.

"He doesn't. He said that he had only admired her looks and had day-dreamed about her off and on. And he admitted that he had occasionally tried to catch her attention, but would own up to nothing else."

"Was he the one who was making those bird calls last night?"

"Yes, he didn't deny that at all. He said he's been able to imitate a thrush from the time he was little and does it often when he's feeling good. About midnight last night, as he was returning home from the Zhus', he saw all the lights on behind the windows of the Gao home. He told the driver to stop, pursed his lips, and let out two or three calls before impulsively taking off his shoe and tossing it up onto the balcony. A shadowy man then opened the window and looked down onto the road. Shen was frightened into momentary sobriety by this and told the driver to take him away."

"He never went upstairs?"

"Never. Lieutenant Fan questioned him a number of times about this, but he stuck to his guns."

"Then he would of course deny that he had anything to do with the murder?"

"That's right. We've interrogated him about it repeatedly, but he wouldn't budge at all on this. He said he could find the driver of the yellow cab to be his witness. It's for this reason that I'm calling Mr. Huo, to ask what we should do with this fellow."

"Fine. I'll let him know as soon as he gets back."

"Thanks, Mr. Bao."

"Hey, there's something else. If Shen Yitian said that he had only tossed the shoe up onto the balcony, then how come it was found later on the carpet in front of the bed?" I paused before asking another question. "Could it be that the man Shen Yitian saw brought it inside?"

"Yes, that *is* the question. In any case, someone has to have moved the shoe. Who could it have been? Was it the murderer? We still have to look into all of this." Ni Jinshou sounded a bit dejected. "So Mr. Bao, if we assume the pretty-boy was telling the truth, we still haven't determined who the murderer is, and the case can't be considered solved."

"That's right. But let me ask you, Jinshou, what is Lieutenant Fan saying now?"

"Him? At first he wanted to force Shen Yitian to admit guilt. But he knows that Mr. Huo is still involved, and his concern for what Mr. Huo might be thinking prevented him from acting on assumptions that have not panned out. Right now, he's as deflated as a punctured rubber ball. I asked him to come with me to consult with Mr. Huo, but he made all kinds of excuses not to. Actually, he's aware himself that he's gone too far with his big mouth to turn back. As for identifying the murderer, Mr. Bao, we'll still have to have Mr. Huo's help, won't we?"

"Yes, but don't you worry. Right at this moment, he's moving ahead on the matter."

The phone call made me glad, but it also unsettled me. I was glad that Huo Sang's conjectures had fortunately proven to be accurate; but I was uneasy about the fact that the murderer was still at large, since Shen Yitian had not confessed to the crime. Huo Sang had said just now that once this young fellow was in custody the issue of the shoe would be settled. But solving the homicide was another matter, as the facts had already shown. For now, Huo Sang was clearly occupied with the murderer, and, moreover, from what he had told me it appeared that he had a good idea of his identity. But I had yet to see what kind of case this really was. Was it a robbery? A love murder? Vengeance? To me, so much still remained so puzzling.

These persistent questions clouded my view of any final solution. Impatient as I was to have everything cleared up, I could do nothing but sit and wait for news from Huo Sang. The sun was obscured by dark clouds, and the weather was dreary and cold. I grabbed a fiction magazine and sat down by a window to read, but grew sleepy after a few pages. Shi Gui woke me just as I was dozing off. He had a telegram in his hand, one that needed a signature of receipt. The telegram was for Huo Sang, so I put his chop on it and opened it up. The sender was Jin Liren, the head detective of the police station in Hangzhou. The telegram said:

> COMMUNICATION RECEIVED. MAN DISAPPEARED
> YESTERDAY AFTERNOON. SEARCH UNDER WAY.
> DISAPPEARANCE AFFECTS SITUATION HERE AS WELL.
> JIN LIREN

VI. A Victim of the Times

Four p.m. came and went, but Huo Sang did not return. Not knowing where he was, I had no way of informing him about the telegram, which I concluded had to have some connection with the ongoing investigation. By leaving it sitting around here, was I missing some sort of opportunity?

The days were short now, it being early winter. Dark cottony clouds were covering the sky. Even before six in the evening, the house would turn gloomy and dark. About seven, Huo Sang finally came back, breathing hard. His eyes were gleaming as he took off his dark-gray overcoat.

"I'm really worn out today, Bao Lang," he said. "Please have Mrs. Su fix dinner right away. After that, let's go unwind at a movie at the Grand Theater."

He flopped down on a comfortable chair, stretched out his legs, and wiped the sweat from his face with a white handkerchief before striking a match to light a cigarette. How could he be so nonchalant as to want to see a movie, I was thinking to myself. Could he have already determined who the murderer was?

"How's the investigation going, Huo Sang? Have you come to a solution of the case?" I asked as I sat myself down in a chair opposite him.

Huo Sang shook his head.

"Then why are you in the mood for taking a break?" I questioned him as I took out a cigarette of my own.

"Well, most of the case can be considered solved. We can at least say that we've done well for our friend."

"If that's so, you ought to let Ni Jinshou know so that he can calm down. Just now he phoned here—"

"Yes, I've already seen him. At the moment, he's busy trying to take the murderer into custody," said Huo Sang before I could finish my sentence.

"Take the murderer into custody? This soon?" I was a bit incredulous.

He nodded.

"So, the case *has* been solved."

"Until the murderer is in our hands, we can't quite say that. Nor can we consider everything over and done with."

"What kind of person is this murderer then?"

Huo Sang stopped to stare at me. "Take a guess, Bao Lang." He let out several puffs of smoke.

I thought before responding. "How can I come up with anything? I can't even decide what the motive was."

"The truth is quite obvious. You ought to have figured it out by now."

Was he deliberately keeping me in suspense? Or was he testing me? I believed it was probably a mixture of both.

"Was it a robbery?"

"Mm, yes—uh, no."

"What the . . . ?"

"The robbery is linked to the crime, but it wasn't the principal motive. So, strictly speaking, it can't be considered a jewelry theft."

"So then it's a love murder after all?"

"No. You yourself have already found that out. The woman was a proper lady, as everyone has testified. And it's clear that the little punk Shen Yitian's infatuation with her was one-sided."

"Oh? Are you saying then that it was really a case of getting even?"

"Not that either. In fact, you're getting colder."

I was at the end of my rope. I felt like thousands of ants were gnawing my insides and could no longer stand it. Huo Sang, however, was coolly dragging on his cigarette, his eyes half closed. He was stringing me along for as long as he could!

I exhaled a series of puffs. "Huo Sang," I said, "I'm ready to give up! Please tell me the final solution!"

Huo Sang put down his cigarette. "What's this?" he smiled. "You're getting upset? Are you saying that you really don't know the killer is the victim's husband?"

"What? So Gao Youzhi is the murderer?" I was shaken.

Huo Sang merely nodded as he slowly released another puff of smoke.

"What about motive?" I wanted to know.

"It was a misunderstanding."

I straightened up. "A misunderstanding—?"

"That's right," he interrupted. "Since it was the husband who did it, many of the details remain hidden. The murderer has not yet been apprehended, so even though I'm confident my theory is essentially correct, it's bad practice to reveal it ahead of time. On the other hand, if I remain silent, you will surely accuse me of deliberately tantalizing you. Isn't that so, Bao Lang?" He let out a few chuckles.

I relaxed a bit. The truth was that these revelations were far, far beyond anything I had expected, and I really couldn't have endured being kept in the dark any longer.

"You're so right, Huo Sang," I said. "Now can I ask you to break your own rule and give me a preliminary explanation? At least you could let me know what you've learned from your investigations."

Huo Sang nodded and flashed me a smile. "Fine. I'll tell you, I'll tell you." He discarded the butt in his hand and settled himself comfortably into his chair.

"There's basically nothing all that mysterious about the case. It only seemed so because of that shoe, which distracted everyone's attention and nearly led the investigation down the wrong path. Fortunately, I was able to break through that initial obstacle right away and not be sucked into a morass. Just consider the situation: If the killer was someone with whom the victim was well acquainted, then she must have let him into her room voluntarily. We can draw two immediate conclusions about the fatal wound. First, the weapon was the kind of utility knife people carry around, which tells us that the killing was not premeditated as much as it was a spur-of-the-moment act. That, in turn, indicates that it probably wasn't a case of a love triangle, in which hurt feelings bring about murderous intentions. Also, as the killer well knew, there was no third person in the room—Xiangling, remember, had been locked in. Neither was there any outcry, nor even the slightest indication of a struggle. So he had little reason to panic and hence to lose a shoe unintentionally. If you were to insist that he did leave it on purpose, then you'd be saying that he was deliberately providing evidence against himself in order to facilitate his own arrest. I don't think such a stupid person exists in the entire world. For these reasons, I thought at the time that there were only two possible explanations for why the shoe had been left there. One was that it had been left by accident. Remember the traces of alcohol on it; a drunk's actions often defy common logic. The second was that the killer had done this to mislead us, to make us think the homicide was the result of an adulterous affair. So, in either case, the shoe was definitely not the killer's. In other words, as the shoe's owner could not be the perpetrator of the crime, we would have to consider other possibilities."

"Looking at it this way then," I said, " the shoe was simply an obstacle to the solution, because it wasn't connected to the crime at all. For his fixating on the shoe as unshakeable proof of a love murder—well, couldn't we now call *Fan* Tong a *fan*atical *fan*tasizer?"

"No, that's not so either. I can't say for sure right now, but I believe that, while the shoe appears to be unconnected in one sense, in another it is perhaps the key to the entire case. Fan Tong's conclusion may be totally unfounded, but accidentally he might have touched on something significant."

"Hmm. What are you getting at?" I was lost again.

"Why don't we set that point aside for now," said Huo Sang. "Let me first recount to you all that happened during my search for the real killer. The most intriguing thing about this case is the fact that the victim sent two people away from the house and then confined Xiangling in her room—the key having been found in a drawer of her dressing table, she must have locked the girl in herself—all in preparation for a clandestine meeting with someone. This someone, then, was without doubt a major player in the case. Who was he? Could he have been the victim's lover? But Wang Four and the maidservant have both told us that the victim seldom ventured out, and never paid attention to the come-ons of those unruly youths. I also noticed she had relatively few cosmetics on her dressing table, and that the clothes and shoes she wore were modest, quite unlike what a seductive woman would wear. At the time, this really threw me into a quandary. But then I hypothesized that the reason for the secret meeting had to do with the letter that had been burned. So the letter became the leading clue in the search for the person the victim was planning to meet. Wang Four said that when it arrived, he had asked her to put her chop on it. That shows the letter must have been registered or was sent via special delivery. When I left the Gao residence, therefore, I made my inquiries at Grass Sandal Cove and then headed straight for the post office. I wanted to find out where the letter had come from and who had sent it.

"As you know, any piece of mail needing proof of receipt must be recorded at the post office. When I inquired there, I learned that, indeed, there had been a special delivery letter for Ding Fangzhu the day before yesterday, and that it had been sent by her husband, Gao Youzhi, from the Bank of Hangzhou. I didn't quite understand right away. Why would a husband's visit home be such a clandestine matter? Why would the victim have needed to send off her manservant and aunt, and even lock in her maid? Could it be that she was after all an adulteress who was secretly preparing to murder her husband? The facts, on the other hand, did not seem to indicate this. So, Bao Lang, it was another conundrum. Can you explain it?"

Huo Sang paused to light up another Golden Dragon. He leaned back in his chair, eyes shut, slowly savoring the tobacco. He was clearly waiting for my explanatory response. It was another test, but I felt this question was not as difficult as the previous one.

"Perhaps the husband had an important matter to take care of," I guessed, "something that required him to keep this particular visit confidential. So his wife got busy right after receiving his letter, preparing for his clandestine arrival."

"You guessed it, Bao Lang!" Huo Sang's eyes suddenly popped open. "I, too, thought so at the time, but then I went a step further. From the letter Gao Youzhi had sent home three weeks previously I discerned the nature of the important matter you're referring to. You've got to be aware that, in current times, the stock market in Shanghai has been experiencing sudden waves of volatility. In one exchange after another, prices have doubled and redoubled in a single day, like bamboo shoots after the rain. So many people have been sucked into the trap. But then, in another blink, prices would start to plunge, sometimes all the way to rock bottom. Those who were duped out of all their financial resources have had no way to recover. So one by one they jump into the Huangpu River,[6] or else they go to the empty lot behind the Great World Amusement Park to hang themselves!"

That was indeed the situation at the time; the papers had been reporting such frightful stories each and every day. That Huo Sang was lamenting the situation in this way suggested a direct connection between the case and what had been happening in the stock market. Sure enough, he went on.

"Since Gao Youzhi is a bank manager, he is likely to be involved in stock investments. He said in the earlier letter that he had recently made fifty thousand dollars in stocks. But buying and selling stocks amounts to nothing more than gambling. Some rich tycoon manipulates the situation behind the scenes; wild gains and steep losses become everyday occurrences. You make a hundred thousand today, lose a million tomorrow. It's all taken in stride,

6. See note 1 to the story "On the Huangpu" (Chap. 5, p. 126).

looked upon as part of the game. Gao Youzhi, though, had probably suffered losses beyond his ability to cover them. Not brave enough to kill himself, he could only try to run away. The trip home, therefore, had to be planned out, kept strictly secret. When this occurred to me, I immediately sent a telegram to Jin Liren in the Hangzhou police station, requesting that he keep an eye on Gao Youzhi's movements—"

"Ah, yes," I cut in. "I forgot about that. I still haven't shown you the telegram from Detective Jin." I pointed to the desk. "It's in the top drawer."

Huo Sang took it out and looked it over. "Hmm. Even though I never saw this before, I could have easily guessed what it says. Because when I heard you tell me that jewelry worth tens of thousands had vanished although the jewelry box was still locked, I could see that my hunch was not unfounded. So I went back to the Gao residence once again and, after a brief conversation with Gao Youhui, secured a photograph of Gao Youzhi. Then I took it over to the Realistic Photo Studio and asked the express service there to print out multiple copies so that once the telegram from Hangzhou reached us, we could distribute the likeness to the police in each station to facilitate their search. I surmised that, after the murder last night, Gao Youzhi probably wouldn't be able to get away from Shanghai in time. I read in the papers that a passenger ship is due to sail to Japan this evening. With his wife's jewelry to pay for his passage, he may very well be planning to leave the country."

"Can you think of any way to stop him?"

"Well, maybe we're not too late. After leaving the photo studio, I returned to the Gao residence. There I learned that Gao Youhui had just received an express reply from the Bank of Hangzhou informing him that his brother was not in the city. So what I surmised had proven correct. Then I returned to the studio to pick up the copies of the photograph and rushed over to the police station to hand them over to Ni Jinshou. Right now, he's busy trying to apprehend the man."

"Why, after all, did Gao Youzhi want to kill his wife? You've yet to give me an answer to this question," I asked after a period of silence.

"I've already said that it was mostly due to a misunderstanding. Once Gao Youzhi is apprehended, the answer will be clear sooner or later."

"What kind of 'misunderstanding'? I still don't understand. Why don't you go ahead and give me your hypothesis."

"It's all about that shoe!" Huo Sang stood up as he answered. "Mrs. Su! Is dinner ready yet? Bao Lang, let's eat quickly. We can still make the nine fifteen movie. We'll talk at length later."

WHEN WE returned home from the Grand Theatre, Ni Jinshou was waiting in our office. He provided us with a most comprehensive report. The remaining details of the case are as follows.

Ni and his fellow officers arrested Gao Youzhi at the train station. Gao knew then that he had been found out. His knife, with its four-inch blade, was still in his pocket; he hadn't been able to bring himself to get rid of it. Traces of blood remained on his sleeves. He was feeling pangs of conscience as well, so he quickly confessed. He said that he had suffered losses in his investments, which he'd covered from bank funds. Once the discrepancy became too great, and he had no way to balance his accounts, he made up his mind to flee. He wrote to his wife Fangzhu to set up a clandestine meeting with her before running off to Beijing to see if he could borrow some money. He'd been home just half an hour, when quite unexpectedly he heard strange calls from outside. Alarmed, he went to the balcony to look out. Sure enough, he saw a yellow taxicab with a young man inside who, once he realized he had been seen, ordered the cabbie to drive off. At the same time, Gao discovered a suspicious shoe on the balcony. He asked his wife and she said she knew nothing about it, even though she appeared both shaken and embarrassed by the inquiry. In his agitation, he was unable to think clearly and mistakenly concluded that his wife had taken up with someone. Now that she had learned he'd had to come home in secret, he thought she would likely inform her lover and he would be trapped. He grew frightened and, concerned for his own welfare, disregarded that of anyone else. As you well know, those who dedicate themselves to profit making are vicious and coldhearted. He stealthily took out his large utility knife and ended Fangzhu's life before she knew what was happening. After moving her body, he decided to place the shoe in front of the bed to make people think the killing was the result of an illicit liaison. Then he opened up the jewelry box to remove the contents and, seeing the letter he had sent inserted between the pages of the novel on the desk, took it out and burned it before leaving the scene.

The veil over the case was thus lifted. I felt like I was finally emerging from my fog to see the light of day. That shoe, which had seemed connected and then not connected to the crime, had turned out to be an important key to its solution after all. The behavior of the young dandy, I felt, should not be lightly dismissed.

"I did make one mistake," Huo Sang added in a regretful tone. "That special delivery letter came the day before yesterday. Had the victim been conscientious about keeping the visit confidential, she would have burned it immediately, in which case the ashes would not have remained there until today. It was really careless of me simply to assume that the victim herself had burned the letter."

"Mr. Huo," said Ni Jinshou, "each and every one of your deductions has been right on the mark. You have no peer. I really can't express to you how grateful I am. One little miscalculation does not detract at all from all that you have done. You need not feel any regret whatsoever."

I sighed. "It's really unthinkable that the primary cause of a murder could hinge to this extent on happenstance. We can see now that the victim was indeed a good, decent woman. It's a pity she was killed in error like that by a husband overpowered by the scent of money. So, Huo Sang, how would you assess culpability in this case?"

"You're right, it's really regrettable that this tidal wave of speculation in the stock market, with big fish gobbling up little fish, eventually swelled to drown this woman as well. Her death is really too heartrending." Huo Sang, too, let out a sigh. "As for culpability, I think that, aside from her avaricious and heartless husband, that young punk Shen Yitian deserves some serious punishment. But that's all a matter of law. Jinshou, I assume you'll see that justice is carried out in this case."

Ni Jinshou stood up and nodded. "Yes, Mr. Huo. You can rest assured. When the case goes before the court, this unconscionable little hoodlum will not be let off lightly. But it's late now, and it's getting chilly. Both of you should get some rest."

② The Other Photograph

I. A Secret Photograph

> Attractive man, 26, high school graduate, family of
> some means, seeks modern, educated woman, about
> 20. Interested parties please write to P.O. Box 167 to
> arrange face-to-face meeting. Wedding plans to fol-
> low if mutually agreeable.

Such personal advertisements for potential marriage partners were appearing almost daily in the newspapers. There were even ads for women seeking husbands—sufficient in themselves to catch the attention of many a young man. Yet this phenomenon should not be considered rare in our twentieth-century civilization, especially in light of current notices such as: "Mr. X and Miss Y have announced that they will begin living together on such-and-such a date," or "Mr. X and Miss Y will be dissolving their cohabitation agreement on such-and-such a date." They clearly show what has become socially acceptable in this day and age. Fifty or sixty years ago, anyone would have been utterly amazed to read such public announcements.

After looking over the news and features in the paper that day, I felt really restless and turned to the personal ads. But I quickly found that they, too, held little interest for me. Tossing the paper aside, I took my cigarettes out of my pocket and lit up. Then I started thinking to myself how marriage had really become a most difficult problem in these "modern" times. The feudalistic practices of marriage by barter or compulsion or parental arrangement—sometimes even before birth—were of course completely unacceptable. But now, self-appointed modernizers had turned conjugal bonds into a farce, where couples could get together on a whim one day and split apart on a whim the next. Such people turn falling in love into a game, and lack any fundamental respect for marriage as an institution. As marriage breaks down, can the family endure? If we abandon the family as well, what sort of society will we have? Is this where human evolution is taking us? Or are we actually regressing? What's more—

"There's no reason to be so serious, Bao Lang. You ought to know that once a massive dike that has held for thousands of years is broken down by overwhelming waves of modern thought, it inevitably releases a powerful burst of wild crosscurrents. So what's the use of getting worked up about it?"

These words came from my old friend Huo Sang who, having just come back from his habitual morning stroll, was seated comfortably on the cushioned rattan chair by the window, puffing on a cigarette.

I looked up at him. "What do you mean by that, Huo Sang?"

"I'm talking about you. You still don't get it? Weren't you just sighing over those notices about couples living together and breaking up? The notices are actually nothing but a waste of time. And for you to be upset by them is to waste *your* time over a waste of time."

"There you go again, trying to guess what's on my mind."

Huo Sang let out a puff. "Why would I need to guess? It was so obvious. I'd read the notices in today's paper and saw you frown, then shake your head and sigh, when you got to that page. After that, you tossed the paper aside and stared vacantly. I well know that the old moralities have left their residue in your brain, so I concluded that you were once again troubling yourself over nothing."

I responded to his smile with my own but did not bother to carry on the discussion. Among Huo Sang's strong points was his ability to see into a person's mind. Just from observing outward expressions and actions he could discern a person's inner musings and thought processes. That he had clearly grasped what I was turning over in my mind just then was hardly unusual.

We both lapsed into momentary silence, enshrouded in a smoky haze, when Shi Gui pushed the door open and came in. "You have a visitor, Mr. Huo," he quietly announced. "It's a young woman who wants to see you alone."

Huo Sang stood up and put down his cigarette as he walked out the office door. "Please come in," he greeted the caller.

I, too, rose from my chair as a slender young lady of seventeen or eighteen looked around the room nervously before hesitantly stepping inside.

It was early fall at the time. The woman had on a padded, dark-colored silk vest, from which extended light-purple satin sleeves. On her legs she wore light-gray silk stockings and dark-brown high-heeled shoes. Overall, her appearance was elegant without being flashy. Her face was oval, the shape of a melon seed, with an extremely fair complexion and sparkling eyes. A curl hung over one corner of her forehead above two slender eyebrows that reminded one of willow leaves. One could imagine that the dimples in her smooth, jade-like cheeks would make her even more alluring when she smiled. At that moment, however, her face was not showing the slightest hint of a smile. To the contrary, fear and uncertainty were written all over it.

I immediately assumed that she had some misgiving about my presence, since she had asked to see Huo Sang by himself. So as soon as she came in, I bowed slightly toward her and made ready to take my leave. Huo Sang, however, pulled a chair over and nodded for her to take it.

"Please have a seat, miss," he said. "I imagine you have some kind of worrisome problem to tell me about. But Mr. Bao Lang here is my good friend, someone I've always worked and consulted with even on highly confidential matters. You can speak frankly and trust the two of us to keep whatever you say to ourselves."

Huo Sang's words were clearly intended to have a double effect—not just to explain the situation to her, but also to let me know that I need not make myself scarce. The woman gave a quick bow and sat down, while I returned to my chair. To tell the truth, this pretty and dignified young lady had made a good first impression on me. The thought of her being in some kind of trouble stirred my sympathies and made me want to help her. But then a contrary thought came to my mind.

I remembered the case of "The Demonic Power," which I had written about a few years back. In that case, I had at first been overwhelmingly sympathetic to the woman Miss Qi before finding out that she was a despicable swindler. Recalling this reminded me that it was very dangerous to rely on first impressions and that I should be a bit more skeptical. So I took up the role of objective bystander, quietly utilizing my powers of observation. The visitor appeared to be the daughter from a traditional household. She might well have received a modern education, but it was evident that she had never broken away from the influence of her parents, and therefore could not be considered basically "liberated."

"Mr. Huo, I believe anything you say would definitely be trustworthy," she said in a lilting voice. "But because this matter affects not only my own future but the good name of my whole family, I have to be extremely discreet."

"You need not worry," Huo Sang responded. "Whatever your problem is, we would never violate your confidence. Please forgive me if I'm too forward, but isn't your problem concerned with an impending wedding?"

The lady's cheeks suddenly took on a deep-red hue, and she involuntarily lowered her head. It was clear to me she had a lot on her mind. In her momentary embarrassment, she wasn't quite self-possessed enough to give a quick answer. So my earlier observation was probably on the mark. No "liberated" woman would show this kind of discomfort on the subject of marriage.

Only after an awkward pause was she able to lift her head and tell us about herself and her family background. In order to honor our agreement of confidentiality, however, I have had to alter certain facts here, for which I must beg the reader's indulgence.

Let us call her Gu Yingfen, and her father Gu Zhibai. He had been a government official, but had been retired for many years by the time of the case. The family had originally resided in Yuyao City in Zhejiang Province before moving to a place on Bubbling Well Road in Shanghai three years before. She had an older brother who was working for lawyers from their home province.

"Mr. Huo, I first have to tell you a confidential story about my late sister, Yingfang," she said as she tried to suppress the grief welling up in her. "But, oh, to tell it still brings such pain to my heart! Four years ago, my sister met this scoundrel from home by the name of Wang Zhisheng; because she had been taught at home by a tutor, she had no experience of the real world. When she met this wicked man at our late aunt's house, she became so infatuated that, in an irrational moment, she agreed to run off with him. This one act led to numerous tragic consequences for my family. We looked everywhere for her without finding a trace. My mother was so grief stricken that she died within a couple of months. My father and brother suffered such humiliation and anger from local gossip that they decided to move here, feeling they could no longer bear to remain in our hometown."

She let out a huge sigh. Great anger was evident in her voice. Huo Sang listened in rapt attention, a serious expression on his face. I was also focused on what she was saying, expecting further drama in her story. Gu Yingfen dabbed at her mouth with a white handkerchief before continuing.

"A year after that, I saw an article in the paper about a woman in Hankou[1] who had killed herself by jumping into the Yangtze River. A picture was included. Her height and general appearance were those of my sister. I thought then that my sister must have been abandoned by Wang Zhisheng and killed herself because she was ashamed to come home. I didn't dare relay this news to my father, as he had vowed never to lay eyes on her again. I was afraid he would be overly distraught by anger and grief. I still don't really know what happened to my sister's remains."

A series of sighs followed. Dark shadows seemed to linger on her powdered cheeks, and her eyes reddened. Huo Sang, however, remained silent.

"That was three years ago," she went on. "We had gradually begun to get over it. Then, last month, I became engaged to Jin Xueming. When it was announced in the papers, the same insidious curse now came down on *me*. Oh, Mr. Huo. That terrible Wang Zhisheng has shown up once again!"

Gu Yingfen's face turned deathly pale. Dread showed in her eyes, which were brimming with tears. It was as if some horrific demon had suddenly appeared before her.

"Has this person been to see you?" asked Huo Sang, visibly moved.

"Yes," Gu Yingfen nodded. "I ran into him unexpectedly on my way home from school a week ago. My immediate impulse was to try to avoid him, thinking at first that he hadn't seen me. But he did see me and followed me to my house on Bubbling Well Road. The next day he was waiting to speak with me when I came out the front door. He told me he had seen the announcement of

1. A city in Hubei Province in central China at the confluence of the Han and Yangtze Rivers west of Shanghai. Connected physically with Wuchang and Hanyang since 1957, the three cities are now known collectively as Wuhan.

my engagement in the paper. Then he took out a photograph to show me. It was of him and my sister, taken in Shanghai after she'd run off with him. I asked him where my sister was, and he said she'd fallen ill and died. Then I asked where she was buried, but he wouldn't give me a straight answer. It was then that I became certain that what I thought had happened to my sister really *had* happened. But I was so afraid of him that I rushed back into my house rather than continue the conversation.

"I then turned the whole matter over in my mind, without daring in the end to say anything to anyone. What Wang Zhisheng had done—ultimately bringing about my sister's death—should be punishable by law. But the whole matter has not been mentioned since we moved. To bring him to legal justice would inevitably affect the good name of my father and brother and be very hard on them. My father is elderly; he definitely wouldn't be able to stand this kind of trauma. So I have to keep matters to myself. Then a note came for me yesterday afternoon. That was when I realized the man will not be satisfied just with having ruined my sister's life; he's out to ruin mine as well!"

Her voice trembled and her breathing quickened. I couldn't imagine a young woman like her reacting in this way if she were not telling us the truth. My sympathies were thus further stirred.

"Is it an extortion note?" Huo Sang asked.

Gu Yingfen shook her head as she put her hand into her gold-embroidered purse to take something out. "I can't really say what this is. Please read it for yourself, Mr. Huo."

As she handed the folded piece of paper to Huo Sang, I quickly went over to read it as well. The note was written on Western-style stationery with a fountain pen. The script was vigorous and elegant, apparently from the hand of one who had been trained in calligraphy. The message was extremely brief—just a couple of sentences. It was unsigned.

Please go to the Gardener's Gazebo in Banhong Park at 10:00 a.m. tomorrow morning, where good news will be conveyed to you. The matter concerns your future marriage, so do not waste the opportunity by declining. 16 October

Huo Sang read the message several times. Then he stared at the stationery, lost in thought.

"The note was received by our servant, Mrs. Cai, sent by special delivery. Even though there's no signature, I'm certain it came from that wicked man. There's no one else in the world who would write me a message like that. What do you think his intention is, Mr. Huo?"

Huo Sang gave no indication that he had heard her question; his eyes continued to seem magnetically affixed to that piece of paper.

"From what I can figure," she went on nevertheless, "he must have had a reason for showing me that photo the other day. It was taken three or four years ago. My sister and I very much resembled each other; the image of my sister in that photograph looks just like me now. Perhaps he's thinking of using the picture to blackmail me. Don't you think that's possible, Mr. Huo?"

Huo Sang seemed to collect himself. "That's possible," he answered. "Since you say no one else would want to make trouble for you, the note most likely came from him. I can't fathom his purpose right now, but there's no doubt he's plotting something evil."

"You're indeed right, Mr. Huo," said Yingfen. "What, then, do you think I should do?"

Huo Sang lowered his head, appearing to be deep in thought, and did not answer immediately. I wanted to interject a few ideas of my own but held my tongue, thinking it would be too forward of me to say anything at the moment.

Gu Yingfen, though, had much more to say. "Mr. Huo, I spent all last night thinking about it. Although it wouldn't be good to meet him, if I ignore him, I'm worried that he will make our private business public and thus ruin my wedding plans. My fiancé, Jin Xueming, works in educational circles, where maintaining a good reputation is absolutely necessary. Even though our engagement came about through free choice, once he hears about this skeleton in our family closet, the engagement will most likely be called off. And that's not all. My sister's rash decision did more than bring about my mother's death; it was a huge blow to my father as well. If I bring further disgrace to the family, the effect on my father and brother will be quite unimaginable. Oh, Mr. Huo! I'm in such a quandary about whether or not to act on this note. When I was at my wit's end I thought of you, a righteous person who is quick to help those in need. I thought that you could surely show me a way to protect my own future and my family's good name."

Huo Sang looked up suddenly. "You're right, Miss Gu. This note makes things difficult whether you heed it or ignore it. Because the man has something he can use to hurt you, and you're afraid he might do just that, we cannot meet him head-on. Neither can we solve the problem by ignoring him."

"What are we to do then, Mr. Huo?" The tone of her voice betrayed her desperation.

Huo Sang remained calm. "Don't you worry, Miss Gu," he said. "There has to be a way out. Let me ask you, though: What kind of person is this Wang Zhisheng? Do you know anything about his personal history or family background?"

Yingfen reflected before giving her answer. "He was my late aunt's neighbor. His father was Wang Boren, a classical scholar in name who was actually a crooked lawyer seeking personal gain through questionable litigations. Anyone in Yuyao City who had dealings with him came away with a headache. Wang Zhisheng took full advantage of his father's notoriety and was considered a spoiled brat. He was actually a shiftless scoundrel as well. After his father died, he came to Shanghai to study law with the goal of becoming a lawyer too. When my sister met him, he had just graduated and returned home. He's very much like his father, having the formidable gift of being able to twist anything to his advantage. My sister fell under his spell and ended up losing her life!" At this point, her voice quavered.

Huo Sang started to mumble to himself. "Hmm. He's an intellectual, is he? Then we'll have to be extra careful in dealing with him." He hesitated just a bit before addressing Yingfen. "Miss Gu, I think it will be all right for you to accept his invitation. Let's see where he's headed before we take any steps of our own."

Gu Yingfen was reluctant. "Do I have to go by myself? I hear that Banhong Park is rather deserted. The meeting is supposed to be in the morning, when there are even fewer visitors than usual. I'm very concerned—"

"No need to be," Huo Sang didn't wait for her to finish. "Since the meeting will take place in broad daylight, I don't think he'll go so far as to attempt anything outrageous."

Gu Yingfen still looked unconvinced. "I just can't feel safe dealing with that man."

Seeing that she was still so nervous, I thought the time was ripe for me to involve myself.

"If that's so," I jumped in to say, "I wouldn't mind going along with you."

She turned her pretty eyes toward me. Her dimpled cheeks reddened slightly as her face took on an expression of shy gratitude. But she didn't respond right away.

"Of course I would do so surreptitiously," I went on. "It should look like you're by yourself. But if he tries anything improper, you can be sure I won't let any harm come to you."

Huo Sang then chimed in. "Great," he said. "That's a very good idea. I, too, want to see what this fellow looks like."

Gu Yingfen was somewhat reassured. "All right," she said. "But it's already after nine right now. Shouldn't we be on our way?"

Huo Sang disagreed. "No, we shouldn't all go there together. You go on home first. You needn't be on time for the meeting. In fact, you ought to show up a bit late. Mr. Bao should be there ahead of you, in order not to arouse suspicion."

Gu Yingfen assented and, with a quick word of thanks to Huo Sang, stood up to leave. She nodded in my direction as if to tell me not to forget the appointment. I bowed to indicate that I understood.

II. Behind the Gardener's Gazebo

I have had quite a bit of experience with bizarre meeting arrangements, but this one was exceptional in that I had no idea whatsoever about what would result from it. In order to be prepared for every eventuality, I took along a handgun, just in case.

"You'll have to change your clothes and start out ahead of me," Huo Sang told me. "Find an inconspicuous place for yourself, where you will escape notice."

"Fine," I said, "but are you planning to be there as well?"

"Yes," he answered. "I, too, want to go take a look at this Wang Zhisheng, to find out what kind of person he really is. I can't go with you, though. You hurry up and get yourself over there first."

Five minutes later, I had dressed myself as a gardener. As I was leaving, I noticed that Huo Sang was going into the laboratory even as he nodded at me in approval of my disguise.

My cab stopped near the gate of Banhong Park; my pocket watch showed it was only 9:35. Another vehicle was already there. Had Wang Zhisheng arrived ahead of me?

I bought an entrance ticket and walked along the winding pathway that led into the interior. The place was completely devoid of visitors. Other than the chirping of birds from the treetops above and the rustle of the windblown leaves near the roots below, no other noises—certainly not the din of city traffic—could be heard. Gentle breezes blew, carrying the scent of chrysanthemums. This kind of early-morning atmosphere was surely beyond anything the late-rising denizens of Shanghai could have imagined. The meandering trail led me through gaps between flowering trees, around a small man-made hill, and toward Gardener's Gazebo. I recalled that it faced the hill and would be immediately visible once I got around to the other side. No one was in the gazebo, so I concluded that Wang Zhisheng must have yet to arrive; the car I'd spotted outside the park must have brought someone else there. I must have been unnecessarily jittery.

I stopped near the gazebo, looking for a place to conceal myself. The hill opposite, thickly planted with chrysanthemums and yellow hollyhocks, seemed to be a good hiding place. But it was somewhat far off, so I might not be able to get to the gazebo in time should I be needed in a hurry. To the east of the hill was a small grove of willow trees, the drooping branches of which were thick enough to hide behind, but it also was too far away. Then I saw that there were several tall rock formations behind the gazebo, as well as a stone fence about shoulder high. This was the ideal hiding place, just three to four meters away and close enough to hear any conversation. So I quickly squatted behind the rocks, first making sure no one was around.

My watch indicated a quarter to ten. Peeping out with just one eye, I could see anything that went on in the gazebo. I felt an indescribable excitement deep inside, a feeling I had experienced many times before without quite being able to put it into words. Perhaps it was like the feeling a fisherman gets when, pole in hand, he sees a big fish slowly swimming toward his bobber.

Three or four minutes later, I heard the crunch of leather soles on the gravel path behind the man-made hill. My heart pounded even harder. In that instant, something came into my line of vision. A young man in a Western suit walked around the side of the hill. Wasn't he surely Wang Zhisheng? He went to the front of the gazebo before turning around to look inside. After taking out and glancing at his gold pocket watch, he walked up to it. At that point I was certain my premonitions had been on the mark.

The man was twenty-six or -seven, and he was sturdily built, even imposing. He had a darkish complexion, a very prominent nose, and flashing eyes. His brand-new suit was of light-gray flannel, and he wore black leather shoes. A gold watch fob hung from his vest pocket, with a pair of pendants, each made from a pound sterling, which clinked together as he walked. His apparel appeared attractive enough, but an artificial fragrance also wafted over on the wind, incontrovertible evidence that he had splashed himself with an excess of cologne. He looked excited, fanning himself vigorously with the gray fedora in his hand as he looked back and forth from one side of the man-made hill to the other.

What I saw confirmed my assumptions. I thought the young man had to be Wang Zhisheng, and that I should take care not to be seen by his searching eyes.

He sat down on a porcelain drum inside the gazebo, as if he were prepared to wait patiently for whomever he was there to meet. But just five minutes later, he was up again, looking at his watch. His lips were moving, though I couldn't tell what he was saying. Was it some expression of impatience? Actually, it was still only five minutes to ten, surely too early for him to lose patience. He continued to stand up and sit down for another seven or eight minutes, as if he could not bear waiting any longer. He walked down from the gazebo and around the hill to the left, quickly disappearing behind it. Because he had thus left my field of vision, I could not help feeling quite uneasy. Had he left because he was tired of waiting? If so, then Gu Yingfen would come here in vain later on. I, too, would have gone through all this for nothing.

Then the tip-tap of high-heeled shoes could be heard from the right side of the hill. So Gu Yingfen was here. She was dressed as she had been earlier, but apprehension was evident on her face. With every step she took, she kept looking right and left. When she drew near the gazebo and saw that it was empty, she stopped, uncertain about what to do next. She forced herself to go up the steps before taking a quick look at her wristwatch and stopping again. I saw her turn around, then lower her head to consider what to do next. It appeared that, since the time of the appointment had passed and Wang Zhisheng was nowhere in sight, she was about to leave. Agitation welled up in me once more. The man really had been there, even though I didn't know where he had gone. But since I couldn't very well speak to her at that moment, I felt completely helpless.

Fortunately, faint clinking sounds and the crunch of leather soles on gravel again reached my ears. The young man in Western attire reemerged from the right side of the hill. I saw Gu Yingfen, who was hesitating in front of the gazebo, begin to come down. When she looked up and saw him, she stopped in her tracks. The young man ran up to her and extended his right hand, as if in greeting. She ignored his gesture but turned to walk back up the steps to the gazebo. The man followed her with a smile on his face.

"Are you Miss Gu Yingfen?" he asked, panting. "My, you're really pretty!"

His voice was rather loud, so I could hear it clearly. As he was speaking, he again stuck out his rough, oversized hand, as if he really wanted to clutch Gu Yingfen's delicate one. Embarrassed and frightened, Gui Yingfen quickly put both of her hands behind her back.

"Who in the world are you?" she asked with a serious look. "And what do you think you're doing!"

Her reaction was so unexpected it surprised me. Could all my assumptions have been wrong? Was this man, then, not Wang Zhisheng? Why else would she be asking those questions? I remained behind the rocks, quietly taking in what was going on. The woman's forbidding look threw cold water on the man's initial eagerness, but the smile never left his face.

"I'm Yang Chunbo," he said. "Even though we have never met face to face, I'm sure my name is already fixed in your heart!"

The situation had changed. The man was Yang Chunbo, not Wang Zhisheng. Yingfen didn't know him, but he seemed to know who she was. I really had no idea what this was all about.

"I don't know who you are!" Gu Yingfen said in a sharp voice.

She looked all around the gazebo, obviously seeking help. What was I to do? Obviously, the matter had taken another turn. Should I show myself and do something about it then? Surely not. I had no choice but to control my impulses for the moment and learn more before I intruded. The man who called himself Yang Chunbo fiddled with the pair of pendants on his fob chain before he spoke again.

"Why are you toying with me, Miss Gu?" he said. "There's nobody else here now, so you don't have to act like this."

Yingfen's face reddened, then paled; she was clearly in great distress. She fingered the edges of her long, dark vest, as she defended herself with a serious expression, wary that the person she was facing might launch some kind of sudden offensive.

"Don't give me any of your nonsense!" she responded sharply. "Who's toying with you, anyway? Who in the world are you and what are you doing here?"

The smile remained on Yang Chunbo's face. "What am I doing here? Strange you're asking me that. What are *you* doing here yourself?"

The last question stopped Gu Yingfen short. She bit her lip, and could not come up with an answer. The situation was highly uncomfortable, but from what I was hearing, I still could not fathom what was going on. Should I jump out then? It still wasn't the right time. But what kind of trick was someone playing on all of us?

Yingfen did manage to respond after a pause. "You—you're here, but—but you're taking the place of—taking the place of—" She could not finish the sentence, evidently at a loss for words.

The man waved his hand. "All right, Miss Gu. Let's start over without any more games. Since it was you who asked me to meet you here, why do you find it necessary to string me along like this?"

"When did I ever ask to meet you? I don't even know you!"

"Right, but you'll surely know me from now on! My name is Yang Chunbo. *Ha, ha, ha!*" He took a step toward her and extended his hand yet again. "Come, Miss Gu, please sit down. We can have a heart-to-heart talk."

The man's hand was close to her chest, as if he were about to invite her to sit down—or attempt something much ruder. Yingfen was somewhat startled and quickly lifted her right arm to fend him off while dodging to one side and taking a step backward. She then circled around the stone table in the middle of the gazebo to the entrance on the other side and started down the steps.

"Hey, what's going on, Miss Gu?" The man sounded both astonished and alarmed. "Are you jerking me around? You're the one who set up the appointment here, and now you're leaving without saying why? What's going on in that head of yours, anyway?"

"I never set up any appointment with you," she said without even turning her head around. "You've got it all wrong!"

She moved very fast, and was outside the gazebo in a blink. Unwilling to let her go, the man rushed to stop her. This was surely the right time for me to come out of hiding. I stood up, but because I had been squatting there for so long, my legs were numb and rubbery. By the time I reached them, Yang Chunbo had already caught up to her. He grabbed her by one shoulder, muttering to himself all the while. I took a step toward him and slapped him on the back.

"Hey, friend, watch yourself," I said. "She doesn't know who you are, so why be so ill mannered?"

The man had clearly not expected a third person to intervene. Quite taken aback on seeing me, he just stood there glaring angrily. He evidently thought I was a mere laborer, and as he let out a loud *humph* from his bulbous nose, his face took on a look of anger and contempt.

"What's this? You're telling me what to do?" He lifted his right hand to strike me across the face.

I was prepared for such a move. Snapping my head to one side, I directed a counterblow to his right wrist with my left fist. The move infuriated him. He clenched his left fist to strike at me again. I ducked and counterpunched him in the ribs. I didn't really hit him hard, just enough to allow me to slip to the edge of the gazebo before he could recover. By this time, Gu Yingfen was long gone. The man was muscular, and seemed to be strong. So even though I had managed to hit him twice, I didn't want to engage him in a serious altercation. He wasn't ready to end it, though, and came after me, pendants clinking away. I didn't wait for him to come nearer but retreated behind the gazebo.

"Hey, friend," I said. "Just think about it. Is it worth your while to get into a real tussle with me?"

"You swine! How dare you cross me!"

Clearly unwilling to stop at that, he rushed toward me, panting with fury. I was able to remain calm in spite of his insult. When he got closer, I played cat-and-mouse with him, running around the gazebo. He couldn't catch me, and, outraged at the smirk on my face, could only unleash a stream of fierce curses in my direction.

It was then that my savior arrived on the scene. A man in a gray silk gown walked quickly up to us from behind the hill, with a black object tucked under his arm. It was Huo Sang, without his customary Western garb.

"Hey, what game are you two playing?" he said smiling. "Is it tag, or cat-and-mouse? *Heh, heh, heh!*"

Approaching Yang Chunbo without regard for his own safety, he blocked his way while he calmed him down with soft-spoken words. Somewhat embarrassed, Yang stopped, his anger slowly dissipating. Huo Sang acted as if he didn't know me, but signaled to me with his eyes. I grasped his meaning immediately and ran around the hill to leave the park. There was no trace of Gu Yingfen at the gate, where I jumped into a cab to go home.

III. The Expected Client

I took a bath and changed my clothes after I got back, but Huo Sang still hadn't returned. So I sat myself down, lit up a cigarette, and began reflecting on what had occurred. Everything was just too baffling. What kind of person was Yang Chunbo? How could he have known Gu Yingfen's name when she didn't know his? We had thought that Wang Zhisheng had set up the meeting because he was after something. But then he hadn't shown up, evidently sending Yang in his stead. Was Yang, then, Wang's henchman? If that was the case, why had Yang been such a smiling sycophant at the meeting, so eager to get on Yingfen's good side? And yet why hadn't he been thoroughly polite to her? Could it be that Wang Zhisheng had not written that anonymous note after all? Was there some other hidden twist to the plot? I had no recourse in trying to solve this conundrum other than to wait for Huo Sang to come home. He didn't do so, however, until nearly lunchtime, and he looked so unusually preoccupied that I couldn't bring myself to ask him any questions right then.

After changing his clothes, it was he who spoke first. "You know, Bao Lang, this case is even more serious and complex than we had anticipated," he said. "Our adversary is without doubt a formidable man with an extremely devious mind, someone we cannot afford to take lightly at all. It's a good thing I was well prepared today, having brought this thing along with me. Otherwise, the trip would have been a complete failure." He pointed at the shiny black camera on the table before taking out his cigarettes.

"You took that camera to Banhong Park?" I asked him.

He nodded as he struck a match to light up a cigarette.

"What on earth for?" I wanted to know.

"Originally, I had a another purpose in mind. But when the situation changed, I found a different use for it."

I did not understand what he was getting at. "What in the world is this all about?" I asked again. "What kind of a person is that foolish devil who calls himself Yang Chunbo?"

Huo Sang let out a puff. "I found out about him by quietly tailing him to his home. He lives at 97 Penglai Road, right in town. His family is decently well off, and he is currently a student at the university. I plan on paying him a visit in a day or two."

"Gu Yingfen doesn't know who he is," I said. "From their conversation, it was obvious neither one had any idea what the other was all about."

I recounted for Huo Sang all I had seen and heard at the gazebo. Huo Sang listened attentively to everything, staring straight ahead while puffing on a Golden Dragon. Even after I finished, he showed no reaction, appearing to be deep in thought.

I waited a while before asking him: "This Yang Chunbo, is he the one you call a formidable adversary with a devious mind?"

Huo Sang shook his head slowly. "No, he isn't. I think he's no more than a supporting actor in the play. The star is someone else."

"Is the star Wang Zhisheng then?"

Huo Sang stood up as he answered. "Yes. Of course it has to be. I don't imagine it will be long before he shows us another move. Be a little patient,

Bao Lang. I've got to get ready for him." He then picked up the camera and disappeared into the laboratory.

I felt like I had been sucked into a most befuddling maze, with no idea of how to get out. Huo Sang had said that Wang Zhisheng was the brains behind it all, but what was his scheme? Was it really worth the serious attention Huo Sang was paying to it? He said that it had been a stroke of luck to have brought the camera along. What had he captured on film? The reason he had not told me was likely more than just old habit. This time he himself seemed to be enshrouded in uncertainty. My incomprehension would have to be borne for five more hours before I would gain a glimpse of the truth.

Toward evening of the seventeenth, there was a genuine development in the case when Gu Yingfen hurried over once more. She had changed into a full-length apple-green sheath, and looked even more upset and apprehensive than she had in the morning.

She sat down. "It's a good thing Mr. Bao got me out of that difficult situation today. I really don't know who that man was, nor do I understand what he was after. But what we were worried about has now come true. Mr. Huo, Mr. Bao, take a look at this. This note was delivered to me just half an hour ago by someone dressed like a laborer." Not only was her voice trembling, but the hand that was holding the note was also shaking uncontrollably.

The note was scrawled in pencil; the calligraphy resembled that of the earlier one in ink, but was written in a much more hurried script. It said:

If you value your reputation and hope to realize your wedding plans, come to Number 19, Alley 3, De'an Lane off Beishan West Road, to talk things over tonight at 9:00 p.m.

Sheng
17 October

Even though the note contained no blatant threat, its tone demanded compliance, and in that way was even more intimidating than a threat.

"This note has to be from Wang Zhisheng," said Huo Sang as he tossed it on the desk.

"Since it's signed 'Sheng,' it most probably is from him," said Yingfen.

"But if the purpose of the first note puzzled me, I can't even imagine what devilish scheme he's up to with this second one."

Huo Sang thought over the possibilities. "I would say that he's now on to something he can really use to blackmail you!" he said.

"What do you think he wants from me? Money? Or—" She looked down without continuing.

"It's hard to say," Huo Sang answered. "But I think we'll have to pay him a visit. Things should clear up once we have a chance to meet him face-to-face." He paused. "Whatever he has, though, has got to be something deadly serious, something we won't be able to take lightly."

"What could it be, Mr. Huo? Isn't it just that picture of my sister Ying-fang?"

"I would say it's more than that. He has something much more formidable."

"Oh? What else does he have?"

"He has a picture of you!"

Gu Yingfen looked doubtful. "No photograph of me has ever fallen into his hands, surely."

"Yes, it has," said Huo Sang with great seriousness. "There's one you don't know about. It's not of you alone. It's a photograph that includes the man you were talking to. You are facing the man-made hill, and the man has his hand extended toward you, as if he were about to touch you. In the background is the quiet gazebo, a most suitable place for a secret rendezvous!"

Gu Yingfen visibly paled as she cried out in surprise. "What? Are you saying that I was just—that I was—" Her lips trembled and she could not go on.

Hmm. Here was a hint at last. I was finally beginning to have a glimmer of understanding about what had happened.

Huo Sang hastened to explain. "Exactly, exactly. During your encounter with Yang Chunbo at the Gardener's Gazebo, a photograph was taken of the entire scene. It's already in Wang Zhisheng's hands at this very moment!"

Gu Yingfen jumped up from her seat, her face white as a sheet. I, too, felt extraordinarily startled.

"Is that really what happened, Mr. Huo?" she asked, quite in shock.

"Yes, indeed," said Huo Sang. "But you needn't be so upset. Sit down and listen to me."

Yingfen sat down with some effort. Her eyes remained wide open as tears welled up in them. "Who took the picture, Mr. Huo?" she asked. "How did it get into this monster's hands?"

Huo Sang remained calm as he answered her. "The photograph was taken by Wang Zhisheng himself. He had concealed himself on the hill across from the gazebo. He waited until just the right moment to surreptitiously take the picture of you and the man talking to each other. That he now ventures to demand a meeting with you clearly indicates he will be using the picture as a weapon for blackmail."

Gu Yingfen's eyes reddened, and she looked as if she was ready to burst into tears. She covered her lower face with a white handkerchief and began to weep softly into it. This Wang Zhisheng was a truly vicious individual, using such devious tactics to extort money from a helpless female. I couldn't help feeling outraged at the injustice of it all.

"What can we do about this, Mr. Huo?" she asked as she choked back sobs. "This monster is really too wicked! How can I possibly defend myself against all that? I'll just have to have it out with him!"

Have it out with him? I could easily agree with that. If we couldn't handle that scoundrel with our minds, I would gladly confront him directly with my fists on behalf of this poor girl.

Huo Sang offered words of comforting advice. "You needn't feel so bad, Miss Gu," he said. "Confrontation is not a good solution. The results are usually not worth it. If you approach him directly, all you're doing is validating his scheme. You will fall right into his trap and will have great difficulty extricating yourself. It would be impossible, moreover, to keep your family's past problems secret. No. Confronting him is not at all a good course of action."

"Then what *is?*" she asked as she looked up at him. "I really can't think of what to do. If he wants money from me, I won't be able to come up with any, since I would never dare tell my father. If he has some other evil intention—"

Huo Sang quickly got to his feet, gesturing her to stop. "Miss Gu, don't you worry. I don't believe we're out of options."

That seemed to lift her spirits a little. She dabbed at her eyes with her handkerchief and stared at Huo Sang, waiting to hear what he would say next. His eyebrows knitted together, Huo Sang paced back and forth in the room with his hands behind his back, as I calmly sat and watched.

"I think we have a way of getting that photograph back," Huo Sang muttered, half to himself. "You needn't worry, Miss Gu."

"Oh! That's wonderful. What are you going to do to get it back, Mr. Huo?"

"I'll have to pay him a visit."

"Won't that bring about a serious clash?"

"No, don't worry. I know how to handle myself in unusual situations."

The young woman's eyes instantly reflected her gratitude; she seemed to smile through her tears. I myself felt greatly relieved.

"Mr. Huo," she said to him in a trembling voice, "if you can really get that photograph back, I will never forget you for the rest of my life!"

Huo Sang stopped his pacing. "You don't have to say that. I'm quite confident I can handle the matter. Don't worry. Just leave that note here and get yourself home."

"I don't have to go along with you?" she asked.

"No. Leave everything to us."

"What if he makes demands?"

"We'll be able to respond to them on your behalf. Just go on home. As soon as we have any results, I will let you know."

Her earlier distress was gone from Gu Yingfen's face, but she didn't appear to be totally convinced. As she stood up to take her leave, she couldn't help cautioning Huo Sang once more. "Mr. Huo, the man's more deadly than a snake. You have to be extremely careful when you tangle with him."

"I know," said Huo Sang as he escorted her out the door. "He's got the upper hand right now, and we of course have to watch that we don't make matters worse. No matter what, we need to proceed with brains rather than brawn. Don't you worry."

With a mixture of relief and apprehension, Gu Yingfen gave both of us a deep bow and walked slowly away. Coming back into the room after seeing her off, Huo Sang stretched, pulled out another cigarette, lit it, and sat down on the rattan chair.

I sat down as well. "I really feel compassion for the young lady," I said. "What are you planning to do, Huo Sang?"

"After we have dinner, let's go straight to see this man" said Huo Sang. "I'll decide what to do after I hear what he has to say."

"What if he wants a huge amount of money before he'll let you have that photograph? Are you ready to meet his price?"

"That would be our final move before we are checkmated. Unless there were absolutely no other option, we would of course not yield to such extortion." He took a quick look at the porcelain clock over the fireplace. "It's getting late. Let's hurry and have dinner now, so that you and I can be on our way quickly."

Quite unsettled by the uncertainties of the task ahead, I did not have my normal appetite. Huo Sang, however, showed no deviation from the usual.

I took the first opportunity to ask, "Huo Sang, how did you know that Wang Zhisheng took that photograph?"

"I saw him with my own eyes," Huo Sang said. "He was hiding under the branches of a potted locust tree behind the hill, pointing his camera lens directly at the gazebo."

"Where were you?"

"I was in a grove of pines off to one side."

"He didn't notice you?"

Huo Sang shook his head as he continued eating.

"You said earlier that you had made use of your own camera," I pressed on. "What did you do with it?"

Huo Sang put down his chopsticks and patted his coat pocket. "I have it in here," he said. "You'll see soon enough."

"What made you think of taking the camera along?"

"I had thought that when Wang Zhisheng met the lady, he might make some kind of threatening gesture, so I took the camera along intending to record anything like that for evidence. What I never expected was that he would be a step ahead of me by having someone else take his place."

"What you're saying, then, is that he set this up in order to invent some sort of false evidence. But didn't he already have that photo of Gu Yingfang in his possession? Wasn't that enough? Why would he need to do any more?"

"That's easy to explain. One of the faces in the former photo is Wang's own. If his threats were ignored and he showed this photo to the world, he would not be able to avoid being implicated himself. So isn't it obvious how the photograph he's now taken can be even more useful to him?"

The explanation was very reasonable. It revealed even more what a shrewd, crafty, and sinister individual this Wang Zhisheng really was. In dealing with a person like that, Huo Sang could never let down his guard. Because he recalled to me Xu Zhiyu, from the case of "The Living Corpse," I couldn't help feeling a bit apprehensive.

"Do you think this Yang Chunbo is his henchman?" I also wanted to know.

"Hmm. I think he probably is. Fortunately, I now know where he lives. Finding him will be no problem."

Well, as they say, the best-laid plans of mice and men often go awry. In my experience, I've seen the truth of that quite a few times, since pure happenstance plays a great role in human affairs. We plot and plan with all our might, but unexpected occurrences regularly bring unanticipated consequences.

After dinner, we smoked for a while before dressing to go to Beishan West Road for the interview, about which I still had my misgivings. Right at that point, Shi Gui brought in the name card of a visitor—none other than Yang Chunbo! That this man would come to us himself was not only beyond my expectation; even Huo Sang was greatly surprised. Had he discovered our identities and come to confront us? Or had he come here to exact some sort of revenge?

He had on the same gray suit he had worn in the morning; the two pendants on his vest were still clinking against each other. There was a trace of anger on his face, although when he greeted us, it was evident from his demeanor that he didn't recognize us. Both of us were dressed differently, and moreover were under lamplight. Since he had no idea of what we had done in the park, he would naturally be unable to recognize us. After the usual words of welcome, Huo Sang invited him to take a seat before calmly addressing him.

"What can we do for you, Mr. Yang?" he asked.

"I need you to take care of a matter for me," Yang Chunbo responded rather directly.

"Hmm?"

"Someone has played me for a fool, and I'm furious. I can't do a thing about it because I really can't figure out what happened. Please find out for me. I'm willing to compensate you well."

I truly believed him when he said he was furious, if only because his nostrils were flaring and his eyes blazing. It was apparent that Huo Sang noticed as well.

"Oh? Someone tricked you? Who would do that?"

"I don't know. That's what I'm asking you to find out for me."

The visitor fished out a letter and newspaper clipping from his pocket. He spread the clipping out and directed our eyes to it. "This is the first part of the scheme," he said. "It appeared in the paper four days ago."

I saw that it was a clipping of a personal advertisement for a marriage partner. This one, though, had been placed by a woman seeking a man. It read:

> Attractive woman of good character with a modern education, alone because her parents are deceased, seeks an educated man under 30 as marriage partner. Interested parties please send personal history and photograph to P.O. Box 256. Meeting will be arranged with the most suitable prospect. All others will not be contacted.

"Is this the ad you answered?" Huo Sang asked.

Yang Chunbo played with his fob chain, appearing rather embarrassed as he nodded his head with some effort. "Yes. After I sent in my letter, I received this reply." Then he took a letter out of an envelope.

The handwriting on it was very small, as if it were a woman's. It said that Yang Chunbo's letter was impressive and asked him to come to a meeting at ten o'clock on the morning of the seventeenth at the Gardener's Gazebo in Banhong Park. It was signed "Gu Yingfen."

The curtain that had hidden everything up to now had at last begun to open; I was finally beginning to see what was behind it. So this "henchman" had not been involved of his own volition but had been manipulated like a puppet. Huo Sang and I had both miscalculated on this one point. Only now did I realize that Wang Zhisheng was the one and only person pulling the strings, like a solitary puppeteer behind the scenes. He had placed the ad that piqued Yang Chunbo's interest. He had also written the letter, in Gu Yingfen's name, inviting Yang to go and meet her. At the same time, he had sent that anonymous note to Yingfen, so that she would also show up at the Gardener's Gazebo in Banhong Park, thus enabling him to carry out his evil plan to photograph them together. This was a man with an unquestionably cunning and devious mind!

Huo Sang frowned before shooting me a sideways glance. I nodded slightly to show him I immediately understood his quiet expression of regret. It was as though he were saying that he, too, had not realized Yang Chunbo was not Wang's henchman, but was indeed no more than Wang's puppet.

"I was delighted at receiving the letter," Yang Chunbo continued. "This morning, I went to Banhong Park, in accordance with the agreement. I actually saw that young Gu woman—ah, she was really pretty! But after we met, she didn't have a thing to say to me. In fact, she tried to avoid me, clearly taking me as some kind of fool. After that, a man showed up and punched me a couple of times. What cursed luck! A person can only take so much. When I got home, I thought everything over carefully and concluded that someone must have been playing some kind of trick on me. Don't you think so, Mr. Huo?"

"Hmm. It's possible," said Huo Sang mildly. "What are you planning to do now?"

The young man clenched his right hand and pounded it into his left. "I just have to get hold of this swine! I've already been to the post office to ask who rented box number 256. But, dammit, the person in charge there just wouldn't tell me. I don't know how I can find out who this swine is, but I'm not willing to just forget it. You are a detective with a sterling reputation, Mr. Huo, so you must be able to help me, right?"

"What do you want me to do?"

"Just find out the identity of the person who did this to me. I'll take care of the rest myself."

Huo Sang looked over at me again, drawing up a corner of his mouth as if to marvel at the incredible coincidence of this man coming to us. He paused for a second before turning his eyes back to the visitor. "Even after going over this in your own mind, you have no idea who this person could be?"

Yang Chunbo shook his head. "No idea. I really can't think of anyone."

"Among your friends, for example, is there anyone who hates you, or who has trouble getting along with you?"

"No, none whatsoever. I don't think I'm a bum. I have never taken advantage of my friends. When we go out, for example, I never leave them holding the check. There's no reason any of them would want to do something like this to me behind my back."

"Would anyone want to do this to have some fun with you?"

"Impossible! Even if you're just having some fun, there's a right way and a wrong way. To make a fool of me like this, how can it be considered just a simple joke?"

Huo Sang took out his pocket watch to check the time. "Fine," he nodded. "I understand. You can take back the clipping and the letter. Just leave me your address. I'll think of a way to find the person who did all this to you and let you know. Right now, I have other business I need to tend to right away."

IV. The Negotiation

Both Huo Sang and I had our guns with us as we headed to Beishan Road. I was thinking in the cab that this Wang Zhisheng was indeed a devious man. Cooking up a diabolical scheme like this and using Yang Chunbo as his pawn clearly showed the kind of mind he had. According to Gu Yingfen, the man had been a law student, hence a recipient of higher education and a member of the intellectual elite. Lacassagne, the French criminologist, has said that "those who possess knowledge, yet lack morality, are truly frightening when they commit a crime."[2] The Belgian Quetelet has also said that training and education are two different matters.[3] Simply being literate or trained is an insufficient gauge of whether a person is more or less likely to become a criminal: It is only a measure of a person's ability to become a higher- or lower-level wrongdoer. In other words, someone who has been through higher education

2. Alexandre Lacassagne (1843–1924) is considered the founder of modern forensic science.

3. Adolphe Quetelet (1796–1874) was a highly influential social statistician. His studies of the numerical consistency of crimes stimulated discussion of free will versus social determinism.

is in no way less prone to break the law than someone who has not. Moreover, when an intellectual commits a crime, his modus operandi is far more formidable. Mr. Hu Zhantang has therefore made the painful admission that "It is fortunate for us that our educational system is not universal!"[4] This remark was of course aimed at education that focuses on providing knowledge and nothing else. We realized from experience that this insight was worth taking seriously. In the case of "The Living Corpse," we had had to tangle with a university professor. Not only was that frustrating to our old friend Detective Wang, but it was almost more of a headache than even Huo Sang could handle. Before us at present was yet another deviant intellectual. It was still an open question as to whether we would be up to the task of dealing with him.

The area around De'an Lane off Beishan West Road was full of recently renovated two-story Shanghai-style apartments. The apartments were cramped, but cheap to rent. They were also noisy, with three or four families packed into almost every unit. We found our way to No. 19 in Alley 3, and Huo Sang went ahead to knock on the door. There was a quick response from inside: Almost immediately, a man opened the door to admit us.

He was perhaps thirty, tall and slender, but shorter than Huo Sang by an inch or two. He was dressed rather plainly in a dark serge outfit with lined pants, black satin shoes, and white socks. Under the lamplight, his facial features were far from ordinary. His hair grew low over his narrow, furrowed brow. Thick, curved eyebrows highlighted a pair of shifty eyes. Although there was a slight indentation at the bridge of his nose, the nose itself hooked out like an eagle's claw. In combination with his very thin lips, his features gave me the immediate feeling that he could not possibly be a good, decent man.

"Is this the residence of Mr. Wang Zhisheng?" Huo Sang asked in a gentle voice.

The man bowed slightly. "That's yours truly," he responded. "To what do I owe your presence here?"

"We are here on behalf of a young woman and wish to discuss a matter with you," said Huo Sang softly.

---

4. Better known as Hu Hanmin (1879–1936), Hu Zhantang was a revolutioinary and close associate of Dr. Sun Yat-sen, the founding leader of Republican China.

The man looked us over. "Very good," he promptly responded. "Please do come in." He stood aside to let us pass, shut the door, and turned to guide us into the place.

In the small, undecorated living room inside, a woman and three men were playing mahjongg under the lamplight, while another man in a short black outfit was sitting at one corner of the table, kibitzing. None of them appeared to be cultured individuals, and none except the kibitzer paid us any attention as we walked past. We followed Wang Zhisheng upstairs and entered the separate quarters where he lived. I realized then that he had opened the door for us so promptly because he had been waiting downstairs.

In the middle of the room hung a bulb of thirty-two lumens, the light from which filled the whole area. Against one wall was a small bed, with a blue serge robe hanging on the wooden frame above it. Across from the bed was a small table and two chairs as well as a small bookcase piled with books. There was also a five-syllable couplet on the wall by the literatus Zheng Banqiao,[5] along with a photograph of Wang Zhisheng himself in full academic regalia on the day he received his bachelor's degree. Although the room was not spacious, it was neat and tidy. He gestured to the two chairs inviting us to sit down, while he himself sat on the bed.

Huo Sang took a name card from his pocket to hand him. Wang Zhisheng glanced at it and smirked before placing it on the table. This was the first time Huo Sang had ever been received with such disrespect. Accustomed to a measure of awe in a potential opponent whenever he handed over his card, he had not expected the quick dismissal it brought on this occasion. Had this fellow been preparing himself to face up to him?

"This is Mr. Bao Lang," said Huo Sang, pointing to me. "He's a good friend who has always worked with me."

Wang Zhisheng straightened up slightly in greeting. "Mm, I've long since heard of you as well." He took out a silver cigarette case, opened the cover, and passed it to us hospitably.

Huo Sang did not accept. "Sorry, no. I have my own." He took out his Golden Dragons and lit up.

5. A painter, poet, and calligrapher, Zheng Banqiao (1693–1765), a native of Xinhua in Jiangsu Province, is known as one of the Eight Eccentrics of Yangzhou.

I followed suit and turned down the offer, since I had also brought along my own cigarettes. Wang Zhisheng then struck a match and lit up himself. I quietly observed him, noticing from his facial expression and his actions that he was extremely self-possessed. It was as if we were his intimate friends, in for a casual chat. There was no hint of either particular deference or extreme negligence. The man was clearly plotting a criminal act, yet in front of detectives he could maintain a cool composure. His devil-may-care intrepidity was really not easy to fathom.

Smoke from the three cigarettes mingled noiselessly in the small room. Huo Sang was the first to break the silence.

"I guess you had not anticipated we would be coming to see you, Mr. Wang?"

Wang Zhisheng's mouth twitched slightly. "Uh, that's right. But it doesn't make much difference who comes."

"Then I would guess that you already know why we're here."

"Of course I know. Excuse me, but I have to ask you this. Has the client you represent given you full representational authority?"

"Yes. We have full authority."

"Even for financial transactions? Are you authorized to do that?"

Huo Sang responded with his own question. "You mean there's money involved in this?"

Wang Zhisheng simpered. "Right. Don't tell me you never thought of that. Do you think I would waste my time making pointless conversation with you?"

"All right. I understand. You are in possession of a photograph that you think would affect the reputation of our client's family. You want to net some kind of windfall from the photograph. Am I correct?"

"*Heh, heh, heh!* If a windfall is not in the cards, I can at least look forward to a goodly sum."

"From our point of view, however, your calculations are probably too optimistic."

"Oh?" There was a trace of surprise in his voice.

Huo Sang remained matter-of-fact. "The photograph has no value. There's no need for us to pay money to retrieve it."

"Is that so? I'm willing to listen to your explanation."

"You've heard of 'shooting yourself in the foot'? It's certainly not what a smart person would do. If that photograph ever becomes public, the persons you think you would hurt would hardly be affected, while you would in effect be getting yourself into a heap of trouble."

"How's that?"

"You're probably not yet aware of it, but Yuyao County has had you on record for the past four years. No action has been taken against you only because the county still lacks enough hard evidence to prosecute. If the photograph were to become available, do you think you could avoid legal prosecution?"

Huo Sang stopped here to take another puff. Wang Zhisheng kept smoking with his eyes shut. He gave no answer and showed no reaction, his face remaining impassive.

"I know you are an extremely intelligent person," Huo continued, "and so would not follow this poor course of action. For this reason, I thought I should tell you straight out to hand over the photograph unconditionally and put an end to this matter from the past. Because it is partly connected to our client, we would of course not make it public once it was in our possession. You would then not have to worry about any resurrection of the old case, which would definitely bring you problems."

Wang Zhisheng's eyes gradually opened. He blew out a long puff of smoke as a weak smile crossed his face. "Mr. Huo," he said, "that was a beautiful speech, one worthy of the verbal talents of a great detective. It's just too bad that you've got it wrong."

"I have? In what way?"

"The financial transactions I was talking about are not based on this one snapshot. Mr. Huo, you are probably still unaware that I have an additional photograph."

Oh, what a fiendish man! What Huo Sang had said to Gu Yingfen earlier was now verified. He really had taken another photo. I was aware that Huo Sang was just leading him on by continuing to pretend ignorance.

"An additional photograph?" he asked.

Wang Zhisheng flicked the ashes from his cigarette. His eyes flashed as he cast a sidelong glance at Huo Sang, indicating that he was well pleased with himself.

"Yes, indeed," he nodded. "This other photo directly involves your client, since it's of a man and a women on a quiet rendezvous by a deserted gazebo! Once that gets out, her engagement will likely be wrecked, but the blame will never reach all the way to me. Just think about it. Would I hand over something like that to you for nothing?"

Huo Sang indicated his understanding. "Oh, so that's it. It's for the other photograph that you seek payment, and not for the original one, right?"

"That's right. That earlier picture is outdated and not really worth anything anymore. If that was all I had, as long as you've taken the trouble to come here I could certainly give it to you for free, just to keep things friendly."

"Can we talk about being friendly with that other photo as well?"

Wang Zhisheng produced another smirk along with a puff of smoke. "I'm sorry, but this later one is a bit more important," he said. "As for friendship, since we have just met, we can't very well talk of such a thing yet, can we?"

His attitude was so cold-blooded, his tongue so keen-edged! Though Huo Sang was able to maintain his composure, I could no longer remain patient.

"Hey, don't be so high and mighty!" I interrupted. "We've been talking with you in a more civil way than you deserve. Aside from us, who would think it worth their while to be friendly with the likes of you?"

He inclined his face slightly. "Hmm. The great writer is talking about friendship with me. That's really paying me a lot of respect! Too bad I'm not respectable!"

That stirred my anger. "Don't you smart-mouth me! Get that picture out now! Otherwise—"

"Otherwise, what?" he said coolly. He shot me a scornful sideways glance before lighting up a second cigarette. His chilly, contemptuous manner was really hard to take.

Unable to contain myself, I leapt to my feet. "You're an evil criminal!" I shouted. "And since you don't appreciate civility, we'll just take care of you ourselves!" As I was speaking, my right hand, which had long since gone into my pocket, now tightened around the handle of my gun.

He remained unperturbed. "Mr. Bao," he said, "you're also an educated man. How can you allow your emotions to get the better of you? What are you planning to do?"

"I'm going to search this place!" I said with determination.

"Oh? That would be meaningless. I'm sorry, but you'd better sit down."

Wang Zhisheng was still seated and composed, but he did incline his head slightly toward the window. One of his hands also reached into the pocket of his black serge jacket to pull out a shiny object. It was a police whistle.

He played with the whistle as he addressed me again. "You need to think about things more objectively. You say I'm a criminal, but I haven't broken any law. It's you, in fact, who are about to break one. Aren't you threatening me with violence? What position or right allows you to do that? Wouldn't that be senseless and dangerous as well? To tell the truth, even though I never thought you two would come here, I'm not totally unprepared. To guard against unforeseen contingencies, I wouldn't of course keep an important thing like that photograph in this little room. I can tell you frankly that I've already made arrangements. If you use force to either detain or injure me, that photograph will immediately be released to the public. Sure, I would suffer some harm if things came to that, but the harm to your client would be incalculably worse. So Mr. Bao, I don't imagine your original plans were as poorly formulated as to include the possibility of using force on me."

I had only wanted to scare him a little and give vent to my own anger. But it hadn't worked. I had failed. This clever little speech of his did give me pause, warning me to consider the consequences of my actions. Of course I could not afford to go on so rashly. Fortunately, Huo Sang was there to smooth things over, allowing me to pull back from my aggressive stance. He had sat back at first, letting me go through my angry display, perhaps wondering whether a more intimidating approach would work. Now that he saw it would not, he was quick to proceed in a different direction.

"Bao Lang," he said to me, "please sit down and talk. We don't need to lose our tempers over this matter. If you think our friend here has broken the law, we can say so in a civil manner. You don't need to upset him by threatening him like that."

After he finished saying this, Huo Sang went back to puffing on his cigarette, casting only a quick sideways glance at Wang Zhisheng with his shining dark eyes. I took the opportunity to sit down, removing my right hand from my pocket at the same time. I could detect a slight change of color on Wang's face; the puffs of smoke from his mouth were not emerging in as orderly a fashion as before.

"Mr. Huo is right," he said. "Even if you think I have acted illegally, couldn't we still have a calm discussion about it, especially since I do have some knowledge of the law? I happen to believe I have absolutely never overstepped any legal bounds! I hear that you've had more than sufficient experience in such matters, Mr. Bao. So how could you have lost your temper as you just did?"

Huo Sang slowly nodded his head. "My original intention was that it would be best for all of us not to get angry. As long as you do your part to cooperate, I am ready to have a civil discussion with you."

"What are we to discuss? Do you still aim to obtain that photograph with no conditions?"

"No, let's set that aside for now. Let's begin again with another topic."

"What other topic?"

"The topic of your violation of the law!"

The situation had changed. Huo Sang was seizing the offensive, forcing his opponent to fend off his attack. Wang Zhisheng stopped short, his face taking on a look of surprise. His sideways glance froze on Huo Sang's face, as if he could not comprehend what Huo Sang meant.

"What law did I break?"

"To ask someone about something you know you have done is not what an intelligent person would do." Huo Sang did not return Wang Zhisheng's look, keeping his eyes instead on the cigarette between his own fingers; his voice remained calm and collected. His opponent, however, was growing ruffled.

"I don't understand, Mr. Huo," said Wang Zhisheng. "Are you referring to our current transaction? But it was willingly entered into on both sides. I have never used any sort of coercion. I cannot agree that I have broken the law."

"There's something else."

"Oh? I can't think of anything. What is it?"

Huo Sang smiled as he answered. "You're pretty forgetful, aren't you? Let me ask you then, what kind of photograph is that other one, the one you're seeking payment for?"

Wang Zhisheng was taken aback. "I've told you. It shows your client having a secret rendezvous with a man in a gazebo. Since their faces show up clearly, I believe it's a very powerful shot."

"Will you let me take a look at it?"

"Sorry, this is still not the time. After the terms are set, you will naturally get to see it."

"How did you come by such a picture?"

"That's none of your business. You don't need to know that."

"It's a basic principle in any business transaction that the price is set only after seeing the goods. So if I don't get to see the goods, you at least have to provide me with an explanation. I need you to make everything clear."

The lines deepened on his narrow brow. He hesitated before he spoke.

"I, too, purchased it for a price."

Huo Sang chuckled. "You're still playing around with us, aren't you?" he said with a disdainful glance.

"It's true," Wang Zhisheng said seriously. "I did pay out money. More over—"

"All right, you did," Huo Sang cut him off. "You paid out money! Let me see how much, though. The biggest outlay for you would have been the one-day personal ad in the newspaper. That would be five or six dollars? Then the cost of the film and photographic paper would be about a dollar. There's also the admission fee to Banhong Park, carfare, and postage expenses—probably not over another dollar altogether. Let's round it out and say ten dollars. So, all right, that's the price you paid and, yes, we really ought to recognize that."

Huo Sang's words were barbed. He fixed his sharp stare on Wang Zhisheng's face, waiting for some kind of response. Up to this point I had not ventured to question Wang's ability to keep his head. Now, however, he was obviously beginning to lose control. A slight tremor went through his body, his bushy eyebrows became even more contorted, and his face paled. It was clear that Huo Sang was getting to him, especially because he had not expected him to have seen through his whole scheme. The situation was clearly taking a radical turn.

He paused a bit before speaking. "Mr. Huo," he said, still pretending, "I don't understand what you're saying."

A trace of a smile graced Huo Sang's lips. "Neither one of us is stupid, so why bother talking nonsense? To put it another way, we have seen through your actions and schemes. That other photograph you took was nothing but a means to carry out blackmail. Since I am not a lawyer, I don't know on the spot what exact statute that violates and what punishment it calls for. But I would say my friend's contention that you have broken the law can in all probability be sustained."

The little room fell silent. Huo Sang took out another cigarette. Wang Zhisheng's eyebrows were now locked together and he bit his thin lower lip. He looked distressed, angry, and resentful all at once. Yes, I was beginning to feel jubilant; victory appeared imminent. This devious person's defenses were at last beginning to crumble.

He steadied himself with some effort, saying coolly, "Legal matters are based on evidence. Your accusation sounds too much like wishful thinking to me."

Huo Sang sat up. "You want evidence?" he retorted. "Of course we have evidence. Let me ask you, when you were snapping your pictures on the hill this morning, did you notice someone in the pine grove to your left with a camera, taking photos of his own? What you took were shots of a man and a woman in the gazebo; what *I* took was a shot of you!"

"Of me?"

"Right! But I'm not as ungenerous as you. If you want to see what you looked like as you were snapping pictures from the hill, I definitely would not seek any kind of payment from you for the privilege!"

Upon hearing this, Wang Zhisheng's face lost color. His eyes dilated with fury, his shifty eyeballs seemingly about to pop out of their sockets. The hook of his nose glistened with moisture. An apparent convergence of astonishment, anger, and resentment rendered him temporarily speechless.

Huo Sang continued speaking, but in more subdued tones. "I said earlier that intelligent people do not want to shoot themselves in the foot. If the photo you took were to become public, you yourself would be in some jeopardy. This other photo, however, is actually a document that incriminates you directly, and could of course be even more detrimental to you. I assure you that the photo can be verified. Once that was done, our client would not be affected at all, but you would have no way to avoid a charge of attempted blackmail."

Wang Zhisheng could not hide his shock. It was evident that he realized what would happen to him. He had expended much effort setting up this extortion scheme. But just like a paper structure held together with paste, it was falling apart as soon as it was hit by a puff of wind. His growing look of distress paralleled the increasing elation in our hearts.

His head lowered, Wang did not answer immediately. But he was not yet willing to surrender. "What you're saying—isn't it all just some clever nonsense you cooked up to outfox me?" he said, still unbending.

"For you to talk like that shows that you not only hold me in low regard, but that you hold yourself in low regard as well. As a matter of fact, we could have used some other effective way to take care of you. But this is our initial meeting, after all, and I know you to be an educated individual. So I was willing to make it easy on you and save you some face by sticking to a gentler approach. I am disappointed that you still seem unpersuaded. The picture I've been talking about is in my pocket. If necessary, I can also go to 97 Penglai Road to ask a man named Yang there to corroborate this evidence."

Ha! Final victory! The wooden frame above the bed began to rattle; Wang Zhisheng was no longer able to sit still. He knew then that Huo Sang had a clear picture of everything he had done before and after taking that photograph. His plan had gone irretrievably awry. He looked up, his face betraying a trace of admiration mixed with fear and doubt. Then he put his head down again, clenching and unclenching his fists. It was evident that his mind was in turmoil, leaving him uncertain about what to do next.

Huo Sang took a white envelope out of his breast pocket. "Here, have a look. My picture's in here. Let's make a trade right now and put an end to this little dispute." He pulled a photo and a negative from the envelope.

I turned to look. The print showed a side view of Wang Zhisheng taking pictures from up on the hill. Even though there were some pine needles in the way, his face was clearly discernible. Huo Sang also removed a ten-dollar bill from his wallet. "Mr. Wang," he said, "this is to cover your expenses. Please accept it. I believe your picture must be in this room; please get it for us. We cannot spare any more time, as we have other business."

Under the light, Wang Zhisheng's appearance was completely changed. His body was trembling like that of a condemned man on the way to execution with nothing whatsoever to look forward to at the end of his trek but death. He pondered a while longer, then let out a sigh.

"Mr. Huo, I am impressed by you," he said as he got to his feet. "The way you do things is really brilliant, really sharp. You can consider that you have won!" He was clearly crestfallen as he shuffled toward the window.

"You flatter me," said Huo Sang. "What I was able to do was fortuitous, so I dare not accept your compliment."

Wang Zhisheng walked to the small window, then turned to face Huo Sang, who was still seated. "Mr. Huo, once we exchange the pictures, we can call it even between us, right?"

"Right."

"You won't seek anything else from me?"

"I won't. I absolutely will not make trouble for you."

"What assurance do I have?"

"Isn't my word good enough for you?"

Wang Zhisheng thought about this, then nodded. He returned the police whistle to his pocket before pulling aside the dark-green window curtain. From behind the curtain, he took out a strip of negatives and handed it to Huo Sang, who stood up to receive it before holding it up against the light for a look. I looked as well and saw that the strip included six negatives: Three were blank, and one was blurry, but the remaining two were sharp and clear.

"You don't have any prints?" Huo Sang asked.

Wang Zhisheng shook his head. "No, just these negatives, which I developed myself. Don't you see? They're not yet completely dry."

Huo Sang nodded, folded the strip over and stuck it in his pocket. He then took out his own print and negative, as well as a ten-dollar bill. But just as he was about to hand them over to Wang Zhisheng, he suddenly stopped. "Oh, Mr. Wang, where's that earlier photograph?" he asked. "It's of no use to you now, so you might as well turn it over to me too."

Wang Zhisheng hesitated, but then gave a firm nod. "Fine. I've made up my mind to get on your good side," he said. "Please stand up, Mr. Bao. The photo is under your seat cushion."

I stood up and flipped over the blue cushion on my chair. Indeed there was a small packet inside, wrapped in newspaper. I picked it up and unwrapped it, exposing a photograph about four inches square in size. Hiding this object in such a place was yet another example of this man's cunning. Huo Sang looked at the picture. It was of a man and a woman. The man, who was standing, was Wang Zhisheng; the woman, who was seated, was Gu Yingfang. Indeed, she resembled Gu Yingfen closely. The photography studio's logo was on the print, which had been produced in Shanghai. Huo Sang put the print into his pocket as well before handing the picture and money over to Wang Zhisheng.

"Mr. Wang," Huo Sang then said, gesturing with his hand, "we can consider tonight's transaction completed. If you will reflect on what's happened now and then, perhaps you can derive some benefit from it."

After that, smiling broadly, he nodded and turned to leave without waiting for an answer. Wang Zhisheng did not see us out as we made our way down the stairs. We were all the way to De'an Lane before Huo Sang came to a stop and let out a breath.

"Bao Lang," he said to me, "our success today was an unexpected stroke of luck! To have gone up against such a devious fellow and not suffered any real loss is well beyond what I anticipated. Just think of what we started out to do. Our original focus was on the first photograph. Had that become public, it would not only have wrecked Gu Yingfen's wedding plans but would have opened up old wounds—enough, perhaps, to bring about her father's demise from anger and frustration. Her brother would also have been affected by the disgrace. Now that we've been able to recover it so easily, we ought to celebrate!"

"This crooked intellectual, however, has clearly violated the law," I said. "Aren't you doing him a great favor by letting him off so easily?"

Huo Sang looked straight at me. "Hmm, are you saying that I ought to have taught him some kind of lesson?"

"Yes. Even though we had to be circumspect and could not control him through legal means, I still can't help feeling uneasy that we let him off as lightly as we did."

Huo Sang mulled over what I said. "You're right. But it's really not a simple matter to teach a person like that a lesson. Consider his crooked eyebrows, his narrow forehead, his shifty eyes, and his hooked nose. According to Lombroso's description of the physical appearance of a lawbreaker, he is a stereotypical criminal.[6] And according to Mendel's basic laws of heredity, the tendency to commit crime is genetic.[7] No matter how you much you want to vent your spleen against a person like that, there is ultimately nothing you can do to keep him from being what he is."

I did not comment, but could not dispel the feeling in my heart that we had let an evil and devious man off too lightly. We walked on until we arrived at the street corner, where Huo Sang again drew to a halt. "Bao Lang," he said to me, "go on home ahead of me. I still have to go to the Bright Lenses Studio to buy back the negative of the original photograph and bring this case to a conclusion."

V. One Last Move

It was already a quarter after ten when I reached home. I lit up a cigarette in the office, waiting for Huo Sang to get back. In one day, I was thinking, we had solved a highly complicated case, and things had definitely gone much better than we could have expected. This Wang Zhisheng was certainly a cunning schemer. It was fortunate that Huo Sang had been ready for him and able to beat him at his own game. He had used a devious plan to harm a helpless young woman after bringing about the death of another. Even though society and the long arm of the law was on guard against social menaces like him, in the end, there was nothing that could be done. I couldn't help bristling at the thought.

By the time Huo Sang came back at 11:00 p.m., the ashtray already contained a half-dozen butts. I could see from his eyes that he was elated.

---

6. Cesare Lombroso (1835–1909), acclaimed the father of criminal anthropology, was known for his controversial belief that criminality could be identified primarily in a criminal's physical characteristics.

7. Gregor Johann Mendel (1822–1884), an Austrian botanist and monk, is credited with formulating the basic laws of heredity, which led to the development of the science of genetics.

"What took you so long?" I asked.

"I got to the Bright Lenses Studio but had to knock on the door for quite a while before I was let in. I wanted to buy back the negative of that portrait of Wang Zhisheng and Gu Yingfang, to make sure he would not be able to use it for some malicious purpose later on. But the picture was taken three or four years ago, and they had to search quite hard before they located it. The negative had become blurry, but I bought it back anyway. Then I also went to—" He stopped abruptly, as if he had just heard something. "Huh? Who would be coming over here at this hour?" he asked in surprise.

I could hear Shi Gui going to open the front door. Before we knew what was happening, Gu Yingfen had rushed into our house. She had changed into a dark sheath. Under the lights, she looked pale and wan. As soon as she saw us, she covered her face with her hands and began to sob.

"Things are falling apart, Mr. Huo! Oh please do me this one favor. Lend me some money right now. I promise I'll pay you back with interest!"

Both the person and the news came so abruptly that I could not help being astonished. Huo Sang also stood up in shock. The high spirits he had displayed just a few minutes before quickly vanished.

"What's this all about, Miss Gu?" he asked.

Gu Yingfen took out a letter. "Take a look, Mr. Huo," she said. "The matter is very urgent. I don't know if I can still make it on time!"

When I looked at the envelope, I saw that it was addressed in Wang Zhisheng's handwriting. The letter, scribbled in pencil, said:

You're quite something, hiring a detective to deal with me. But I'm not so stupid as to have gone through all my trouble for nothing. I'm informing you that I still have one more photograph; there were two copies of the picture of Yingfang and me . So even though that man Huo has taken away one of them, the other is still inside my trunk. Because my own likeness is in it, I had not planned on using it. But since I have now been thwarted, I don't want to stay in this place any longer but have made up my mind to have one last tilt with you. If you come to me with three thousand dollars to buy back the picture within an hour of receiving this letter, we will call it even. Otherwise, after the

hour has passed, I will send the picture to Jin Xueming on Beihai
Road, to avenge the anguish I have suffered. If you go to consult Huo
again, I swear I will wreak vengeance on your person. Decide what
you want to do.

After we had read the message the room fell silent. I looked over at Huo Sang and saw that his eyes were staring, his lips trembling slightly, and his breath coming rapidly—indications of his anger and surprise. So this wicked man was making one last move! Who would have thought it?

Huo Sang began mumbling to himself. "That's despicable! That's really despicable!"

"Please, Mr. Huo," Gu Yingfen begged tearfully, "you have to hurry."

"Oh, don't be so afraid of him. He might be bluffing."

"No! Don't think like that, Mr. Huo! It's just too risky! The letter was delivered by someone in a dark jacket at ten fifteen. It's now after eleven, and I might not make it even if I go there right away. Please, Mr. Huo, please help me out *right now!*"

Huo Sang remained still, biting his lip. The color of his face darkened and veins started bulging on his forehead. He seemed regretful, but also busy pondering a course of action. What were we to do? That this criminal could not be trusted went without saying. Why had Huo Sang just let him off? He had held to his promise not to make more trouble for the man, and now came this new move. How was he to deal with him now?

Letting out a sigh, Huo Sang finally made up his mind. "How much do you need, then?" he asked.

I couldn't help sighing and shaking my head. Huo Sang had lost after all! There was nothing he could do other than submit to the demand.

"After I got the letter, I secretly snuck out and pawned all my jewelry for a thousand. Then I went to a classmate's house and borrowed another thousand. So I'm now still a thousand dollars short of what he's demanding."

Huo Sang gave a nod and headed straight to a corner of the room where he took out his keys to open up the safe, from which he took out a stack of bills. He was ready to hand the money over to Gu Yingfen when he abruptly stopped.

"Do you have the two thousand with you?" he asked her.

"It's in my purse," said Gu Yingfen. "I had planned to hurry over there as soon as I got the cash together. But time's running out. It'll probably take at least a quarter of an hour to get to Beishan West Road from here."

Huo Sang thought this over, then hastened to the telephone in the other room and asked the Great Dragon Taxi Company to send a couple of cabs. He returned to convey his decision to Gu Yingfen.

"Miss Gu, I think it's best for me to go in your place one more time. Wait here for further news. Let me have your two thousand dollars."

"But he said that I have to bring the money there in person. Mr. Huo, you—you can't very well go!"

"No. It'd be too risky for you. Who can say this wicked man won't have something else up his sleeve? It's best that I go."

"Then this won't—this won't mess everything up?"

"No, it won't. Trust me. Everything connected with this case will be my responsibility."

Gu Yingfen looked dully at my friend, still unconvinced.

"Come on, we have to get moving," Huo Sang urged her. "I will definitely take care of everything for you."

Gu Yingfen removed two large rolls of bills from her gold-embroidered purse and handed them to Huo Sang. "No matter what, Mr. Huo, please, please don't clash with him," she again warned. "You know that if this picture comes out, my whole family will be ruined."

Other than giving her a nod, Huo Sang did not respond. He quickly put on a beige woolen overcoat and grabbed his hat. "Bao Lang," he said to me, "take one of the cabs to Jin Xueming's house on Beihai Road. If you see anybody delivering a photograph there, do everything you can to stop it. Under no circumstances can it reach Jin Xueming's hands within the hour. But if nothing is delivered within an hour, you can come back here and we'll consider another course of action." With that, he strode swiftly out of the room.

By this time, the cabs were honking in front of our house. I didn't dare tarry and went out soon after delivering a few words of comfort to Gu Yingfen and checking with her about Jin Xueming's house number. There was only one taxi still waiting; the one carrying Huo Sang had already driven off.

I jumped in and headed toward my destination. In about ten minutes, we were at Beihai Road.

I got out and found No. 108, a Western-style house with an iron front gate. A dark bronze plaque on it read "Jin Residence." I looked at my watch; it was already 11:25—a full ten minutes beyond Wang Zhisheng's one-hour deadline. Was Huo Sang meeting with him at that very moment? If the picture had been sent before Huo Sang got to Wang's place, it would already be at the Jins' house by now. I looked through the iron gate; the house was brightly lit, but it was totally silent. I didn't want to knock on the door and disturb the family, so I just waited outside, hoping that the picture had not yet been delivered and that I would have a chance to intercept it if it came.

I paced back and forth between the house and the corner of Beihai Road for perhaps fifteen minutes. There weren't many pedestrians around; no one came to make a delivery. Down the road to the west, I saw a policeman looking time and again at me pacing, which made me nervous and restless. If Wang Zhisheng had sent the picture before Huo Sang got to him, it should have been here by now. On the other hand, if Huo Sang had reached him in time, Wang probably would not have been able to send it, and I would be waiting around for nothing. So after enduring the wait until midnight, and observing the policeman advancing slowly toward me, I turned to leave to save myself the trouble of having to explain what I was doing there. The cab had been waiting all along, and I took it home.

Gu Yingfen was still by herself in our office, waiting for news. It had grown very late and she was curled up in a chair, trying to ward off the late-night chill.

"What happened, Mr. Bao?" she asked as soon as she saw me.

"I didn't see anyone delivering a picture," I answered. "Huo Sang will take care of everything."

"Could the picture have arrived there before you did?"

"I don't think so. It couldn't have gotten there that quickly."

She stopped briefly before asking another question. "Why hasn't Mr. Huo come back? He must be in some sort of trouble."

I tried to calm her. "Don't get yourself worked up. He absolutely won't fail you."

"It's just that I'm truly worried," she said, still anxious. "You would think that obtaining the photo and paying the money would be a matter of just a few minutes. Why is it taking this long?"

What she said was of course reasonable. I was also secretly concerned about any unforeseen turn of events, but all I could do was try to comfort her with encouraging words.

"Don't trouble yourself, Miss Gu. Mr. Huo has already promised he would handle the whole matter, and you can trust him completely."

Gu Yingfen fell silent. She looked down, as her willow eyebrows tightened with anxiety and the crimson drained from her lips. She dabbed at her mouth now and then with the white handkerchief in her hand, abruptly lowering her face, then lifting it to gaze absentmindedly at the electric light, never ceasing all the while to listen intently for sounds outside the window. I empathized with her restlessness, but there was nothing I could do for her, since I was as anxious as she. What had happened? Had Huo Sang actually agreed to buy back that photograph? Or had he tangled directly with that scoundrel? If he had chosen to be expedient and make some kind of deal for the photograph, he definitely should have been home by now, but he still wasn't back. Could it be that he had opted for a hard line, precipitating some other result? That crooked intellectual was full of tricks, evil to the core. If we failed to deal him a decisive blow, not only would we not be able to vent our anger, but we would be allowing a social boil to fester and to infect other innocents in the future.

It seemed forever before half past twelve, when honking sounds from afar startled me out of my reverie. A car was approaching the house!

"Mr. Huo is back!" Gu Yingfen exclaimed.

How did she know Huo Sang was in the taxi? Could she be delusional? Nevertheless, I was intensely hoping that she was right. But the car went right past the house, continuing on its way westward.

Gu Yingfen was greatly disappointed. "Oh, no! It wasn't him!" Her voice shook. She was on the verge of tears.

"Don't be distressed. I think he'll be here presently." I was talking nonsense, which was not comforting to her in the least.

Both of us lapsed into silence—assuredly a rather unbearable silence.

More time passed before she leapt up again. "Listen to that, Mr. Bao! Another car is approaching!"

She was right. It was another car. I nodded my head as it came closer and closer, its horn beeping continuously.

"Yes, it's him!" I said. "Listen to that, Miss Gu. The repeated honking is for you, to tell you that the transaction has been successfully completed. You don't have to be despondent anymore!"

Gu Yingfen's spirits were indeed lifted. She rose to her feet and went over to the window to listen. This taxi did indeed stop outside the door. Then we heard the sound of a man's rapid footsteps entering the house. Gu Yingfen rushed over to open the door to the office. First to enter the room were clinking noises, followed by a strapping fellow in a Western-style suit. It was not Huo Sang; it was the man who had met her in Banhong Park that morning— Yang Chunbo!

"Oh, no!" Gu Yingfen cried out, staggering back several steps. Had there been no chair there to prop her up, she would most likely have fallen to the floor. Extremely unnerved, she leaned against the back of the chair, her upper body bending slightly backward, her eyes betraying her fright. It was as if some menacing devil had suddenly appeared to prance wickedly before her. To have this pawn of Wang's reappear, and at this very time, was both unexpected and incomprehensible. He wasn't at all surprised to see us, however. After standing by the door for a moment, he took a step inside and made a deep bow toward Gu Yingfen, murmuring apologies all the while.

"Miss Gu, I'm so sorry, *so* sorry. I regret so much what I did, and I've come now to apologize. Miss Gu, please forgive me."

Still leaning against the chair, Gu Yingfen did not straighten up. I, too, had no idea what the apology was for.

I took a step forward. "What's this all about, Mr. Yang?"

Yang Chunbo answered, taking a thick square package he was carrying under his arm and placing it on the desk. "I've come to beg Miss Gu's pardon. This morning someone made a fool of me, causing me to offend her. Mr. Huo will come and tell you the rest. He's outside right now taking care of the cab fare."

The sound of familiar footsteps told me that Huo Sang was indeed back.

Coming through the office door, he nodded and waved to Gu Yingfen. "Miss Gu," he said, smiling, "please sit down and don't fret any more. Your problems are finally over. But it was not my doing. You ought to thank Mr. Yang here." He took out a huge roll of bills from his pocket, counted out a stack, and returned it to Gu Yingfen. "These two thousand dollars are yours. They were not needed."

Gu Yingfen straightened up, but she still seemed in a fog, her eyes flitting back and forth between Huo Sang and Yang Chunbo. She neither took the money nor sat down. She just stood there, unable to utter a word, her eyes staring straight ahead, her mouth agape. The fog, of course, hovered over me as well.

Huo Sang put the bills down on the desk. "Fine," he said smiling. "Let's all sit down and have a chat. Excuse me, Miss Gu, but I'll have to light up a cigarette or two."

So, one after the other, the four of us sat down. Only then did Huo Sang give us his explanation, puffing on his cigarette.

"The final act of this play seems rather complicated on the surface," he said, "but actually nothing could be simpler. When I took the cab just now to Wang Zhisheng's place on Beishan West Road, his four neighbors had resumed their mahjongg game, though without the kibitzer in his shorts and sleeveless shirt. They told me that Wang was no longer up there. I couldn't help being taken aback at the news, thinking he had already run off. But when I pressed them, I learned that someone had taken him to the hospital. That startled me even more, so I asked how that had come about. I learned then that a tall young man in Western garb had been upstairs to see him, but had come down and left a short while later. They thought nothing of that until they had finished their session and gone upstairs, when they heard moans issuing from his room. They pushed open the door to look and saw Wang Zhisheng lying on the floor. His bedding and the contents of his trunk appeared to have been packed away and then rifled through again; they were in a huge mess. By then, Wang Zhisheng was no longer able to say anything. His neighbors concluded that he must have had an altercation with the young man who had just been there. He was obviously injured, so they took him to Charity Hospital. As soon as I heard this, I thought it must have been the good work of Mr. Yang here. So then I hurried over to his residence on Penglai Road and learned right after I saw him that my conjecture had indeed been on the mark." At this point, Huo Sang gave Yang Chunbo a slight nod. "You should tell them yourself what happened."

Some light had broken through a gap in the fog, but it had not completely lifted, because the transaction with the photograph had yet to be explained. Gu Yingfen still looked dazed.

"About two hours ago, Mr. Huo came to see me, to inform me of the results of his investigation," said Yang Chunbo, continuing the story. "It was only then that I realized the ins and outs of the whole scheme. This evil man had toyed with me, turning me into his puppet and then including me in his photograph. He even dragged me into his plot to harm Miss Gu, which was despicable indeed. So as soon as Mr. Huo left, I rushed right over to that blackguard's place.

"Downstairs from where he lived four people were playing mahjongg. When I went upstairs to his room, I saw that he had just put a photograph into an envelope and was writing a name and address on it. He was greatly startled to see me and stood up, thrusting his hand into his pocket to fumble for something. I thought he had a gun and punched him in the chest. I didn't realize that, tough though his mind may be, he's physically extremely fragile. He didn't even cry out when I struck him that one blow, but staggered to his left and crumbled to the floor, making neither a sound nor any further movement.

"Then I remembered having sent him a picture of myself when I answered his advertisement and thought it must still be in his possession. Seeing that he had packed his bedding, as if he had been getting ready to move away somewhere, I searched the trunk that held his bedding, but couldn't find the photo. Then I noticed that the wastepaper basket in the corner of the room contained a great number of photos, clear proof that many people had fallen for his ruse and sent him their pictures. I found mine among them, and took it, along with the photo on the table he'd been getting ready to send off.

"As I was leaving the place, the people downstairs were still concentrating on their game. No one suspected me of anything. Only when Mr. Huo came to see me again did I learn that the photo this evil man was about to send out was connected with Miss Gu, and that it was very important. Miss Gu, I have it here with me." He stood up and opened up the large envelope he had placed on the desk. Taking out the photograph, he presented it to Gu Yingfen with both hands.

From the two accounts, I had pretty much come to a full understanding of the final twist in this case. Everything having turned out as she had hoped, Gu Yingfen was of course sincerely grateful to Huo Sang. But it was through Yang Chunbo that the crucial photograph had been retrieved. Due to his behavior at the Gardener's Gazebo, she could not help feeling a bit of aversion toward him. Still, hesitant and blushing, she did manage to utter a word of thanks to him before taking her leave of us with her two thousand dollars. Yang Chunbo offered to escort her home, concerned that it was late and she had a long way to go, but she would not hear of it. In the end, Huo Sang called the Great Dragon Company for a taxi to take her home.

As Yang Chunbo was leaving, I heard Huo Sang giving him words of advice about not letting the pursuit of the opposite sex wreck his youth and his future. But because the lighting by the door was not very bright, Yang's face was not well illuminated and his reaction was indistinct.

When we were alone again, Huo Sang happily lit up another cigarette and settled down to discuss his ideas about the proper punishment for criminals.

"Bao Lang, earlier on you were dissatisfied about the kid gloves with which I handled that evil man," he said. "How do you feel now?"

"That one punch of Yang Chunbo's was surely better than nothing," I answered. "At least it made me feel a little better."

He nodded. "Right—its only practical effect was to make somebody 'feel a little better.' There's hardly any other reason for it." He took a few more puffs. "Bao Lang, do you know why I chose to handle Wang in this way?"

"You had to be careful to preserve the good name of the Gu family and therefore could not use the law to take care of him. So you used Yang Chunbo indirectly to teach him a lesson. Am I right?"

"Yes. But there's another factor. I couldn't do anything to him directly because I was constrained by the promise I had made to him when we exchanged photographs."

"Yes, I understand that point as well," I replied. "But I still feel that this punishment is briefer and less stringent than this heinous criminal deserves—."

Huo Sang abruptly removed the cigarette from his lips. "Stringent?" he interjected. "What kind of stringent punishment would you suggest, Bao Lang? Tell me!"

I looked up at the light and did not answer him. In truth, I could not come up with an answer.

He emitted a heavy sigh. "Bao Lang, you've got to agree that the way to deal with a criminal is to punish him. You're also acquainted with penology and so must understand that the punishment of criminals follows the evolution of social systems, leading to the formulation of various ideologies and justifications. In the very beginning, punishment had to do with vengeance— 'an eye for an eye, a tooth for a tooth.' After that, it focused on intimidating the criminal with harsh physical punishment. Later on came the idea of reform through nurturing both the mind and the body. At present, these ideas have made a huge advance by taking the path of prevention through anticipation. In your opinion, in dealing with somebody like Wang Zhisheng, which of these practices would have been most effective—or most thorough?"

I thought about this for a while. "Are you saying that there really was no effective way to have dealt with him?" I asked.

"That's right. There really wasn't any, because the criminal tendency in him had already hardened. Neither intimidation, persuasion, or prevention would have had the least effect on him, and so, at the end of my rope, I chose the most barbaric of methods. I knew that Yang Chunbo was a rough-and-tumble person with a lot of anger in his belly. It was unnecessary to give him subtle suggestions. I knew he would just naturally take care of the matter for me. Still, as I have said, it was only to vent our spleen. It was not meant to be effective or thorough."

It was almost 3:00 a.m., but Huo Sang didn't look at all fatigued. He remained deep in thought, his eyebrows drawn together, puffing on one cigarette after another. In terms of handling the case, we could surely say that he had succeeded. But he was still troubled by his inability to mete out proper justice to this scoundrel.

"That's enough, Huo Sang," I tried to soothe him. "It's very late, and you ought to get some sleep. Don't tax your brain any further."

On October 24, I saw an article in the paper about an injured patient in Charity Hospital who had died six days after suffering a heart attack. The man had been taken there by his neighbors around midnight on October 17. He had been injured in a fight, but it was not known by whom.

In the middle of February the following year, Jin Xueming and Gu Yingfen were married in a ceremony held in Grand Central Hall. Huo Sang and I were both invited. At the banquet, we noticed a strapping, heavily built person—Yang Chunbo—also in attendance, his fob pendants clinking away as always.

3 The Odd Tenant

I. Suspicions

The gray-haired woman had just settled into the easy chair reserved for guests in Huo Sang's study when she suddenly leapt up again. Flailing her thin, wizened hands about, she panted between sentences. "I'm so terrified, sir! . . . My husband works in a textile factory. If he misses a single day of work, we go without food for a day. We can't survive an emergency. . . . Anything bad happens and the whole family's done for! . . . Sir, I'm really frightened! . . . You've got to figure a way out for us!"

This is only a brief sample of what she actually said—and hereafter I shall present her utterances in the same way, for to write down faithfully every word that came out of her mouth at the time would fill up more than a page. Her endless railings were without any order whatsoever. Breathlessness permeated her speech, and her many exclamatory interjections added to the overwhelming feeling of chaotic verbosity she conveyed.

The woman gave Ma as her family name, and Daqing Alley, Baotong Road, north of the city gate as her address. In her late fifties, she was wearing a dark padded jacket of synthetic fabric with a number of grease stains on the front. It was evident that this garment did double duty: It was worn at home as well as when she ventured out. In place of a skirt, she had on faded blue padded trousers. Her appearance alone made it evident to us, well before she opened her mouth, that she was of the working class. From the time she arrived, she rambled on nonstop about one thing or another, repeating herself over and over while interjecting a number of non sequiturs. Unless one listened to her very attentively, one could easily become befuddled.

Huo Sang usually dislikes talking to older women, because doing so often takes up an inordinate amount of time and moreover demands concentration to catch the drift of their verbal meanderings. On that day, he was at first pleased to be receiving a client who was a common worker. He listened to her patiently, showing no trace of annoyance. But the old lady was punctuating her statements with sprays of saliva, some of which landed on Huo Sang's face. This brought his forbearance near to the breaking point. Using a handkerchief to wipe himself with one hand, he guided the woman onto a chair with the other. He sat her down with much effort, but she bounced up again like a spring the moment he released her, only to repeat the same barrage of words I've summarized above. Seeing there was probably no effective way to calm her down, Huo Sang retreated a step to keep at a safe distance. It was evident he wanted to stay outside the range of her rainy emissions.

I was quietly chuckling to myself at the situation when an amusing thought crossed my mind. Had this woman been some twenty years younger and dressed more fashionably, even if she scattered spittle when she talked, there would surely have been a goodly number of eager young men who would call it "fragrant dew" and gladly submit to the moistening.

"Mrs. Ma, please get hold of yourself. No matter what you have to say, you've got to sit down to say it. Why don't you listen, and let me tell you what I know about you. You live at 7 Daqing Alley in a two-story building rented out to four households. You sublet part of the space you occupy, staying behind the living room downstairs. Recently you rented out the rear room upstairs to a man named Ye. You say that this person is very odd, and you've grown somewhat afraid of him. Is that correct?"

The old woman still couldn't control her hands, which kept moving jerkily up and down as she spoke. "It's more than just 'somewhat afraid.' Actually, I'm terrified! You know that my husband's a factory worker. He leaves early in the morning, comes back late at night, and never asks about the goings-on at home. Also, I'm just a woman, and I'm truly panicky about what's been happening! Sir, nowadays when a kidnapper or a robber is arrested, doesn't the law also come down on those who sublet to him? I'm really worried about legal hassles, sir! If that tenant's not a kidnapper, he's got to be a murderer or a robber! I'm so upset, and can't think of what to do. Luckily, Mr. Mao in the front building told me to come here and ask you to figure a way out for me. I'm poor and have no money to pay you. But I beg you, sir. Please do this for me as a good deed!"

Huo Sang waited until she had finished and calmed down before he un-hurriedly responded. "It's not a hard problem at all. If you think the person's not a decent sort and might get you in trouble, just tell him to move out."

"Oh, no! Oh, no!" the woman kept shaking her head. "Even I could have thought of doing that. It's only that he just moved in ten days ago and paid a whole month's rent in advance—that's five dollars. If I were to ask him to move out, not only would I have to return the money to him but, according to the rules, I'd also have to pay *him* another month's rent. So with him mov-ing in and moving out like that, I would lose ten dollars altogether. Where would I come up with that much money?"

"Then why don't you report him to the police and ask them to help you evict him? It wouldn't cost you anything to do that."

"That wouldn't do, either. Even though I suspect him of wrongdoing, I have never seen him commit murder or robbery. Besides, how would some-body like me dare to trouble the gentlemen in the police station? Wouldn't doing that also cost me money? Sir, you're my only hope. Please help me figure out how I can get out of this mess without any losses."

Huo Sang frowned as he walked over to his desk to take out a Golden Dragon cigarette. He lit it slowly while saying with a nod of his head: "In that case, go ahead and tell me. How odd is this person really?"

The old woman again expended a good bit of saliva chattering meaning-lessly around the subject before she got to the point. "The man has a northern accent and claims to be a teacher. But he doesn't look like one to me. He wears a padded cotton robe that is really old and tattered, along with a well-worn, ill-fitting vest of Venetian cloth. He never gets up before noon, and once he goes out, never comes back before midnight. Just think. How could he be teaching school so late—if he's a teacher at all?"

"That may not be so strange. There are a lot of night schools now."

"No, no. Mr. Mao in the building in front is also a teacher. His school has night classes too, but he's always back home by ten every night. This strange Mr. Ye, though, never returns till past midnight. Also, Mr. Mao, thinking he was in the same profession, tried to speak with him on several occasions to learn the name and location of his school. The man hemmed and hawed and never came up with an answer. Mr. Mao has also peeped into his room through a crack in the wall and has said that there were a few chapbooks on his desk, but nothing one would find in a school. So it's clear he's not really a teacher."

"Well, then," Huo Sang said, nodding his head, "he may just be pretending to be one. Is there anything else suspicious about him?"

Having gained what she took to be Huo Sang's agreement, old lady Ma was somewhat encouraged. As her spirits lifted, the spray from her mouth also increased in intensity and range.

"There are so many things!" she answered. "He never greets anybody when he leaves his place. The third day after he moved in, I saw him coming out and asked him in a friendly way where he was going. He merely rolled his eyes and walked past me without saying a thing. Ever since, he's kept his mouth shut whenever he appears, never exchanging a word with anyone.

"And that's not all. Whenever he goes in or out, he always carries a small, rectangular package under his arm. One time Genfu, the nine-year-old boy who lives above the kitchen, touched it, and the man went crazy, threatening him and cursing at him. Apparently no one is allowed to touch that thing of his. Don't you think that's strange?"

"All people have idiosyncrasies. Perhaps he's merely a bit eccentric. You don't have to make a mountain out of a molehill."

"Hmm. So you still think there's nothing unusual, sir? Fine. There are a lot more strange things about him! Three days ago, he came back after midnight and, suddenly, clear and loud, *ding-dong ding-dong* noises came out of his room, like he was rattling silver dollars. This went on for more than an hour, so that Mr. Mao in the front building was unable to get to sleep. He had clearly gotten hold of quite a few silver dollars and was trying to see for himself whether or not they were genuine. Think about it, sir. If it took more than an hour to count up all that cash then it had to have been over a thousand dollars, don't you see? Just think about it sir—a person like that! Where would he have gotten so much money?"

On hearing this, Huo Sang seemed to become a little more attentive. He lowered his eyes and flicked ashes from his cigarette before slowly asking her a question. "The clinking sounds of silver dollars—did only Mr. Mao hear them?"

"No, I heard them as well. But I was extremely drowsy at the time. The clinking sounds came to me as I was turning over in my bed, and I didn't realize it was him and drifted unconsciously off to sleep again. But since there's only a single wall between him and Mr. Mao, I'm sure the noise would have kept Mr. Mao up."

Huo Sang nodded. "Is there anything else that has aroused your suspicions?"

The old woman's hands started to flutter wildly as the rainstorm once more emitted from her mouth. Fear showed in her eyes.

"Yes, there's more! There's more! The night before last, he suddenly hung a piece of black cloth over all the cracks and holes in his wall. Surely he was trying to prevent anyone from spying on him in secret! Think about it, sir. If he didn't have anything criminal to hide, why would he do that? . . . And another thing, the most peculiar of all! Yesterday afternoon the small pointed knife we use for slicing vegetables suddenly disappeared from our kitchen. We looked everywhere but couldn't find it. While we were cooking dinner, I searched all over the kitchen for it for quite a while, but I still couldn't figure out where it had gone. By then that strange man Ye had already left the place. Auntie Wang, who lives above the storage room, said she had seen the knife on the table at twelve-thirty, before he went out. Also, Ye seems to have run into the kitchen just before he left. That's why we thought he must have taken the knife. Then, this morning, we found out we were right. The knife reappeared in the kitchen!"

His interest piqued, Huo Sang discarded his cigarette butt. "If, as you say, he stole the knife, then why would he return it afterwards?"

"He didn't want to steal it," the old woman replied. "He was only borrowing it! I figure that, since he took the knife, he must have wanted to do something criminal with it, like commit a murder. If he somehow failed and was arrested by the police, wouldn't we be in trouble? The knife is ours, after all."

"How do you know for sure that he was the one who borrowed it?"

"I have proof. I've had the knife for a long time. We don't have a sharpening stone at home, so it had grown very dull. Now, though, it has been honed to razor sharpness, surely sharp enough to kill somebody with. I don't know whether he used the knife to do that yesterday, but I'm really frightened now."

The woman's voice trembled a bit at this point. Her face turned ashen, and the movement of her scrawny hands became more jerky. It was evident she was gripped by fear.

"There's no use being afraid, Mrs. Ma," Huo Sang told her in a calming voice. "I understand now. There's definitely something odd about that tenant of yours. But you need not torture yourself like this. I suggest you go home for now and not let this matter bother you any longer. You see, once you begin to suspect things, you will find something suspicious in everything that happens. As a result, you end up troubling yourself needlessly. If you come across anything else suspicious about this man, please come back and tell me. I will help you without fail."

"Can you tell me what I should do now, sir? I still can't make him move out?"

"Of course not. I can, however, quietly find out for you what he's up to. After that, we'll see what we can do about it."

"Please do that quickly. I'm afraid he's about to do something really awful!"

"Calm down. If he does anything criminal, I can go talk to the police for you, and you will not be blamed in any way."

II. The Investigation

Huo Sang stood up right after the old lady left, stretched himself, and yawned.

"Bao Lang," he smiled at me, "you've got to compliment me today. Usually I hate talking with someone like that. Today, though, I patiently spent an hour and a half doing so—and ended up with this tiny problem. Can't say it's not worth it, right?"

I knew it was Huo Sang's cherished principle to take on a job for the sake of the job itself. So when he asked whether something was worth it, he was decidedly not talking about monetary compensation.

"Do you think the case *is* worth looking into?" I asked him.

"I feel there are several points about it that are challenging," said Huo Sang. "First, why does he want to pretend to be a teacher? Second, since he's subletting a back room, you can imagine what his financial situation must be. Then where did all that cash come from? And third, what's most bizarre is the question of his purloining the knife. Was he really going to commit a violent crime with it? Since he did have money, why couldn't he have bought one for himself? If he didn't steal it, then the knife's disappearance was odd indeed. Besides, how did it come to be sharpened?"

"Hmm, that's indeed strange. I was thinking the knife had perhaps been taken and used by someone else living there and that the man had simply been wrongly accused by the old lady."

"I was thinking the same thing. Since you're not doing anything right now, why don't you run over to Baotong Road? You can consider it a fun trip."

"Fine. After all, this is a rather minor case, and it's quite unnecessary for you to handle it yourself. I'll be glad to do it for you."

Huo Sang smiled in response, and all seemed settled for the moment.

After lunch that day, I went over to Baotong Road by myself. Daqing Alley was a narrow little pathway with lower-middle-class dwellings on either side. Filthy water covered the ground, so that it seemed all but impossible to walk down the alley without dirtying one's feet. All over the walls of the buildings hung wet clothes drying in the sunlight, and the people living there kept up a constant din. When I got to No. 7, I suddenly caught sight of old lady Ma, who had just visited us. She was at the gate conversing furtively with an elderly neighbor woman. She greeted me as soon as she saw me approach.

"That strange person hasn't gotten up yet," she whispered to me. "Do you want to see him, sir?"

"That's not necessary," I said, waving my hand. "Don't bother him. If I want to see what he looks like, I'll do so inconspicuously. Right now, I just want to take a look at that knife. Have you been using it today?"

"Yes, we have. Even though the knife belongs to me, it's used by just about everybody. Everyone in our three families, except for that man, has used it today."

As soon as I heard that, I realized that my previous conclusion was no longer valid. Since the knife was regularly treated as common property, other residents would have no reason to steal it for personal use. "Have you examined the knife?" I asked further. "Were there traces of anything suspicious on it?"

"Are you asking whether there were bloodstains on it, sir?" she answered with a question. "All of us looked and found nothing. You can go into the kitchen now, and I'll let you take a look for yourself."

I followed her to the kitchen in back. She picked up a pointed knife from the tabletop for me to examine. The blade was about seven inches long and attached to a wooden handle. Half of it had been ground away, but the edge was extremely sharp. As for the knife's value, it would be worth twenty coppers at most to a second-hand vendor. So the idea that it might have been stolen was really rather ridiculous.

"Do you think someone else could have taken this knife for personal use?" I asked in a soft voice.

The old woman shook her head. "No, it's got to be him. It's definitely got to be him. Ordinarily, in the mornings, every one of us uses this knife, and we always put it back on the table afterwards. Yesterday afternoon, it was clearly gone. When I went to bed, there was still nothing on the table. But when I got up early this morning, the knife had reappeared right here! Everyone else around here goes to bed early. It's only *him* who doesn't come back until midnight. There's a muddy shoe print in here as well. I forgot to mention that to you earlier." She then pointed to the concrete floor.

I looked down at the place she had indicated and, indeed, there was the blurry outline of a shoe's sole, although it was less evident now because it had been repeatedly walked upon.

"It was raining last night. Obviously, he came straight to the kitchen when he got back and returned the knife to the table. Sir, there's definitely no doubt about it—"

At this point, the woman suddenly stopped speaking and looked momentarily startled. I also heard footsteps on the stairs. Someone seemed to be slowly walking down them. The woman made a quick gesture as if to tell me "*He's* coming!"

I quickly hid myself behind the kitchen door and looked out surreptitiously. Before long, the footsteps reached the bottom of the stairway, at which point the man turned and went out the front door.

In the brief glance I had of him, I could see that this tenant Ye was a short fellow with a sallow, weathered face and sunken cheeks, though his small dark eyes sparkled with energy. Pale, straggly whiskers were scattered around his mouth. It was hard to tell right then whether he was in his thirties or his forties. He was dressed in the manner described by his landlady. I noticed that he swaggered as he walked toward the front gate, much like an old-fashioned scholar. Overall, he was a rather comical sight.

Once I saw that he had left, I spoke to the old woman in a low voice. "After you came back, did you do anything to make him suspicious of you?"

"Nothing at all," she said. "He always goes out at this time every day, and he always comes back at midnight."

I didn't ask any more questions but hurried out the front door myself, intending to tail him in order to see where he was going. When I got to the mouth of the alley, I saw him strolling down the sidewalk along the thoroughfare. There was indeed a rectangular package tucked under his arm. It was wrapped in a black-and-white handkerchief and seemed to be some kind of small box.

I followed him all the way across the streetcar tracks, almost to Baotong Road, where there were a number of tobacco shops and vending places for lottery tickets. (At the time, lottery tickets, with such names as "Charity Prize Tickets" or "Disaster Relief Tickets," were still highly popular.) The man stopped, seeming to peruse the signboards there. Quite unexpectedly, a large delivery van pulled right in front of me, and I quickly retreated to get out of its way. By the time it had passed me, the strange man was nowhere to be seen.

I hurried ahead a short way and looked into a few of the lottery ticket stores, but there was no sign of him. Could he have slipped into Hede Alley over there? But if he hadn't known he was being followed, he surely wouldn't have slipped away so quickly. I rushed down the alley anyway. It had quite a few Shanghai-style two-story residences as well, but I could not find a trace of him. Greatly disappointed, I reminded myself that I had come just to look into the matter of the lost knife. As for learning about where he always went, I thought I'd go home and talk to Huo Sang about it first.

When I arrived back home, I learned that Huo Sang had also gone out. Our servant, Shi Gui, said that he had changed and left less than ten minutes after me, and that, no, he had not said where he was going. It wasn't until almost 3:00 p.m. that he returned, whereupon I reported to him about my encounters during my investigation.

"As far as I can see," I said, "he definitely did take and return the knife."

"You really believe that?" said Huo Sang with a frown. "That is the stickiest point. I had originally concluded that the matter of the knife was the result of some misunderstanding."

"How so?" I asked him.

"From all I can ascertain, I feel that this man Ye does not at all seem to be a vicious sort of person. That old woman has been misconstruing everything."

"What?" I cried out in surprise. "You've already gone and investigated the case yourself?"

Huo Sang nodded. "Exactly. Even though this is a minor case, I felt that, since the old lady came so trustingly to ask for my help, I couldn't very well not look into it myself to learn the truth about that man and solve this puzzle for her. So after you left I made up my mind to join you in the investigation. Now it is completely clear to me who this man really is."

"That's strange. How did you find out about him? Why didn't I see you?"

"When I hurried to Baotong Road, I saw you tailing the man from a distance. Since he was dressed as the old woman had described, I could pick him out right away. But I was ahead of him while you were following behind him, so I couldn't very well make contact with you. Then later, when he was standing in front of the lottery ticket places, I was already waiting for him at the mouth of Hede Alley. I never expected, however, that once he went down the alley, he would go straight into the No. 3 building. I happen to know that place is an opium den. So I went in after him, pretending I wanted a smoke and using the opportunity to find out what the man is really all about. He turned out to be a regular customer of the place. By spending a bit of cash, I learned the whole truth about him."

"So that's what happened!" I said happily. "No wonder I didn't see you. What kind of person is this man? Why is his behavior so bizarre?"

"Don't be impatient," Huo Sang said in a measured voice. "I'll explain everything to you step by step. This man's full name is Ye Shixian. He makes his living analyzing written characters to tell fortunes. He's somebody who shouts at you to 'Find out what's ahead for you and your business!' along the roadside or inside teahouses. With such an occupation, he's of course free in the mornings. Then, every night, after all the teahouses have closed, he goes back to the opium den for one more smoke. That's why he never gets home till after midnight."

"Then that's also why he claims to be a teacher. It's just to save face, right?"

"That's one reason. But at one time he did open his own school and lived the simple life of a schoolteacher for a few years. He feels that even though he is addressed as 'sir' while he works as a fortuneteller, the appellation only carries a minimum of respect. So that's why he trots out the title of 'teacher' as his profession. This explains another question about him. The rectangular package he carries is what he earns his living with. It contains such objects as a writing brush, an inkstone, and a scroll full of characters. Since he keeps quiet about his actual profession, he of course wouldn't want anybody to touch the tools of his trade. Moreover, his cold reluctance to engage in conversation with anyone on his way out is attributable to a traditional superstition among itinerants who earn their livelihoods by their wits. When they are about to do their business, they detest engaging in casual chitchat. But since old lady Ma doesn't know the truth, we can't blame her for having all kinds of suspicions about him."

"But there are more questions. Why did he cover up the holes and cracks in his room? And how did he come by all that money?"

"Even though I haven't finished investigating those questions, I think we can deduce the answers to them as well. Didn't you notice that when he walked past the Profit Lottery Shop, he paused there for a while? I would say he is somebody who likes to buy lottery tickets, and one time he got lucky. I would say that the silver he has came from a lottery prize. As for covering up the cracks in his wall, it's simply because he was afraid someone would peek in. You ought know that once a poor person comes into some money, he sees everyone as a potential robber and sets up all sorts of needless defenses against them. That's a common mind-set, almost too obvious to point out."

I could not help breaking into a smile. "I really hand it to you, Huo Sang," I said. "Things always go so well for you. For a few cents, you were able to solve this little case. The whole thing really couldn't have been any more economical. But that kitchen knife is still an enigma. What do you think is the reason the knife was first stolen and then returned? What could be the reason for that?"

Huo Sang could not come up with a plausible answer right then. He knitted his eyebrows and thought to himself for a while before giving me a measured reply. "I think that has to be some misunderstanding; perhaps the knife was never really stolen by anyone. Or maybe the thief was not our man at all. At any rate, I've decided to pay him a visit tomorrow. Then we'll have all the answers for sure."

III. "He's Killed Somebody"

Even when a case appears to be unexceptional, something unexpected almost always comes up as it unfolds. We have experienced that many times. Most of the questions in this case involving old lady Ma were answered by Huo Sang, and seemingly little mystery remained. So how was I to anticipate that before I even got out of bed the following morning Shi Gui would be rushing into my room in a dither?

"There's an old lady downstairs who's terribly upset. She wants to see you."

As soon as I heard it was an old lady, the events of the day before came back to me.

"Do you recognize the woman?"

"It's the one who was here yesterday."

I knew right then that the case had taken another turn. "Where's Mr. Huo?" I asked.

"He's gone out for his usual morning walk. I only came in to wake you when I saw how desperate she was."

I nodded and jumped out of bed without saying anything more. I wiped my face, pulled on some clothes, and hurried downstairs. When I got to the living room, the woman was standing there trembling. She appeared deathly pale, her eyes wide open and her hair disheveled. The state of her agitation was far more severe than yesterday.

"What's happened?" I asked as I greeted her. "Please sit down and tell me about it."

"Sir, the matter's gotten way out of hand!" she said in a quivering voice. "I really can't take it anymore!"

If her legs had seemed like springs yesterday, today they had become steel poles. There was absolutely no way I could have persuaded her to sit down.

"What's the matter?" I asked her. "Tell me."

"He's gone and killed somebody!" the woman said.

"What?!"

"I'm really scared about the law coming down on us. I beg you, sir, please save me!"

I couldn't help being startled, but had to maintain my composure. "Don't be rattled. Tell me clearly. Who killed whom?"

"It's that tenant Ye. He killed—I don't know who!"

"Is that so? Where did he do it?"

"Upstairs in the back room, where he lives."

"Oh! In that case, give me all the details."

"When he came home late last night, he brought along another person," said the woman, her voice still quavering. "I was already in bed at the time and never saw who it was. I only heard them talking upstairs. The other person spoke in a very low voice, so I couldn't tell whether it was a man or a woman. I felt uncomfortable about the situation, but since I've already rented to him, he has tenant's rights. If he wants to share the place with another person, I can't very well object. Beside, it was late at night, and so I felt I should just as well let things go.

"Then, early this morning, as my husband was headed to the factory, a neighbor from the house at the entrance of the alley asked him whether our tenant upstairs had moved out. This took my husband by surprise, and he answered no. Then the neighbor said that he had seen that odd person leaving at dawn carrying a large bundle that looked like a bedroll. That's why he thought the man had moved out.

"My husband couldn't help but be surprised. He's often heard me say that Ye never gets up before lunchtime. So why would he be going out so bright and early? My husband came back inside to tell me about it. By then, I had already discovered a frightful thing in our room. There were quite a few drops of blood on top of our mosquito net! When I looked closely, I realized that they had come from between the boards in our ceiling!

"I was beside myself when my husband suddenly came in to tell me what the neighbor had said. Then, when he saw the blood on the netting, he gasped in surprise and rushed upstairs to knock on the man's door. But the door was locked; the strange man had really gone. I went into the kitchen right away to look for the knife, but it had disappeared to I don't know where!

"Only then did I realize the tenant had murdered somebody for sure. According to Mr. Mao in the front building, he also had heard two people talking last night in the room above ours. Just about dawn, he thought he heard some kind of outcry. All indications are that the strange man had lured someone upstairs last night, then used our knife to do the person in. Early in the morning, he had wrapped the body up and taken it away. Since this is a murder, we're so afraid that the authorities may think we had something to do with it. My husband has already gone to the police to report everything. I hurried over here to beg you to talk to them and stand up for us. Tell them we had nothing to do with what happened."

I have of course edited and abridged the foregoing. The thought that occurred to me, however, was that the explanations Huo Sang had given the previous day had undeniably been arrived at too quickly. He had not been able to account for the knife, and never foresaw that the case would turn into a homicide. Since he still hadn't returned and the old lady was so upset, I couldn't very well refuse to see what I could do for her myself. So, in a quick five minutes, I finished my morning toilet, told Shi Gui what was going on, and hurried off with the old woman.

When we got to No. 7 Daqing Alley, Baotong Road, there were already quite a few people gathered in front of the Ma residence, jabbering to each other in twos and threes. It was only when I entered the place that I learned the police had already sent someone to investigate. The detective, Xia Bingsheng, was someone I knew. We greeted each other, then went together to the old lady's room to look at the bloodstains.

The netting over the bed was not new, but it had been recently washed. There were indeed numerous bloodstains evident on top, concentrated in a small area perhaps the size of a silver dollar. I looked up directly above the stains and saw that, sure enough, there was blood coagulated between the ceiling boards as well.

Xia Bingsheng touched the stain on top of the netting and nodded. "Yes, it's clear that the blood dripped down from above. The stains are still very fresh."

We then hurried upstairs. There was indeed a small, Western-style lock on the door. I looked through a crack in the paneled wall and saw that the inside was all draped with black cloth, so that nothing was visible. The lock was of the lowest quality and gave way once Xia Bingsheng applied a bit of pressure to it. The door now being open, I followed him inside.

There was a small bed in the room with a mosquito net hung above it as well. The net's color, though, had turned from the original white to gray. The bedding was in a tangled mess, as if it had never been straightened out. There was a decrepit old leather suitcase under the bed, along with cardboard cartons, hatboxes, and a small, thoroughly rust-covered container that used to be a kerosene can. There were a bedside table and a couple of chairs. Aside from a stack of old books and a square paper-wrapped package, something else caught my eye: It was none other than the knife I'd seen yesterday!

The detective was also drawn to this object. He hurried over, picked the knife up, and examined it in the light. "Hey, there's still blood on it!" he cried out in amazement. "Even though he tried to wipe it off, it's still stained. Take a look, Mr. Bao. Aren't those bloody traces along the blade?"

With one glance, I saw that the detective was absolutely right. I held the blade up to my nose; sure enough, the odor of blood was still distinct.

"Come look, Mr. Bao," Xia Bingsheng called out once again. "There's more indisputable evidence here."

I turned my head, saw him leaning over examining the floorboards, and did the same. "You're right," I said. "There are traces of blood here as well. The blood on the netting downstairs surely came from up here. There's not a shred of doubt about it."

The detective then picked up a crumpled piece of paper by the bed. "There's more," he announced in a loud voice. "This is what he used to wipe up the blood."

Just then, shouts from downstairs caught our attention. When we listened closely, we could hear Mrs. Ma's crying out triumphantly: "We got him! We got him!"

Police detective Xia seemed to grasp the situation. "Good," he said to me. "There's not much more to this case. Soon everything will come out. My partner Cao Shengbiao and I came together. He was waiting for the man at the entrance to the alley, and the shouting downstairs tells me he must now have him in custody."

"But if this Ye Shixian committed such a heinous crime," I said, "why would he come back to be caught?"

"I would say he never expected us to be on to him so soon," replied Xia Bingsheng. "Since he's disposed of the body, he'd naturally think he could come right back here as if nothing happened."

Before I could respond, various sounds of footsteps could be heard from downstairs. When I looked down, I saw that the person coming up the stairs was Huo Sang.

"So you're here too?" I said right away. "This is developing into quite a major case."

Huo Sang seemed not to have heard me. He came up to where we were, appearing calm and self-possessed as usual as he gave Xia Bingsheng a nod in greeting.

"I saw your partner Cao Shengbiao just now; he wouldn't wait and has already taken Ye Shixian to the police station."

"What do you mean?" I jumped in to ask him. "Are you implying that Cao Shengbiao was overly hasty?"

"I feel that if he had listened to me and come with me to look around here, then perhaps we could have verified what Ye Shixian was telling us. What have you two come up with so far?"

Xia Bingsheng picked up the knife from the table and handed it over to Huo Sang, who looked it over. "This knife surely is a challenge. But what I am looking for right now is something else."

Xia Bingsheng pointed to the floor. "There's blood here," he said. "This crumpled piece of paper was used to wipe it up."

Huo Sang took the paper ball and opened it up carefully, only to discover a small white down feather inside. "Ha!" he nodded. "This is an important piece of evidence." Then he took a quick glance at the tabletop. "Bao Lang," he told me, "go and unwrap the package on the table from the China Modern Publishing House. See if what's inside isn't a complete collection of books on Daoist incantations."

I opened the package as he had directed. The contents were exactly as he had predicted. I was quietly amazed. Did Huo Sang have X-ray vision? This extraordinary discovery left us all baffled.

Then Huo Sang leaned over, pulled out the converted kerosene can from under the bed, and removed the cover—to lift out a dead white rooster! A happy exclamation escaped his lips as he plopped the chicken back into the container. Turning around, he grabbed the books from my hands, flipping open to the tables of contents in first one, then another. When he got to the third volume, he pointed out something to us on the first page.

"Here, Bingsheng, is the key to the whole case. Take a look too, Bao Lang. It can add to your general knowledge."

What was it all about? I was really in a fog. The passage Huo Sang was pointing to read: "The way to attain wealth and good fortune: Consume no meat for three days. Before the break of dawn on a propitious day, shut the world from your mind. Slaughter a rooster and draw the charm below with its blood. As you do so, chant the following incantation and then carry the charm on your person. You will then surely win out in any game of chance." Below that followed the outline of the charm, along with four rather unintelligible lines of incantations.

Xia Bingsheng and I could only gape at each other. "You now understand, Bingsheng, that Ye Shixian didn't kill anybody," said Huo Sang to him. "All he did was slaughter a rooster. And he did that because he wanted to get rich by indulging in this wild fantasy of performing a ritual and then going off to play the lottery. If you hurry back to the station and search him, you will undoubtedly find a charm just like this on him—and maybe a lottery ticket as well!"

Only then did everything suddenly become clear to me. So it was nothing more than some ludicrous scheme! I could never have imagined anything like this; I, too, had taken illusions to be realities.

"This whole thing has really proven to be unimaginable. How did you manage to see through it?" I asked Huo Sang.

"When I heard what Shi Gui said and hurried over here, I was just as startled as you," Huo Sang answered. "But Cao Shengbiao was right in the act of arresting Ye when I got to the mouth of the alley. On learning he was a murder suspect, the man was frightened out of his wits, so he quickly disclosed everything. Once I heard his story, I never had the slightest doubt that he was telling the truth. Cao Shengbiao, though, thought he was making it all up. Now that you have seen the whole picture, Bingsheng, will you go back to the station and clear up the case, so that the misunderstandings will not continue? Before they release Ye Shixian, on the other hand, they should set a short time limit for him to move out of this place. Otherwise, his overly imaginative landlady might find something else to suspect him of and really bring him grief."

Xia Bingsheng still seemed to be less than totally convinced. "Then what about the person who spent last night with him?" he asked Huo Sang. "Do we know his whereabouts?"

"That was his friend," Huo Sang replied. "This friend had asked him repeatedly to let him stay there for the night before he agreed. Early this morning he was carrying his friend's bedding to the train station to see him off. He also told us that while he was performing his ritual before sunrise, his friend was having a nightmare, making all sorts of grunts and squeals from the bed and almost spoiling everything. He said the friend has now gone to Wuxi.[1] You can easily verify all this, should you need to."

Huo Sang turned to go downstairs after gesturing me to follow him, which I did. He paused to offer a few words of explanation to old woman Ma before we left the house together. When we got outside, Huo Sang finally turned to me. "All this trouble occurred because Ye Shixian wanted to save a little bit of money. So it was his own fault," he said.

"I don't get what you're saying. What 'little bit of money' did he want to save?"

"He thought he didn't need to buy a knife just to kill one chicken. So he decided to borrow the knife that belongs to his landlady. But then he was too conscientious, and took the knife out to have it sharpened. Since what he was going to do was secret, he naturally didn't tell anyone, and that's what led to all the trouble. If he had only gone and quietly bought a knife for himself, wouldn't the subsequent fuss have been completely avoided?"

Ye Shixian's testimony at the police station also helped to wrap up the remaining loose ends. He was indeed carrying a charm drawn in chicken blood.

---

1. An industrial and resort city eighty-seven miles west of Shanghai.

Moreover, after he had seen his friend off at the train station, he'd gone and bought a five-dollar lottery ticket. His fanciful desire to get rich quick had been sparked by an enticing advertisement he had seen in the newspaper on charms and incantations, which had greatly aroused his interest. Then, three days ago, after unexpectedly winning ten dollars in the lottery, he made up his mind to use the charm-and-incantation method and buy a number of tickets, fully expecting to attain instant wealth. As for the large number of silver dollars he was supposedly rattling for quite a while that one night, it was in actuality just the ten he had won earlier. So this seemingly comical and yet socially meaningful case had thus been totally cleared up. I couldn't help feeling some lingering regret, however.

"The lottery arouses people's natural yearning for good fortune as well as their greed, causing them to pursue the fantasy of getting rich without having to expend any effort. This is extremely detrimental to society," I said with a sigh.

Huo Sang was thinking the same thing. "That's right," he said, "but there's another fundamental problem here. In recent years, disasters and famines have threatened the livelihood of so many, making it easy for people to fantasize about possible solutions to their problems. Even in our day, the power of thousands of years of superstition still holds sway over our entire society, over which incantations, spells, and fictional accounts of ghosts and spirits continue to wield formidable influence. Our educational system is so deficient that most people still lack basic knowledge. It's only for these reasons that something as ridiculous and ludicrous as we have seen in this case could actually occur. Oh, I don't know how long it will take before such ridiculous practices disappear from our society! What a pity they're still with us!"

④ The Examination Paper

Because I have been writing about my friend Huo Sang's cases for so long, many of you readers, perceiving the depth of our mutually supportive relationship, have expressed the desire to know how it all began. In looking through my old bamboo chest recently, I came upon my diary from college days, which contains an abbreviated record of a bewildering and disheartening case, one that involved me personally and that Huo Sang solved. Up to that point, even though we were both students at Zhonghua University, Huo Sang and I had yet to become close friends. Only later did our friendship grow deeper by the day, to the point where we can now be considered soulmates. Thus what might have been just a negative experience for me actually turned out to be the start of a deep and lasting friendship.

On that particular day I had been hunched over my desk, writing nonstop for two hours until my head was spinning, my wrist ached, and all the joints of my hand seemed afflicted with sudden stiffness. The cause of this agony was a philosophy examination. After presenting us with his question, the professor had given us special permission to write our answers in our dormitory rooms, so long as we met his preset time limit. But the question was so complex and difficult to analyze that I was having trouble deciding how to frame my answer. Not long before, I had heard someone say that writing an essay is like unraveling a silk cocoon: However hard you try, if you don't find the right starting point you'll never get anywhere. Once you locate it and follow the natural path of the thread, however, smooth success will follow. That was a good way of putting it. When I had started wrestling with the problem, my mind had been blank, my hand frozen, and my brain numb; I could hardly set a single word down on paper. It wasn't until something ignited my train of thought that the words came flooding into my head and I was able to complete my task in one fell swoop.

Putting down my pen, I looked over my essay and could not help being pleased with myself. Such a brilliant answer would surely propel me to the top of the class! When the news of my success reached home, I could imagine how proud my family would be. After reading it over, I casually placed my paper on the righthand side of the desk before taking up my pen once again to answer a letter from my mother. The letter had come just as I was agonizing over the exam. Its contents had so cheered me to the core of my being that I had been able to zip right through the difficulties posed by the exam question, quite like a gust of wind clearing away fallen leaves. (When I wrote just now that something had unloosed a flood of words in my brain, I was referring to what my mother's letter contained.) You readers must be somewhat skeptical at this point. What could my mother have said to cause me to write her such a prompt reply? As the matter was very personal, I wasn't inclined to blurt it out at the time. I was also afraid that if I revealed its contents, it could elicit the envy of my companions.

After I'd finished writing my reply, I sealed the letter in an envelope, addressed it, and put on the proper amount of postage. At that moment I was bubbling over with happiness. My exam was over and good news had come my way. In my excitement, I restlessly tapped on the desk with my fingers, then stole a glance over at the two seated on either side of me, neither of whom seemed aware of my unusual state of mind. The three of us shared a dormitory room. One, named Cheng Deng, was in my class; the other, Fei Dezhi, was younger. Each of us had his own desk, which we had arranged in the shape of a T. With Cheng to my left and Fei to my right, we were at right angles to one another. I could see that Cheng Deng, pen in hand, was still deep in thought, while Fei Dezhi was clutching a book, reading it to himself under his breath. Neither one, luckily, was aware that I was trembling with elation as I sealed the envelope. I stood up when I was done and went outside with the letter to call out for Bei Four, the janitor.

Bei answered me instantly. I handed him the letter and told him to pass it on to the gatekeeper. "What time has it gotten to be, Bei Four?" I also wanted to know. "Will the mailman be here soon?"

Bei took out his bronze pocket watch. "He's scheduled to come again at ten thirty-five," he answered. "It's now ten fifteen, so he'll be here in another twenty minutes."

I nodded at Bei as he left. Then I went back to my seat, still brimming with elation, intending to give my answer one final going-over. To my astonishment, nothing was on the desk. The examination paper had somehow disappeared!

At first, I thought there was a problem with my eyes. But nothing was there even when I steadied my gaze. The paper had flown to the clouds like a yellow crane! I was shocked, and the joy that had overwhelmed me the moment before instantly disappeared in a puff of smoke. The exam I had written had been truly inspired; I had been jubilant over it as I had placed it on the desk with my own hands before turning to write the letter to my mother. But in an instant, it had somehow vanished. What else could have happened but that someone had taken it? I looked over at my two roommates. Which of them could have done the deed? By then, Fei Dezhi was already noticing my agitation. As he put his books away, he had a strange expression of uneasiness and apprehension on his face. The fellow had a questionable past, having once picked up another person's books and hid them away to sell. When this came to light, he received an official reprimand from the university and was ostracized by his schoolmates. Recalling this, I instantly suspected Fei Dezhi and could not help staring accusingly at him. Fei's face flushed all the way to his ears, and it seemed that even before I announced my loss he had already admitted his guilt.

I was just getting ready to question him about it, when Cheng Deng, seated at the desk to my left, suddenly threw down his pen, stood up, and rushed out the door, thus drawing my attention to him and away from Fei Dezhi. Cheng Deng was normally a rather close-mouthed individual who preferred to be left alone; it was not easy for anyone to get close to him. Even though we were classmates as well as dorm mates, we never had much to say to one another. Since I had just lost my examination paper, the abruptness of his departure could not help but make me suspect him too. But as I couldn't very well have asked him to stay, or otherwise prevented his departure, I could only stand and watch him go. Overwhelmed by a feeling of helplessness, I breathed heavily and my heart pounded. Just as Cheng Deng left, someone else I knew came in. It was Huo Sang.

Because he was intellectually gifted with outstanding discernment, everyone said that Huo Sang had uncanny deductive powers and considered him a great detective. Seeing him, I felt a little less anxious and thought that I could perhaps seek his help. Huo Sang was smiling as he came up to me, but instantly turned serious when he saw my agitation.

"What's going on, Bao Lang?" he asked, rather startled.

"My paper has disappeared," I told him straight out. "It was a philosophy exam that I had worked hard on and felt good about. Now it's been stolen. So how can I not be upset?"

"Really? Could that really have happened?" Huo Sang asked me seriously.

"Why would I joke about something like this? If you think you can help, I'll tell you all about it."

"Please do. Maybe I can solve the problem for you. Why do you think your examination paper was stolen?"

"It's obvious. The paper was on the desk there. In an instant it was gone. If it wasn't stolen, it would have had to magically take wing and fly out of here."

Because I was staring right at Fei Dezhi, he was starting to be alarmed. His face turned pale, making him look more guilty. I then told Huo Sang everything that had occurred from the time I took up my pen to the disappearance of my paper. I didn't hold back anything except my own suspicions about Fei and Cheng, which were hard to talk about with Fei right there. Huo Sang listened with rapt attention, without uttering a single word. He looked around only after I had concluded.

"This is indeed strange," he said. "But your desk is next to the window, where an occasional breeze may blow in. Have you looked around?"

"I have," I answered, "and there's nothing anywhere. The window may be open, but there's no reason to believe the wind blew my paper somewhere."

Huo Sang pondered momentarily in silence. "After you finished writing, did anybody come in here?"

"Only the three of us—Fei, Cheng, and myself—were in the room. Cheng just left. You probably saw him. He . . ."

"How can you say no one's been in here?" Fei Dezhi interrupted. "Just now, Qiao Yilei was here to borrow a pen from me; he was standing right next to your desk. How could you not have noticed him?"

This made me recall that, while I was writing my letter, there did seem to have been someone standing near me. But because I was so wrapped up in what I was doing, I never looked up to see who it was. That's why I didn't quite remember the incident.

Huo Sang suddenly looked up. "Is this so, Bao Lang?" he asked. "Did you really see Qiao Yilei in here?"

"It seems to have happened," I said haltingly. "I wasn't paying attention, and he and I haven't been getting along—," I admitted reluctantly.

"What?" Huo Sang was quick to ask. "Has there been some kind of rift between you two?"

"Yes," I answered him. "A week ago, we got into an argument over a game of badminton. We haven't spoken a word to each other since. Whenever we run into one another we merely exchange glares."

Huo Sang lifted his eyebrows. "I didn't know about this," he said. Then he looked over at Fei Dezhi. "How long was Qiao Yilei here? Did he just borrow a pen? Was there anything else?"

"He was here about five minutes," Fei said. "As soon as he got the pen, he left. There was nothing else he wanted."

"But the examination paper is gone, " said Huo Sang. "Do you think he had anything to do with that?"

"How . . . how am I to know?" Fei Dezhi stammered. "Why are you grilling me about this?"

"I'm not grilling you," said Huo Sang. "I consider this just a private discussion. In your view, what do you suppose happened?"

"In terms of position, Qiao was standing right behind Bao Lang's desk, and therefore it wouldn't have been difficult for him to make off with the exam. But he's in a different class and has a different exam question to answer. What good would it have done him to steal the paper?"

"Who can say he wouldn't secretly destroy my paper if he knew we suspected him? Or maybe he just wanted to settle his grudge against me," I said.

"That's right," Fei Dezhi jumped in. "What you just said hits the nail on the head. But we've got to get evidence in order to be certain. Are you up to the job, Huo Sang?"

Huo Sang stroked his chin, without answering. "Dezhi," he said after a while, "please leave the room for now, and let me have a little private discussion with Bao Lang. Meanwhile, you must keep this whole matter strictly confidential; don't talk about it to anyone else."

At this, Fei Dezhi, like a high imperial minister assigned to proclaim an edict, assented without hesitation and immediately left the room. I remained anxious and unsettled—and unhappy with Huo Sang's seemingly unwise course of action.

"Settle down, Bao Lang," Huo Sang said to me. "Think back. Can you say the exact time the examination paper disappeared?"

I pondered for a while. "I'm so rattled now I can't recall anything that would pin down exactly when that happened. But for you to send Fei Dezhi off like that was not exactly the right thing to do."

"Why? Isn't he the one you suspect of taking your paper?"

"Yes, you're right. You know that he has not always been trustworthy in the past. It's possible he stole my exam to sell to somebody, who knows?"

"In which case, Qiao Yilei would not have anything to do with it."

"Well, that's also hard to say. I'm rather befuddled at the moment and can't make up my mind. But you were wrong to let Fei Dezhi leave so quickly. If he's the one who took my exam, haven't you just given him the opportunity to stash it away someplace?"

Huo Sang smiled. "If that's what you think, why are you blaming anyone but yourself? Weren't you the one who let Cheng Deng get away just now?"

Stunned, I was quite unable to answer right away. "Okay, I was stepping over the line to criticize you," I said after a while, flushing. "Cheng Deng and I are in the same class and had the same exam question. So I can't say he had no possible motive in this situation. He was really agonizing over the exam question just now and seemed unable to finish his answer even after a long while. After my paper was gone and I was looking for it, he suddenly left the room. So there is certainly reason to suspect him as well."

Huo Sang knitted his eyebrows in thought for a moment, as if he too was unable to get to the bottom of the problem.

"So what's your conclusion, Huo Sang?" I said, impatient for a quick solution. "Who stole my exam?"

"According to what you've been telling me," he said methodically, "it seems that we have not one but three suspects. Let's not jump to any conclusions right away; first, would you clear something up for me?"

"What is it?"

"You said just now that you had been able to finish the examination because a letter from your mother had set off your train of thought. Can you give me some idea of what was in that letter?"

I was hesitant. "Why do you need to know?" I said finally. "Are you thinking that there's some connection between my mother and my losing the exam?"

"Even though that may not be so, you must have heard that it is the proper responsibility of a detective to get to the bottom of every question," said Huo Sang. "If you're serious about having me help you find your paper, please don't hold out on me in any way."

So there was nothing I could do then but reach into my vest pocket after a short pause, pull out my mother's letter, and hand it over to him. Huo Sang grinned as he took the sheet out of the envelope, and began to read aloud.

My dear son Lang:

    Your letter telling me that the school term is ending and you will be taking your exams came yesterday. I hope with all my heart that you will make every effort to do well, not forgetting the high hopes all of us have for you. Your aunt came to visit at the beginning of the month and I disclosed to her your intention to ask her daughter Huizhu to be your wife. Your aunt was delighted, and immediately assented. She also told me that aside from her own joy at having you as her future son-in-law, Huizhu herself has also indicated great interest in the prospect. So it appears that this matter will come to a successful conclusion. In this way, my own wishes will be fulfilled, and your happiness will follow as well. Moreover—

By the time Huo Sang got to this point, I was too embarrassed to let him continue and grabbed the letter from his hands.

Huo Sang was silent for a moment before letting out a loud laugh. "That's terrific!" he said. "With news like that, no wonder you were so overjoyed. But why haven't you said a word of this to anyone? Don't you want your good friends to celebrate with you?"

"Please don't make fun of me," I said. "The examination's still missing, and if we don't get it back very soon, what will I hand in? Besides, my mind's so muddled at the moment I can't recall a single word of it. If you've any sympathy for me, shouldn't you be changing your congratulations to condolences?"

Abruptly, Huo Sang took out his pocket watch to check the time. "I've got it!" he said as he leapt from his seat. "Don't worry about it! Don't worry! Just sit tight for a while, and I'll clear everything up for you."

Before the echoes of his voice had even faded, he was gone from the room. The whole thing seemed rather crazy to me, and I remained in a huge quandary. Was Huo Sang telling me the truth? How could he have claimed success in an instant like that? Was he simply trying to comfort me, seeing how distressed I was? I pondered the whole matter but came up with no answer. In fact, the more I thought about it, the more downhearted I became, until my skull seemed to be splitting apart. Then, with a bang, Huo Sang burst back into the room in a state of excitement, as if he was on to something. My heart was pounding in my chest like a wild animal, and I was unable to calm it down.

"What's going on, Huo Sang?" I asked him in a trembling voice. "Did you find out what happened to the examination paper?"

"The whole case is solved!" Huo Sang crowed. "It's more than just what happened to the paper."

"Really?" I cried, overjoyed with the news. "Who took it? Can you say who it was?"

"Why not?" he said, smiling. "I've got both the culprit and the spoils."

I was astonished. "That's incredible," I said. "You've really lived up to your reputation! But who's the thief? Could it be Qiao Yilei?"

"No, your idea is unfounded. Just think about it. Even though he had that argument with you, the paper was right next to you. How would he have dared take it? It was just too risky, and he's not dumb enough to try something like that."

"What you say makes sense. So Fei Dezhi has got to be the one."

"Not so either. Even though his past behavior may have been questionable, he's not going to go as far as to steal an examination paper to sell. Pitifully cowering about as he does—it's surely because of his bad reputation, which must give him a feeling of inferiority and constant dread that people are suspecting him of things. You don't seem to have noticed this, so you thought it could be him. But if you think about it again, you'll realize how ludicrous it is to consider him a suspect."

At this, I stared at Huo Sang in bewilderment, as if I'd entered a maze. Huo Sang looked back at me out of the corners of his eyes, smiling to himself all the while.

"I was at my wits' end and let the real thief get away without a thought," I said, blushing. "Now I know my mistake."

"Let's consider what's behind your statement just now," Huo Sang said a chuckle. "You assume there is a thief. Now who might that person be? Can you enlighten me?"

"Since the one who stole the paper was neither Fei nor Qiao, who else could it be but Cheng Deng?"

"I knew you would say that," said Huo Sang, rubbing his hands together. "Actually, it's none of them. I know for a fact that Cheng Deng is a serious and upright sort for whom any act of thievery would be out of the question. When forming conclusions about people and events, we must keep the broader picture in mind and not just focus on a single point. Your speculation here was shortsighted indeed."

I was both ashamed and startled, quite unable to understand his point. I felt somewhat bewildered and lost.

"That's strange," I responded. "I really cannot see, if all three of them are innocent, where the real thief could have come from. Could it have been the wind that blew in from the window, which then—?"

Huo Sang suddenly inserted one hand into his coat pocket, motioning with the other for me to stop talking. "The thief is you yourself!" he declared. "Here's what you stole!"

He placed a letter in my hand. Dazed and feeling like I was in a dream, I took a look at the envelope. It was none other than my letter to my mother that I'd just asked the janitor to mail. I was puzzled at first, until I noticed that the letter was quite heavy and must contain more than a single sheet. I opened up the envelope to look, and—sure enough—the examination paper that I had produced with such painstaking effort was inside!

At that moment, surprise, joy, regret, and shame intermingled in me. I felt like the peasants who, during times of famine, eat a stew of yams, radishes, beans, and barley—I could not distinguish the bitter from the sweet. This whole thing had turned out to be the result of my momentary lapse, when I had blithely placed the examination paper in the envelope, then accused others of having stolen it. Now, though, there was nothing I could do about it.

"That was a big mistake, Huo Sang," I said uncomfortably. "Fortunately, you have come to my aid and solved the problem. Otherwise, I would never have known how to break free of my preconceived notions. I truly admire your mental prowess."

"What's so extraordinary about what I did? As the proverb says, 'Players in a game of chess never see as well as kibitzers.' It was because your mind was in such turmoil that you made a mistake like that. Since I was a bystander, I was able to keep my head more than you could. That's why I could unravel the mystery."

"Absolutely! How did you figure it all out? Can you tell me?"

"Sure. When I heard just now that you'd lost your examination paper and suspected it had been stolen, I disagreed right away. Then, when I heard your highly reasonable speculations, seemingly plausible as they were, I felt even more that you had begun with a wrong premise. While I was pondering as a bystander about what could have happened, I thought about the letter you had received from home. After I was able to read it out loud later on, I learned that the unexpected good news had arrived at the very time you were under great mental stress, so you would of course be unable to contain your feelings. In hurriedly sealing your letter in an envelope, you must have put in the exam as well. You told me earlier that after finishing your exam, you had casually placed it on the righthand side of your desk. Right after that, you wrote the reply to your mother and addressed it. From these facts, I could surmise that, as you started to prepare the letter for mailing, it must have been lying right on top of your exam. Then, as you rushed to pick up the letter, fold it, and slip it into its envelope, you must not have realized that you had picked up the exam paper as well. When I asked you later exactly *when* you had lost the exam, you told me you had no idea. When a person is overexcited, his thinking processes can become unconsciously muddled.

"Once I had considered all this, it became clear to me what had happened. You know, however, that it would have been useless for me to have said anything to you; it would only have added to your confusion. Moreover, it was urgent that I act immediately. So I ran off without asking you any more questions. The mailman had just come as I got to the gate. By explaining to him that your examination paper had been mistakenly sealed inside the envelope, I was able to retrieve the letter. It was heavier than usual, so I knew as soon as I felt it that I had been right. Now that the case is solved, how are you going to thank me?"

"My friend, you're really the smartest," I said, praising him in a loud voice. "That's why all our schoolmates consider you a great detective. Wait until the holidays, and I'll take you on a boat ride. It'll be my treat, all right?"

"Is that all the thanks I'm going to get?" said Huo Sang smilingly. "No. Oh no. That's far from what I would like."

"What? What is it you want?"

"What I wish is that, on your wedding night, you have your beloved bride fill a goblet from a jug of wine with her own pretty white hands and present it to me personally. Only then will I be fully satisfied."

At these words, I blushed deeply and my ears felt hot. I raised my hand to take a swipe at him, but he dodged to one side. We looked at each other and laughed, and neither of us said anything for quite a long while.

5 On the Huangpu

I. The Ransom Notes

I've often said that the two words "detective" and "danger" are inextricably intertwined, and that the compensation for detective work—excitement—is simply the result of facing danger. This story records an instance of "No pain, no gain," a time when the danger we had to face was extreme: I nearly lost my life!

But I have no regrets. Even at this moment, as I take up my pen to set down what happened, the feelings I had then still color my recollections.

It was ten o'clock one morning when, quite without warning, an old man of perhaps sixty came to our residence to see Huo Sang. The man was dressed very plainly in a padded, dark silk robe. He had kindly eyes and a square face, which added to the overall impression of genteel honesty he conveyed. He was clean-shaven, but his thick eyebrows were starting to gray. That day, anxiety tinged with sadness showed on his face, which immediately aroused our sympathy. Huo Sang politely offered him a chair and then asked the reason for his visit. The old man succumbed to a series of coughs before he could answer. He reached into his pocket and took out a picture and newspaper clipping. Spreading the clipping out, he directed our eyes to the local news article it contained with an unsteady finger. "Another Case of a Missing Child," the headline proclaimed. I read on:

> Our report last Saturday on the case of the disappearance of Hao Qizhen caught the attention and elicited the concern of the public at large. Unexpectedly, however, before the furor over the first case has had a chance to die down, a similar case has come to light. The day before yesterday, Yu Huibao, the son of Hongyuan Yard Goods proprietor Mr. Yu Shoucheng, was also

reported missing. Huibao, only nine years old, is a student at Dahua Elementary School. After leaving school that day, he disappeared before reaching home. The Yu family notified police authorities, who sent detectives out searching everywhere for him without success. Mr. Yu is advanced in years, and the disappearance of this boy, his only son, has naturally caused him much sorrow and consternation.

Mr. Yu is an honest and principled businessman who has contributed greatly to the public welfare. He takes special care to promote national products. When his business boomed last year, he set up two new public schools with his own funds. For this reason, he has enjoyed wide trust and respect. Now that he has suffered this unexpected calamity, surely many people will be eager to express their sympathy for him.

I glanced at the old man when I had finished reading and felt a genuine tugging at my heart. Then I looked at the photograph, which showed a handsome youngster in a boy scout uniform.

"I suppose that you, sir, must be Mr. Yu Shoucheng," said Huo Sang, quite deferentially.

The old man indicated he was with a nod.

"I'd seen the article already—the day before yesterday. It really caught my attention at the time. And because you, sir, are an honest businessman, I felt especially concerned for you."

The old man hurriedly stood up and bowed. "I don't deserve your flattery. I just try to fulfill the obligations of my profession."

Huo Sang extended a hand. "Please sit down. There's no need to be so formal. Am I right in assuming that you, Mr. Yu, want me to look into this matter?"

Yu Shoucheng nodded once more. "That's right," he said, his voice tinged with grief. "Right now, I'm unsure whether my son is dead or alive. I can only hope I may rely on your great abilities to try and get him back." Then he put his hand again into the pocket of his padded robe.

"It's the twentieth of November today. The day your son disappeared, wasn't it the sixteenth?" Huo Sang asked.

"Yes, exactly," said Yu Shoucheng. "My son was on his way home from school late in the afternoon when he met up with the kidnappers. I didn't know the particulars at the time, and sent people to look everywhere—"

"Then, you know more about it now?" Huo Sang couldn't wait to be informed.

Yu had by then fished a letter out of his pocket. He handed it to Huo Sang as he answered, "Yes. Please take a look."

Huo Sang removed the letter from the envelope. I moved up close to him in order to read it aloud.

> *Mr. Shoucheng: After getting this note, you should feel somewhat relieved. Your son Huibao is on our boat at this very moment. Rest assured we do not intend to harm him. We have learned that your business is prospering, and so have gone ahead and taken your son into temporary custody. We would like to borrow $20,000 from you. From the moment you get this note, you will have a total of twenty-four hours to deliver the full amount to the Five Blessings Boat opposite Poplar Beach on the Huangpu River, in order to ransom him back.[1] Understand that this is a good-faith gesture on our part. Should you take us lightly and seek out other solutions, do not blame us for the consequences. Be forewarned that we do kill for our livelihood, and that we are neither fools nor cowards. You should have no doubts about what you're dealing with.*

Huo Sang examined the envelope as he was folding up the letter. "According to the postmark, this letter was mailed at 2:00 p.m., November eighteenth. It's now 10:00 a.m. on the twentieth—well past the twenty-four-hour deadline. Why have you put off coming here till now?"

"There's a reason for this," Yu Shoucheng quickly replied. "I wasn't purposely holding off. After I got this ransom note toward evening the day before yesterday, I was both relieved and fearful. Someone suggested that I take it to the police and let their inspectors find a way to get my son back. I considered

---

1. The Huangpu, a branch of the Yangtze, is a large navigable river running along the southern and eastern edge of what used to be metropolitan Shanghai.

that too much of a risk and absolutely refused to act on the idea. I'd rather lose the twenty thousand than endanger my son in any way. Even though I'm not actually all that old, I'm so worn out that I'm just not up to handling demanding tasks any more. I was greatly concerned that if I went there myself to pay the ransom, something might go terribly wrong. So I went to see my younger brother Shoujin to ask him to deliver the money to the boat. He agreed at the time, and was going to do it on the morning of the nineteenth." The old man then lapsed into a fit of coughing. Huo Sang stood up to pour him a cup of tea.

I waited for him to stop before asking, "Did your brother actually go?"

The man shook his head, then spoke up angrily. "He did not! He talked to his wife and declined at the last minute. Oh, what a good sister-in-law she is, and what a loving and upstanding brother he has turned out to be! I was at my wits' end, because the deadline was approaching without anyone dependable to carry out the mission. I became really desperate every time I thought of the threat to Huibao's life. Then, last night, another note came, which I have brought with me as well. Please take a look at it." As he was speaking, he took out the slip of paper, breathing hard all the while.

Huo Sang read the note aloud:

You really don't know what's good for you, missing that first appointment. We're extending the deadline another twenty-four hours. If you ignore that also, you might as well forget about coming and just retrieve your son's body from the Huangpu.

As Huo Sang finished reading, the old man's face suddenly paled, his hands and feet trembled, and his breaths came even more rapidly.

"Mr. Huo, do you think my son is still alive?" he stammered.

"This second note was sent yesterday evening, the nineteenth," Huo Sang replied with a serious expression. "The deadline has not been reached, so your son is of course not yet in danger. Don't worry. Since you're here now, however, are you asking me to deliver the ransom for you?"

Yu Shoucheng nodded repeatedly. "Exactly so, exactly so. Because I never had any intention of capturing the culprits, I never thought of you. But now, after mulling things over, I know I couldn't find anyone else I could entrust with the job. So I'm here to ask you to deliver the ransom. I am also imploring you not to make trouble for the kidnappers, so as not to bring harm to my son. You must, I beg of you, be compassionate on this point and comply with my request, so that I can put my anxieties to rest."

Huo Sang folded up the note and fiddled with it. "Since you're willing to spend twenty thousand dollars to get your son back, of course I won't put his safe return in jeopardy. But there is an important matter that we need to clear up beforehand. I understand your son is only nine and most probably cannot write you a proper note. Because both these notes are unsigned, how do we know that the person who sent them actually has your son? Could it be that someone who read the news article has set out to bilk you? We've got to determine this before we proceed."

This was indeed of crucial importance, I was quietly thinking. Any hope of recovering the boy might not only be dashed, but the twenty thousand dollars, not to mention Huo Sang's efforts, might also be expended for nothing.

"What you're saying is true," Yu Shoucheng explained. "But the first message came with a gold locket, and the second one included a shirt, both of which belong to my son. It's clear that they're not bluffing."

Huo Sang pondered the situation again. "In that case, I'll see what I can do. But I'll have to ask my friend Bao Lang to come along. And when I go, I'll need to pretend to be your brother Shoujin."

A ray of light seemed to break out of the despondent gloom on Yu Shoucheng's face. "Thank you, sirs," he said happily. "I will be eternally grateful if you can bring my son back safe and sound, so that I can reunite with my flesh and blood. I will definitely compensate you well for your efforts."

The necessary arrangements were quickly settled. Yu Shoucheng was to return home to fetch the ransom money. Once that was delivered to us, we would set out for the kidnappers' boat so that the second deadline would be kept and Huibao would not have to face further danger.

As he took his leave, the old man earnestly enjoined us to proceed as we had agreed. "You've already promised me, Mr. Huo," he said. "You must get my little boy back safely this time and not make trouble for his captors, no matter what. You know that this is why I refrained from involving the police. If anything catastrophic happens to my son, then not only will my ancestral line be ended, but I will have no reason to go on living." The tender love he had for his heir was evident in his tone of voice. He then fell into another paroxysm of coughing. We were genuinely moved.

"Don't you worry, Mr. Yu," Huo Sang tried to comfort him. "Your aim is simply to get your son back safely. I will do my utmost to carry out your wishes by seeing that this happens. Anything else will be my responsibility, and you need not concern yourself about it."

The "anything else" Huo Sang mentioned here seemed to suggest that he had other intentions. So I waited until Yu Shoucheng had left and we were re-laxed and smoking after dinner to ask him for an explanation.

"Huo Sang," I said, "what are your real plans for this case? Are you simply going to deliver the twenty thousand to the boat—"

Huo Sang answered before I could finish the question, shaking his head all the while. "No. No. A large sum of money like that, why shouldn't I use it for some other purpose? You're really rather simple-minded if you think I'd just go and hand it over to those crooks."

"Are you planning to keep it for yourself?" I asked with a laugh.

Huo Sang remained serious as he shook his head once more. "Of course not. You should know that a ransom of twenty thousand dollars is of little im-portance when measured against the menace of that outlaw gang. We just can't let them go on bringing harm to our society."

"So you want to capture them?"

"Absolutely. We ought to catch ourselves a few big fish, just for fun."

"Then some sort of clash will be inevitable. Can you guarantee that their little hostage, Yu Huibao, will not be affected?"

Huo Sang slowly let out a puff of smoke. "I don't think he will be," he said solemnly.

He sounded like he wasn't sure. "What do you plan on doing?" I asked him. "Are you going to get the police involved?"

"No. To do that would be to declare open war, in which case Yu Huibao would definitely be affected."

"Are you saying, then, that there'll just be the two of us going on that boat?"

"That's right. I'll be Yu Shoujin, and you'll have to eat a bit of humble pie and play my servant."

"Just the two of us?"

"Right."

"Isn't that too dangerous?"

"Are you afraid of danger?"

"Of course not. It's just that this case involves the lives of a father and son, and so we have to be that much more cautious."

"If we keep our heads when we get on that boat, there's every chance we'll be successful."

"By 'successful,' do you just mean getting Huibao back?" I pressed him. "Or do you include apprehending the crooks?"

"You're getting into too much detail," Huo Sang said smilingly. "But, to tell the truth, the success I am planning on wouldn't stop with accomplishing only one task, but would, I hope, include the other."

Our conversation was brought to a sudden halt by the ring of the telephone. Huo Sang stood up to answer it, tossing away what was left of his cigarette.

II. The South-China Swallow

I continued smoking as I thought over Huo Sang's plan. I felt that it was too risky. In detective work, taking risks was part of the job and nothing especially to shy away from, but we did have to be reasonable. Admittedly, Huo Sang's was an outstanding intellect, and he didn't usually go wrong. Still, the outlaws' base was on a boat in the middle of the Huangpu. Once the two of us ventured out there, wouldn't it be difficult to get away if things didn't go as planned? In that case we could very well fall into their hands, as they outnumbered us by far. Wasn't the risk much greater than we should take?

Huo Sang took a while to hang up before returning slowly to the office. He had a very serious, coldly detached expression on his face.

"Who called you?" I asked him in surprise.

Huo Sang pulled out another Golden Dragon cigarette from the can. "You'll never guess."

"Could it be that another case has come up before this one has even been settled?"

"No. It was the South-China Swallow."[2]

I couldn't help jumping up in surprise, quite unconscious of the half-smoked cigarette slipping from my fingers.

"So the great, magical South-China Swallow has turned up again?" I said. "What did you talk about with him?"

Huo Sang sat down and lit up. "He told me to take care and not involve myself with the kidnapping case."

"Ah, so he's connected to the case we are about to be involved in."

Huo Sang nodded.

"What else did he say?"

"Nothing important, really. Mostly that one sentence."

"So even though this call seems to be a greeting on the surface, it's really a threat. Wouldn't you say so?"

"That surely is the obvious conclusion, but he kept insisting that he meant well in saying what he said."

"So how do you plan to deal with it?"

Huo Sang quickly exhaled a thick cloud of smoke. "What uncertainty can there be about this? He can threaten all he wants; we'll just go ahead and do what we're going to do."

I paused for a second before asking him, "So you mean that you've decided to take on this Yu family kidnapping case?"

Huo Sang fixed me with his gaze. "That's right. I decided that from the start, so why bring it up again? Since I already promised to carry out Yu Shou-cheng's wishes, why would I now go back on it?"

"But now that the South-China Swallow has contacted us—"

"No, no. Not only does this not deter me from carrying out my plans, it energizes me. As you know, Bao Lang, we have always acted on the fundamental principles of satisfying our curiosity, practicing our spirit of service, and maintaining our integrity. So even if we have to lay our own safety on the line, we'll just have to take our chances. Don't worry about what's nonessential. Just get dressed so that as soon as the money from the Yu family arrives, we can be on our way to the boat." At that, Huo Sang hurried upstairs to change.

2. The South-China Swallow is the master thief who appears in this and other stories as Huo Sang's potential nemesis. See especially "At the Ball" (Chap. 7).

I sat down on the sofa once more to mull things over. The more I did so, the more I feared what we were getting ourselves into. Even though we had yet to learn about them, people who would kidnap someone for ransom were probably nothing but bloodsucking devils. The two of us would have our hands full just dealing with them. But now this mysterious South-China Swallow had also entered the fray. Wouldn't that make the task overwhelmingly difficult? The intervention of the South-China Swallow clearly showed some kind of link between him and the gang. Or worse, it was not outside the realm of possibility that he was the prime mover behind the entire scheme.

The South-China Swallow had always proved to be a devious and clever fellow. We'd almost been bested each time we'd met up with him. Now that we were about to tangle with him again, I was not all that confident we could prevail. Still, since Huo Sang had expressed such strong resolve, I couldn't very well back down. There was no recourse but to join him, perilous as the enterprise might be.

After lunch, Shi Gui ushered in a middle-aged man who appeared to be a servant. He turned out to be the one Yu Shoucheng had sent with the ransom money and also had with him a picture of Yu Shoujin, to help Huo Sang disguise himself properly. I took the delivery, sent Shi Gui upstairs to give Huo Sang the photograph, and wrote out a receipt for the man to take back with him.

Soon enough, Huo Sang was ready. He'd put on traditional attire—a dark satin Manchu jacket over a squirrel-gray robe of Ningbo silk along with thick-heeled leather shoes—and looked the picture of an up-to-date member of the gentry. His square face was extended somewhat by a wisp of dark whiskers on his chin. A pair of dark glasses covered his piercing eyes. As I had to disguise myself as well, I changed into an old robe and a black woolen vest to masquerade as his attendant.

Huo Sang was amused by my appearance. "Be alert," he chuckled, "especially when we talk to each other. Don't you forget the class difference between us and ruin the whole operation."

"I should remember to call you 'young master' then?" I asked.

Huo Sang shook his head. "That won't do. It's probably better to forget about the 'young' and put in 'old' instead. *Your* name is now 'Xilu'—'Happy Prosperity.' Now, take care not to forget it." As he was speaking, he handed me a pack of Pagoda cigarettes. "We're both smokers, but we have to maintain the master–servant distinction now. When we get on the boat, you can light those up, but I will be smoking these cigars."

Each of us put our own tobacco away. Huo Sang took Huibao's picture and the ransom notes from the gang. He also divided the paper currency that had just been delivered to us, putting half in his pocket and locking the other half in the metal safe.

"You're just going to give half of it to them?" I asked.

Huo Sang shook his head. "The half is just a kind of bait. Why in the world would I give them good money?"

I was quietly amused. He was actually planning not to spend anything, to ultimately hang onto the entire amount! I thought he had gone well beyond simple wishful thinking and wondered what kind of capacity he had for stomaching disappointment.

Huo Sang quickly called our servant, Shi Gui, over and whispered a few words in his ear. Then he asked me, "Bao Lang, do you have a white handkerchief on you?"

"I always do. What do you need it for?"

"We might get sweaty. Then we would certainly need it."

"Sweaty? I—"

"Let's just stop gabbing and be on our way."

"We're leaving now? I still have to go upstairs to get something important," I said as I turned around.

Huo Sang grabbed me. "What are you getting? What's the need?"

"I still don't have my gun. I can't be without it."

Huo Sang did not release his grip. "Ah, that's not something we'll need. Don't bother with it."

I was greatly taken aback. Since we were now entering the robbers' lair, shouldn't we even take along a gun to protect ourselves?

Seeing my consternation, Huo Sang quickly added: "Don't worry, I've long since gotten everything ready for you. Let's just get going."

III. Boarding the Boat

As Huo Sang and I rode along on the Poplar Beach tram, I couldn't help feeling very uneasy. I was thinking that once we boarded that boat there would be no way of knowing whether success or failure, good or bad fortune, awaited us. Yet Huo Sang was as quietly confident as always, as if he already had everything well in hand. He had planned not only to get Yu Huibao back cost-free but also to capture some of the culprits. While I had always admired his courage and capabilities, what he was attempting this time seemed somewhat foolhardy, as I could not for the life of me imagine what his planned course of action might be.

Huo Sang puffed on his cigar for a while. "Bao Lang," he said to me in a low voice, "this time you must follow my instructions to the letter in everything you do. Don't ever act on your own. You should realize that one little false step could ruin everything."

I indicated my agreement.

"After a while, if things go well, have no qualms about taking Huibao off the boat by yourself," Huo Sang added.

"And leave you all alone? Are you telling me you really figure on capturing the kidnappers?"

Huo Sang gave a slight nod but no answer. He started again to puff on the cigar. "You know the kind of people you're up against, don't you?"

Huo Sang was deliberate in his response. "They're probably quite formidable."

"Do you think the South-China Swallow is their leader?"

"I was thinking perhaps not. It's probably closer to the truth if we just say there's some kind of link."

"Let's hope you're right. Otherwise, the danger will be much greater."

Huo Sang's eyes quickly widened. "What do you mean by that?"

"For one thing, the South-China Swallow has encountered us before," I said. "He could see right through our disguises. In that case, not only would all our plans be dashed, but we would also be putting ourselves in grave danger."

Huo Sang smiled. "Bao Lang, you're really too naive. Do you think that just because he recognized us we'd have no way of defending ourselves? Pull yourself together now, whatever you do. Above all, don't be so weak-kneed, or people will see that we're up to something. Hey, we just passed the Santai Textile Factory. The tram's coming to the last stop. Watch yourself, now."

We got off the tram at Poplar Beach and turned south to Mansha Road. The entire area was rather desolate, devoid of either residential buildings or pedestrians. Off in the distance, we could hear the faint din of workers in the factories and the *ding-dong* of the departing tram. We walked to the beach and saw that, indeed, there was a small steamboat moored in the middle of the river, several hundred yards away. Could it be the Five Blessings Boat?

Huo Sang walked along the shore ahead of me. As we approached Tengyue Road, he suddenly came to a halt.

"Did you notice that the boat is flying a small flag?" he asked me softly.

We were drawing closer and closer and could see the boat more clearly than before. I saw that there *was* a little white flag fluttering above the stern. On it were five red bats in a circle.[3]

"I guess that has to be the boat," I answered.

Huo Sang did not respond, but his face suddenly took on a serious expression, as if something had just occurred to him.

"Do you remember the case of the haunted villa?"[4] he asked, his mouth next to my ear.

With this prompting, I immediately recalled an out-of-town gang called Five Blessings. Its members were active all over the Yangtze delta. Kidnapping and extortion were their principal stocks-in-trade. When they got to Shanghai they had wanted to turn a villa belonging to a man named Hua in the town of Zhenru into their headquarters, before their plot was ultimately thwarted by Huo Sang. It was rather evident now that they were up to their old tricks, with the boat as their base of operations.

"I do remember," I answered. "And I still recall you telling me that you had met their leader, Hairy Lion."

Huo Sang nodded without answering.

"Now that you're going on the boat, aren't you concerned that he might recognize you?" I said.

3. In China the bat is a traditional symbol for "blessing" because of the similar sounds of the two words.

4. The story, entitled "The Ghost in the Villa," is translated in my book *Stories for Saturday: Twentieth Century Chinese Popular Fiction* (Honolulu: University of Hawai'i Press, 2003), pp. 175–189.

"If we take proper care," replied Huo Sang, "that won't happen. But don't bother to go on about that. Look, there's a sampan over there."

I saw the small vessel as well as an oarsman standing up in the rear, looking over at us. I waved at him, whereupon he rowed right over.

"Take us over to that boat, please," Huo Sang said to him.

The man seemed to know already why we were there. "Please get in," he quickly nodded in response. Huo Sang turned his eyes toward me and reached out his hand to hold on to my shoulder, deliberately acting like a weak, apprehensive old man uncertain about how to climb into a water craft.

We were all silent as the sampan began to move. The oarsman rowed hard, and we headed directly toward the small steamer. As we drew near, Huo Sang took out a silver dollar to give to the man.

"This is a little payment for using your sampan," he said. "In a while, when we come back, we'll have to call on your services again."

The man mumbled a brief word of thanks as he rowed the sampan alongside the boat. Another man in seaman's garb came up, and they signaled each other with their eyes. Huo Sang pretended not to notice while switching his attention to the sailor.

"Is this the Five Blessings Boat?" he asked.

The new man nodded a brief yes.

Huo Sang looked over at me. "Xilu, you go on ahead and pull me up."

So I stepped onto the boat first, turned around and reached out to help Huo Sang over the side.

"Where did you come from?" the seaman asked after he looked us over carefully.

"I came to see your captain," said Huo Sang. "Please pass the word to him."

The man took us into a small, dark cabin near the stern and left us there.

When my eyes had readjusted, I saw that the cabin was extremely cramped, with only the one entrance. A round table was placed in the middle. Some of the cups on it still had wine in them. There were also five stools. One in the corner of the cabin had a leg missing, as if it had been used in a fight and had thus suffered a debilitating injury. The single window, on the side facing the shore, had iron bars on it and was covered with a curtain, so that the room remained sunless. The place was unbearably close and stuffy.

Just as I was about to lift up the curtain to peek outside, I suddenly heard heavy footsteps coming ever closer and almost jumped in surprise. Huo Sang quickly indicated to me to remain still, implying that looking around nervously could give away our identities.

The cabin door opened with a bang and a man bulled his way in. He was big and tall and had to duck a bit to get through the door. When I looked up at him, he appeared daunting indeed. He had a dark complexion, along with extremely prominent cheekbones. Add to that his large unkempt mane and his bushy eyebrows, and one can see why he was so aptly called the Hairy Lion. Most menacing about him was the glare of his pair of triangular-shaped eyes. His upper body was covered by a short black jacket of silk crepe. There were two large pockets, one on either side of the jacket, with the shiny nickel-plated handle of a revolver hanging out from each. Shutting the door behind him, he made his way down the steps into the cabin and stared at us with those menacing eyes. We stared back without moving a muscle. Soon, his eyes focused on Huo Sang.

"Aren't you Huo?" he asked abruptly.

My heart nearly stopped when I heard the question. Those strange eyes were indeed formidable; they had seen through our disguises immediately! Were our very lives now in danger? I quickly looked over at Huo Sang, who, very much maintaining his composure, calmly looked up at the man from his seat. He shook his head ever so slightly at the question.

"No," he answered in a low voice. "My surname is Yu."

Quite surprisingly, the large man nodded. "All right," he said. "Then you're probably Yu Shoucheng."

Huo Sang shook his head once more. "No again. I'm his younger brother, and I'm called Shoujin."

The man scratched his head, then appeared to understand. "Oh, right. I heard Shoucheng had a younger brother. I suppose that's you, sir."

Hearing the two of them warming up to each other, my anxiety subsided somewhat. I could see now that the man's first question had not arisen from recognition but from Huo Sang's reputation, which he obviously feared; he had just wanted to make sure we were not connected with him. Good thing Huo Sang, wise to such a possibility, was able to maintain sufficient calm to get us past a potential calamity. I imagine that, had we switched places, I might very well have blown our cover.

Huo Sang already had the two ransom letters in his hand, having just taken them out of his pocket. "Didn't these letters come from you? Then you should already know the reason we're here."

The man laughed heartily, his mouth wide open. "How could I not know? I've been looking forward to this for a long time. Why didn't you come yesterday? Had you waited a few more hours, your son—uh, your nephew— would have been playing in the Huangpu River." He turned to open the cabin door to say something to someone outside before turning back.

"My brother is rather advanced in age and could not withstand the elements. He therefore had to stay home," said Huo Sang in reply. "I was in Hangzhou when I got his telegram and hurried back on the night train last night."

"So that's why you're late," said the gang's boss. "If you've got something up your sleeve, on the other hand, you'd be looking for trouble for yourself."

Right then, I heard the voice of a child outside the cabin calling out "Uncle!"

"You hear that?" the man grinned. "Where's your money? Hurry up and hand it over!"

Huo Sang then took out the currency from his pocket. "Now, mister," he entreated, "there's something I need your indulgence on. My brother is a minor merchant, and recently his business—"

"I know about that," the man quickly cut in. "Last year, he netted seventy or eighty thousand in profits."

"How could that be?" said Huo Sang. "It's all just rumors. Actually, he lost money last year—"

The man did not let him finish. "Fine, fine. Whether he made or lost money, who's going to look at his books? Just hand over the money, and all will be well." He seized the cash from Huo Sang's hand even as he was speaking.

IV. Our Detention

I couldn't help being alarmed. Huo Sang had said that the ten thousand in cash was nothing more than bait. But now, with the fish yet to be hooked, the bait had already gone into its stomach! Hadn't Huo Sang lost the first round?

Huo Sang stared at the man, apparently upset but helpless. The man counted the currency and stuck it into his pocket. Then those eyes of his grew large with anger as they stared directly at Huo Sang.

"Hey, there's just ten thousand here. Where's the other ten?" he wanted to know.

"I'm so sorry, mister," Huo Sang stammered. "My brother really couldn't come up with the whole amount, and so he's offering you half. I ask you to forgive us."

"Forgive you?" the man screamed. "How dare you just go ahead and violate my terms! You really don't know what's good for you."

He hesitated, then pushed open the cabin door and stuck his head out again to shout an order. Acknowledgment was immediate as a pair of fierce-looking men came inside. Both were sturdily built, and each had a gun in hand. Shaken by the situation, I stuck my hand into my pocket but found no weapon there. I was utterly helpless.

What Huo Sang had said about having taken care of my gun came to mind. Wasn't this a good time to use it? Why were we just sitting there like a couple of goggle-eyed dopes? He had never been without a plan, and I couldn't imagine him just waiting to be done in. Could it be that he had worked out something in his mind after all?

As soon as his two subordinates entered, the gang's boss took his pistols out of his jacket pockets and pointed them at us. Then he barked out further orders: "Hu Xing, Li Seven, search them carefully. See if they have any more money on them."

It was only at that point that I realized we would be searched. I didn't have anything on me and so was not concerned for myself. But didn't Huo Sang have my gun? If they found it on him, we would not only lose our only means of defense, but chances were our true identities would be revealed as well. Yet when I stealthily looked over at him Huo Sang still appeared unperturbed.

He stood up slowly. "No problem if you want to search me," he said. "I actually only have a bit of loose change. I would never hide any money entrusted to me."

"I don't believe you," the Hairy Lion said. "We're going to frisk you no matter what you say."

The two lackeys went up to Huo Sang, ready to begin, when he cooly responded: "Fine, but you don't have to touch me. I'll take off my clothes and show you myself." So he unbuttoned his outer clothing and flipped over each pocket for their inspection.

So Huo Sang really hadn't brought along any weapon?

"Hey, what's making your vest pocket bulge like that?" the gang's boss suddenly barked in a sharp voice. "What have you got in there?"

Huo Sang had to smile. "Oh, that's just a cigar case."

"A cigar case? Why have you got it hidden like that? We've got to take a look," said the boss.

Grinning, Huo Sang took out the case; there was indeed nothing else in the pocket. He even opened it up for inspection.

"The tobacco is rather delicate, and I don't want to overexpose it to air. So I keep the case in my pocket. Do you want to try one?" He handed a cigar to the Hairy Lion.

The man was not at all shy. He stuck it between his lips and lit up before turning his attention to me. Not having anything on me to worry about, I let them go through the motions of a search. When the boss saw that nothing was being found, he turned once more to Huo Sang.

"You listen to me!" he roared. "My commands mean more than imperial edicts. No one ever dares to defy them! I placed a price of twenty thousand dollars on that child, so don't even dream of getting him back for anything less. Since you've come in place of your brother, you tell him that he must pay me every last cent!"

Huo Sang appeared to ponder the idea. "You mean you want me to go back and then bring another ten thousand here to you?" he asked with some trepidation in his voice.

The boss squinted, his eyes becoming fearsome slits. "No need for that," he said, shaking his head. "You can just stay here a few hours while we send someone there in your place."

"You want my servant Xilu to go?" Huo Sang said as he pointed to me.

"That's no good either," the boss said. "Don't worry, we've got our own messengers. I only need you to write a note."

Huo Sang appeared surprised. "Write a note?"

"That's right."

"That's—that's—"

"That's very simple. Write it to your brother. Make clear what I've just said to you—that he cannot be so much as a cent short. Also, tell him that you and your servant have now become hostages. If the ten thousand doesn't get here immediately, the two of you will die too. That way, we don't have to worry about your brother ignoring your note."

Huo Sang suddenly stood up, trembling. "I can't write it," he said, gesturing with his hand. "Please, mister, forgive me."

"Forgive you? Stop dreaming!"

"My brother really has no more funds. It won't do any good for me to write to him."

"Nonsense!"

At this point, I feared it would indeed be difficult to emerge from all this unscathed. If Huo Sang were to really write the note, he of course couldn't sign his own name to it. Would Yu Shoucheng then believe his message? Yu, moreover, had already supplied the twenty thousand dollars, but now he would be told to make up another half of that amount. That would make no sense to him. So how could he not become suspicious? Even if he did go along, wouldn't he then be aware that Huo Sang had squirreled away half the ransom money? So even if we got Huibao back home safely, Huo Sang would lose his reputation for trustworthiness, and that would be the worst of all. For if Yu Shoucheng were to seek out the whys, he would of course realize that everything had come from Huo Sang's machinations. Wouldn't Huo Sang then be held responsible?

At the time, Huo Sang looked completely cowed. He seemed dumbstruck, unable to utter a word.

The boss man put down the cigar he'd been smoking. Baring his teeth, he said in a cold, threatening voice: "Have you forgotten already? I told you that my orders mean more than imperial edicts. You're really clueless! You have no idea what you're up against!"

Huo Sang looked at him blankly as before. I detected a sudden, almost electric, flash from behind his spectacles, as if he were about to get into a physical fight. The fact was that, ever since taking up detective work, Huo Sang had never suffered this kind of disrespect from anyone. The time he fell into the clutches of the Finger Choppers, he never showed the slightest submissive attitude, even when threatened with a knife and saw. At this moment, he had to continue pretending to be someone he was not. But once the role he was playing became strained to a near breaking point, he naturally couldn't help reverting to his true character. Still, he was unarmed. So even if a fight were to ensue, what could he fight with? Wouldn't he be putting himself at an impossible disadvantage? He probably felt just then that he had erred when he failed to listen to me about taking along a handgun.

Quickly, though, Huo Sang seemed to regain his self-control. He clasped his hands together politely and spoke to the Hairy Lion in a low voice. "Please, brother. I have something to say to you."

The man glared. "What is it? Speak up!"

"If you want me to write that note to get you the other ten thousand, then you should send Huibao back right away," said Huo Sang. "We'll wait here until the money comes. That's my only condition for writing the note. What do you say?"

The anger on the Hairy Lion's face did not subside. "That's nonsense!" he screamed. "What's all this drivel about your 'only' condition for writing? I've said it already. The sum is twenty thousand. If it's a half-cent less, don't even think about getting the boy back."

Huo Sang lapsed back into dumbstruck silence.

"You've got to smarten up," the gang's boss went on. "I would suggest you write that note right now. Otherwise I'll have to teach you a lesson or two, to show you that disobeying my orders will do you no good at all!" He waved his pistols about, glaring again at Huo Sang.

At that moment, Huo Sang looked to be in such a sorry state that I simply had to turn my eyes away.

But then he quickly assented with a nod. "All right. I'll write it. I'll write it."

The two lackeys standing alongside already had pen and paper ready. Huo Sang leaned over the round table and scribbled a note in a hurry.

The Hairy Lion was evidently able to read. Picking up the slip of paper, he recited the contents out loud:

My brother Shoucheng:
Huibao is currently on the boat. But the captain feels that the ransom
is insufficient, and that you need to add another ten thousand dollars.
Xilu and I are now being held as hostages here. I hope you can quickly
turn over the money to the person who delivers this to you, so that the
three of us can return home.

—Your brother,
Shoujin

The Hairy Lion nodded, apparently satisfied. I felt that Huo Sang had been greatly clever in his wording, which seemed to conceal the fact that he had put aside part of the original funds.

The man then addressed his two orderlies. "Hu Xing, Li Seven, you two stay here. In a while, when this matter is settled, I'll have the cook give each of you an extra portion of booze. If these two want any tobacco, tea, or food, don't hesitate to get it for them."

"Yes, sir!" the two responded with evident subservience.

Hairy Lion then nodded at Huo Sang. "Just settle down here. We'll talk again when we hear from your brother." With that, he turned and left us.

The cabin door slammed shut. The two of us were now detained.

V. Huo Sang's Plan

I was really on pins and needles sitting in that place. Every move we had made since getting on the boat seemed to have backfired. Huo Sang had yet to show any semblance of resistance. The note, cleverly crafted as it was, did not say anything about making the sum add up to twenty thousand dollars. The messenger, though, had to be another orderly from the ship. If Yu Shoucheng were to ask about why more money was needed, the person would surely tell him. In that case, the fact that Huo Sang had stashed away half the money would no longer be concealed.

While I was worried for Huo Sang on the one hand, I felt unusually depressed on the other. Huo Sang, though, continued to appear untroubled.

"Xilu, as things have come to this pass, let's just sit still for a while," he unexpectedly said to me. "We'll most likely be able to get home before sundown."

On hearing this seemingly self-comforting babble, I could hardly contain myself at first. Then I looked over at him and felt that he was perhaps passing me a message—that the case should be wrapped up before evening. But upon what magical insight would he be basing that assumption? How could we escape from these ruffians and accomplish our primary mission?

Then he started to mumble to himself. "In this cabin, we can ask for things like cigarettes or drinks to keep us comfortable. But the boy Huibao, we have no idea where he's being kept. Is he hungry? Is he cold? Isn't it a pity that he doesn't have anyone to look after him?"

One of the two orderlies, the shorter one with the dark complexion, interrupted to reassure him. "Don't worry. Someone's taking care of him. He's definitely not suffering."

Huo Sang slowly brought out his cigars, removed one from the case, and lit it. "Ah, but it's so chilly today," he said. "If he is held in a windy place, how can he take it?"

"They're in the second cabin in the bow," the shorter man promptly told him, "right next door to our boss's cabin amidships. It's very cozy there, not a bit of wind."

"Oh, then, that's fine," said Huo Sang. "I feel better."

His eyes flashed again at me behind those spectacles, as if to say that we now knew the boy's location. He then picked up his case of cigars, pulled them out halfway, and offered them to the two orderlies.

"These are first class," he said. "They have a really good aroma. Your boss was smoking one just now. Why don't you each try one? Don't be shy." He pulled out a couple and passed them to the men, who accepted them happily, each immediately striking a match to light up.

"How many of your comrades are on the boat altogether?" Huo Sang went on to ask.

The dark man did a brief calculation. "Aren't there thirteen now on the boat?" he asked the fat one.

The latter only shook his head in answer, as if to tell his partner to shut his mouth. Whereupon the dark man did stop talking as he continued to smoke.

"Hey, brother," Huo Sang then addressed the fat man. "Have you got any liquor? I could use a little to warm myself up."

The fat one pointed his thumb toward one of the walls. "Liquor? Every night we drink to our heart's content. Lots of it behind there. Too bad I can't let you have any."

"The boss never said they couldn't have drinks," the dark one interjected. "Why don't you ask our cook next door for some?"

"Then you go get it," the fat one said. "It'll be even better if you come back with a whole bottle."

"No. Li Seven, it's better that you go," said the dark-faced man, shaking his head. "With my reputation, he probably won't believe me."

All of a sudden, Huo Sang stretched and let out a yawn. "Oh, I'm so exhausted," he said. "Didn't get any sleep on the night train. Getting old and can't take it anymore. Hey, brothers, I actually don't feel like a drink just now. Let's wait a while before I trouble you to go get the liquor." He extended his arms in another stretch, as if he was really worn out.

I was feeling quite on edge. Remembering those Pagoda cigarettes in my coat pocket, I thought I might as well have a smoke. As I was taking one out of the pack, I suddenly heard Huo Sang cough. I then saw him look me in the face and knew he had a reason for doing so, even though I couldn't figure out what it might be. When he redirected his stare to my hand, I began to understand. Right away I took out one of the cigarettes and gazed closely at it. It felt very loose, as if it had been rerolled. Putting it alongside another one from the pack, the difference was evident. So I smoked the one that was more tightly rolled and marked with a black dot.

By now, eighty or ninety percent of Huo Sang's plan had become clear to me. The two cigars he had given away most likely contained foreign substances, and our two guards would be his first prey.

When I looked again, Huo Sang had already put down the cigars and laid his head on the round table. The dark-complexioned man had long since passed out. Only the fat one was still sitting upright. It wasn't long, though, before he too threw the cigar he held to the floor, put his hand to his head, and looked over at Huo Sang, who had sat up meanwhile to look back at him.

The fat man opened his eyes wide, then suddenly put his hand into his pocket to take out a gun. I knew we were in trouble then, since he had likely noticed a peculiar smell in the tobacco and realized that Huo Sang was up to something.

I stood right up and lunged at him, intending to get his gun. At the same time, Huo Sang jumped up from where he was seated and in one quick motion snatched the man's weapon. I put my hand over the man's mouth to prevent him from shouting out. By then, actually, he had long since lost most of his strength and was hardly able to resist. All he could do was lean weakly against me.

The mounting depression that had been overwhelming me was at that moment all but dispelled.

Huo Sang opened up his case once more to take out the four remaining cigars. He also removed a small bottle from the bottom of the case, uncapped it, and waved it under the noses of the two men. I knew that it contained chloroform.

I smiled and spoke to him in hushed tones. "The things you brought along are actually much more effective than any gun."

Huo Sang pointed at the pocket of the dark man. "You want a gun? Well, there's one in there. I've said all along that I had everything ready for you."

"I didn't think you meant it that way."

"Which do you think is better? Getting what you need like that or bringing it along with you?"

"You're right. For what you were planning to do, having a gun along would have been a problem for us."

"I knew from the start that there would be no shortage of firearms on the boat. It was only a matter of us getting hold of them."

"Let's be serious. How do you want to proceed now?"

Huo Sang frowned. "For what's going to happen from now on, I'll have to depend on your help."

"I really want to do my part. What are you thinking of?"

"Look at these two men—one's too short, the other's too fat. Neither is at all like me. But you look something like that dark-faced Hu Xing."

"Fine. I'll be him. Then what?"

"First, after disguising yourself, you'll go over to Huibao's cabin and take him out. Then you'll signal to the river police to come."

"Oh? Have you already contacted the river police?"

"Yes, I called the station from home and told them to assemble quietly on the east side of the river and mix in with passengers on ferries or workers on transports while patrolling the area. I considered the fact that the gang's attention is focused only on the west side. All you have to do is think back to the sampan we took as proof. In fact, if you look over to the east right now, you'll surely be able to see them waiting."

"What's the signal, then? Did you talk that over with them?"

"It's really simple," said Huo Sang. "Didn't you bring along a white handkerchief for your sweaty brow? All you have to do is to go to the east side of the boat and wave it three times, and they'll come right over to assist you. Now, if you foresee any problems about doing that, you must first arrange to get Huibao safely off the boat. After that's done, we can move on to Step Two."

"What's Step Two?" I asked.

"Don't worry about that just now," said Huo Sang, shaking his head. "Wait until Step One's finished. Go change your clothes, and I'll put the disguise on you."

I hurriedly took off my own as well as the dark man's clothes and changed into his. Meanwhile Huo Sang unscrewed the tall heel on his shoe. I knew that the heel concealed a rubber-wrapped metal container that could hold small articles. Now he took some dark makeup from it and rubbed it on my face.

He examined me closely. "You look very much like him," he said, "but you've got to modify your southern accent, since he speaks like a northerner—"

Huo Sang abruptly stopped speaking and craned his neck to listen, and I became aware of slow footsteps coming our way. After looking all around, he hurried over to stand next to the cabin door, the fat man's pistol in his hand, ready for anyone who might enter. The situation in the cabin was rather topsy-turvy at that point; if any gang member were to come in, it would be immediately obvious what we were up to, and we would be thwarted before we could even begin.

When I listened carefully, I could tell that the footsteps were coming from the cabin amidships; they were getting closer and would be outside our door any moment.

I tightened my grip on the gun, holding my breath. I could feel a tingle all over my body as my heart pounded so hard in my chest it seemed it must be audible. But the footsteps did not stop. They slowly went on past us, heading toward the stern.

"That was probably someone on patrol," Huo Sang said softly.

"I was afraid it was the Hairy Lion himself," I said. "Ah, but I remember now. That boss man also smoked one of your cigars. So he must be unconscious at this moment."

Huo Sang shook his head. "No, the one he had was as clean as the one I was smoking. Had it not been so, our haste might very well have turned out to be our waste and nothing would have worked out. You have to remember this fellow on patrol, though. Before you give the signal, be sure you take care of him."

"How should I do that?" I asked. "Should I leave it to the cigarettes I have?"

"Right," said Huo Sang, "if the opportunity presents itself. But you don't have to settle on the particular means. . . . Hey—can you handle this?"

"Sure I can." My answer was quick and firm.

But even though I sounded confident, I did have my doubts and was worried lest my enthusiasm overshoot my capability, since I was actually uncertain I could do the job. And that was because, in every case we had worked on so far, it was always Huo Sang who took the lead. I only tagged along, giving what help I could. This time, though, I would be on my own. Moreover, the tasks I would have to carry out were so fraught with danger that my faith in my own abilities was insufficient for me to be confident about my chances of success.

Huo Sang quietly opened the cabin door to look around. "Hey, take a whiff," he suddenly whispered to me.

I then stuck my head out, to be greeted by the smell of alcohol as well as a refreshing cool breeze that entered my nostrils and awakened my senses.

"That's Shaoxing rice wine being warmed up," said Huo Sang. "I guess that means they're about to have dinner."

I nodded my head. It was now early evening; the fading sunlight was tinging the sky. As far as the eye could see, the river was shrouded in mist. The dinner hour was drawing near.

Huo Sang withdrew into the cabin. He lowered his head to think before abruptly saying to me, "I'm changing the plan."

"In what way?" I quickly asked.

"At first I wanted you to do everything by yourself, which is really too risky. Now I think we ought to take advantage of the wine they're going to drink and knock them all out. *Then* we'll be able to do what we want in safety. What do you think?"

"Are you going to drug them all with wine?"

"Yes, indeed. The fat man said they drink every evening. If you can sneak the drug into their wine, the rest will be simple."

I readily agreed.

Huo Sang then carefully picked out one of the remaining four cigars. "This is the one with soluble drug in it. You'll only have to get that into their drink and everything will work out."

I took the cigar and broke it in half. There was indeed a powdery substance in its core, which I removed and put away.

"Shall I be going now?"

Huo Sang nodded. "Take care of yourself," he said.

VI. The Bloody Battle

When I stepped out of the cabin, the fresh air that greeted me was invigorating. I looked out and saw that the sun had already set and there were no other vessels nearby. The man on patrol had gradually moved from the other side of the boat to the bow. There was no one else in sight. I felt somewhat reassured. For even though I was disguised as that dark-complexioned Hu Xing and might roughly resemble him in looks, I had seen neither his walk nor his body language, and I couldn't possibly mimic his accent. So if I ran into anyone who really knew him, I would definitely be in trouble. Fortunately, no one saw me as I went along, led on by the smell of the wine wafting over from the stern.

Just a few steps later, I was in front of the window of the rear cabin. I saw at a glance that it was the kitchen, with someone in it busily preparing the evening meal. On the stove was a pot of wine emitting steam and wave after wave of fragrance. The cook looked up randomly and saw me peeking in.

"Who're you?" he shouted at me. "What are you doing sneaking around like that?"

It was a critical moment. I had to get in there, whatever the consequences. I went over to the door, and bravely announced, "Cookie, it's me."

The man threw me a glance. "What are you doing here, Hu Xing?" he asked.

I didn't dare say much of anything else and, not knowing how to respond, merely shrugged my shoulders and made a clicking noise with my mouth. I tightened my throat and somehow squeezed out a series of sounds that could be taken as chuckles. That turned out to be the right move, as it was unexpectedly effective.

The cook made a face. "Hah! So you're here to bum another drink? Too bad I can't accommodate you today."

I put on a mischievous look as I eased myself into the place. Taking one last step inside, I suddenly raised a hand to grab a cup off a wooden shelf while taking the cover off the wine pot to scoop some out. I was putting the cup to my lips when the cook punched me between my shoulder blades. "You boozer!" he yelled at me. "How dare you come in here and just help yourself!"

I took the blow as I concentrated on getting the wine into my mouth. I had downed about half when the cook wrested the cup from my hand. I then ducked my head to run out, but unexpectedly banged full bore into someone coming in the door. The man had been holding a long tray, which went crashing to the floor. My ears rang with their shouts as I made my frantic escape.

"That Hu Xing has been getting worse and worse," said the cook. "Just because he had a new assignment today, he thought he could come in here and help himself to whatever he wanted."

I did not hear what the other man said because I had already returned to the small cabin where we were confined. Huo Sang was tying up the two orderlies in the dark there when I entered.

"How did it go?" He asked as soon as he saw me.

"I guess the job's done," I answered with a nod. Then I told him about pretending to sneak a drink while slipping the powder into the wine pot.

"Outstanding," said Huo Sang, smiling. "When everything's over and done with, you'll get the lion's share of the credit."

"Don't talk about credit right now," I said. "Let's just wait and see what happens."

We shut the cabin door and sat down in silence. Then I heard murmuring voices from amidships and knew that the outlaws were probably gathering there for their evening meal. I was still unsettled, since I worried that they would somehow discover what I had put into the wine pot. Soon enough, quickened steps were again heard approaching our little cabin. Even though the place had grown quite dark by then, anyone who came in would see what we were up to. Huo Sang gave me a little shove, and I knew what he meant. I got up and went over to the door, which someone was soon pushing against. I opened it and went out, positioning myself in front of it on the outside.

Someone handed me an oil lamp. "Hu Xing," he said, "you've been awarded another portion of wine for today."

I took the lamp, and let out a harrumph. "You jealous?"

"Why should I be?" the man said. "You've still got to swallow your own spit for now, and wait until we're done eating before any of the stuff can get into your piggish mouth. The drunken worms in your stomach might chew through your throat by then!"

I clenched my fist and acted as if I wanted to hit him. Sure enough, he turned and ran off. So—whew!—we had cleared another hurdle.

We purposely turned the lamp down and listened in silence to the commotion from the middle cabin. The ruckus went on for a time. Within about twenty minutes, however, things began to quiet down bit by bit. Was that because the wine was working?

"Why don't you go take a look," Huo Sang said to me, "to make sure success doesn't slip away because of some small oversight."

When I came out of the cabin this second time, the river was shrouded in darkness. I plodded my way toward the middle of the boat slowly and deliberately. The scent of liquor again entered my nostrils, and I secretly rejoiced. They had indeed been drinking over there. When I reached the door to the compartment, hardly any noise was emerging from it. I still did not let down my guard, but leaned forward to direct my gaze inside the window.

The middle compartment was very spacious. Two gas lanterns were hung in the center, illuminating the large round table below. Eight or nine people were seated there, some of whom—apparently the engineers—had faces blackened with grease. They flopped this way and that, as if they were thoroughly inebriated. Among them was the Hairy Lion, their leader.

I could hardly contain my joy at the sight and almost let out a whoop. Our final success was there, right before my eyes. I counted the number of people and hurried back to Huo Sang to tell him everything.

"Nine have been overcome by the wine," I told him. "Hu Xing said earlier that there are thirteen in all. Add the two here to the nine and we have incapacitated eleven of them; all that's left are the two in the kitchen. If we can subdue them both, the entire boat will be in our hands."

"In that case, let's hurry and get over to the kitchen," said Huo Sang. "Any delay and they might wise up to what's happening."

I turned to lead the way directly to the kitchen window. I looked in and saw that only the cook was inside. "I saw the assistant a while ago," I whispered to Huo Sang. "But he's not here now."

"In that case," said Huo Sang, "you take care of him. I'm going amidships."

I assented and took out the handgun, thinking I would rush the kitchen. Just then, the cook grabbed an iron rod and ran out the doorway, probably having overheard our conversation. I jumped to one side to avoid his attack, lifted up the gun, and shot him in the leg. The man cried out before slumping to the floor. He gritted his teeth in anger as I walked up to him. "So you're a damn secret agent! I've been so blind!"

"Do you really know who I am? Since you were nice enough to let me have that half-cup of wine, I'm going to spare your life." Then I went into the kitchen, found some rope, and tied up the man's hands and feet. I also took a rag and stuffed it into his mouth.

By the time I got back to the middle of the boat, Huo Sang had already tied up the kitchen assistant I had crashed into. He had also found a large coil of rope and was in the process of binding the Hairy Lion's arms, showing great elation as he did so. I didn't want to put a damper on his high spirits, as I was getting ready to go to the cabin nearest the bow. Our primary purpose had been to get Yu Huibao home. Now that we had subdued the entire gang on the boat, we should of course see about getting Huibao out.

I went past a cabin that was lit up, ducking down as I looked into the

Hairy Lion's bedroom. Not a soul was inside. I recalled that Huibao was supposedly kept close by, probably right next door. I was no more than a meter away from the next cabin, so I was immediately aware of sounds from within. Startled, I quickly came to a halt, as I heard someone getting up, yawning, and inquiring in a sleepy voice, "Who's there?"

Only then did I realize that at least one person had not been drugged. When the dark-complexioned man had said there were only thirteen comrades on the boat, he had been imprecise, or perhaps he hadn't included the captain Hairy Lion among the members of the crew. This man was probably the one who had been patrolling the bow. He must have fallen asleep, so that he hadn't even heard the gunfire from the stern.

At that moment, I crouched down silently.

"Who goes there?" he asked once more. "Why aren't you answering?"

His voice was much louder this time. I remained immobile, hunched over in the darkness.

The man began to sound alarmed. "Who the hell are you?" he shouted. "Are you an intruder or something? I'm going to shoot!"

I could see his silhouette. Naturally, in that kind of situation the rule was to strike the first blow. I took aim and fired once. The man fell over without making another sound. Concerned that he might just be pretending, I waited a while before crawling up to him on my hands and knees. My bullet had hit him in the throat, so he was unable to cry out.

I was just about to enter the cabin when I heard chugging sounds. I directed my eyes to the river. Amid bits of reflected lamplight and starlight bobbing on the waves was a motorized dinghy heading toward our anchored vessel. But the transports and ferryboats Huo Sang said the river police would be on were nowhere in sight; my white handkerchief would remain unused. A frightening thought came to me: The dinghy must hold other members of the gang returning from shore. Aside from the two who had gone to collect the other half of the ransom and who ought to be coming back about that time, there could be others. I came to a quick decision and, putting all my faith in my handgun, fired a shot at the oncoming craft. Even though I probably didn't hit anything, the dinghy came to an immediate stop. Several of the passengers on it shouted something resembling a password. I paid no attention to them as I fired again, expecting them not to come any closer.

I then ran over to the forward cabin. Even with the door closed, the dim lamplight was visible from the outside. I pushed open the door, which was unlocked, and started down the steps, calling in a loud voice: "Huibao, come up right now. I'm here to get you out!"

Sure enough, an eight- or nine-year-old boy, answering from a corner of the cabin, came running toward me. I was overjoyed, as if I'd stumbled upon some sort of treasure. I leaned over immediately with my arms outstretched, ready to embrace him. But just then something else unexpected happened.

Bang! A bullet flew toward us, hitting the back of Huibao's head! He crumpled immediately to the floor, blood spurting out like a fountain. With his skull shattered and his brains spilling out, he was unquestionably dead.

This was something I truly could not have anticipated. I had not been on guard against a fifteenth person on the boat, whose one shot could wipe out everything I thought I'd accomplished. I became almost crazed with anger. With my gun at the ready, I searched the corners of the cabin with my eyes, wanting so badly to find the one who should be cowering somewhere there.

Bang! A second shot rang out. I felt a cold shock to my left shoulder, which staggered me. My mind was clear enough for me to realize I'd been hit. Even though I couldn't straighten up, I was nevertheless able to fire back in the direction of the shot. Then the pain in my shoulder intensified greatly as the blood gushed out. My head started spinning and my knees buckled. After that, I lost consciousness.

VII. Two New Articles

When I came to, I was aware of being in a cozy little room I had never seen before. It was a clean and quiet place, with cheerful sunlight glittering on white window curtains. I, however, was lying on a bed without a canopy. Seated next to it was a young woman in her twenties, clothed all in white. When she saw that my eyes were open and I was looking around at everything, she smiled at me.

"Are you comfortable?"

I could only look her up and down, unable to answer right away.

"Are you feeling strange? Well, this is a hospital," she said.

"Oh? How did I get here?"

"You don't remember, do you? Last night, you suffered a gunshot wound on that gangster boat. Your friend brought you in here. While you were still unconscious, Dr. He removed the bullet, cleaned your wound, bandaged you, and left you to rest. You've been asleep until just now."

Her words brought all that had happened last night back to me. I also felt a stiffness in my left shoulder that prevented me from moving it. My arms and legs were dog-tired. "You said it was my friend who brought me here," I said. "Is his surname Huo?"

She nodded. "Yes, he sat by you all night and left only at dawn."

"He wasn't wounded, was he?"

She shook her head, the warm smile remaining on her face.

I thought that, even though I'd been shot, Huo Sang was fortunately unarmed, so we could at least say there was good news with the bad. But then I remembered the boy Yu Huibao had been killed by some unknown culprit just as he had been on the verge of being rescued. All that effort for nothing! We had done everything we could, but still failed in the end. I was horribly distraught. Thinking back, I concluded that the reason for the failure was my own carelessness brought on by some kind of mental lapse after I'd shot at that approaching dinghy. Now Huibao was dead, I was wounded, and moreover, because of me, Huo Sang had fallen short of his primary charge: We hadn't returned Huibao to his father. All these mishaps, I thought, were still unexplained. What had happened in the end to those drugged gang members? How had Huo Sang extricated himself from danger? These were questions I wanted immediate answers to. I felt so in the dark.

"Are you in any pain?" the nurse suddenly asked me.

I knew that her question was prompted by the dejected expression on my face. "No pain," I said. "But I'm very thirsty."

She gave a quick nod and tiptoed out of the room. I shut my eyes during the short interval before she returned with a glass of water. Holding my head up, she helped me drink a few mouthfuls.

"Feeling better?" she asked me once more.

I was very grateful for her solicitous care. The job of nursing should really be reserved exclusively for women. I remembered the last time I had been hospitalized; a male nurse had made an impression of callousness and impatience that had never left my memory. The difference between his treatment of me and the warm and caring solicitude of this woman was like night and day.

"Much better." I smiled at her.

"In that case, there's someone named Yu waiting outside to see you," she said. "Should I invite him in?" She took out a card to show me. On it was the name Yu Shoucheng.

I mulled over the possible purpose of his visit. Would it be to grill me about what had happened to Huibao? Even if he didn't go as far as that, he had nevertheless lost an only son in his old age. The grief and despair of the situation was beyond what I could bear.

"I don't want to be troubled right now," I said. "Please tell him I'm unavailable."

She said she would and left. I remained greatly unsettled, afraid he might just barge his way in and make it highly awkward for us both. In about five minutes, however, she returned to tell me that the guest had departed. Only then was I able to relax.

"There's no need for you to stay here with me," I then said to the nurse. "I'll take a quiet nap." She acceded to my wish and left.

As soon as I shut my eyes, however, scene after scene of our failed mission invaded my brain. As I tossed and turned, I heard the door open quietly. I looked up and saw that my visitor was Huo Sang slipping into the room.

He grinned when he saw that I was awake. "Hey, you're up," he said. "How are you feeling now?"

"Glad you're here," I said happily. "I'm physically all right, but my spirits are down."

"Why so?" said Huo Sang. "Was that the reason you didn't want to see Yu Shoucheng?"

My face flushed. "Have you seen him already? What did he say?"

"He only wanted to know how you are. He already came once last night."

"To ask after me?"

"That's right. He's grateful for what you did, and just wanted—"

"You're still kidding me."

Huo Sang's face turned serious. "Nobody's kidding you. You got yourself wounded rescuing his child. Who wouldn't be grateful for that?"

"Rescuing his child?" My voice got louder. "Don't you know what happened to Huibao?"

Huo Sang nodded his head. "Sure I know. The two of them have already been reunited."

I was flabbergasted. "What're you saying? What do you mean 'The two of them'?"

"I mean Yu Shoucheng and his son Huibao, of course," said Huo Sang.

I couldn't stop myself from sitting right up. "Really? Huibao didn't die?" The sudden movement, brought on by my joyous surprise, jarred my wounded shoulder and sent a painful spasm through my body.

Huo Sang helped me back down to a reclining position. "Don't get overexcited," he said. "Let me read to you from the paper, dated today, November twenty-first." He took out a roll of news clippings from his vest pocket, selected one, and said, "Look at the headline: 'Wonderful Work from the Dr. Watson of the East.'"

Then he read the article out loud:

The disappearance of Yu Huibao, reported previously, has now been determined to have been the work of the Five Blessings Gang, which has been operating from a small steamboat on the Huangpu River. Yesterday afternoon, the great detective Huo Sang and his assistant, Bao Lang, boarded the boat and captured alive the leader, Hairy Lion, and more than ten of his underlings. They also got Huibao out safely. In the operation, Bao Lang took enormous risks and contributed greatly to the final success. He suffered a bullet wound in his left shoulder and has entered Bo'ai Hospital for treatment. Mr. Bao has a strong sense of civic duty as well as the courage to carry out his tasks. He is perfectly suited to be Mr. Huo Sang's only assistant. The danger he was willing to face in this case resulted in ridding our society of a great menace, and he deserves our gratitude and respect. Details will be forthcoming as we learn more about the case.

I was embarrassed on hearing all this. "They've really laid it on this time. But what happened last night was so strange. I clearly saw a gang member kill a child by shooting him in the head. How on earth could it be—?"

"What you say did occur." Huo Sang smiled at me. "There was indeed a child killed, but it wasn't Huibao."

"Were there two children on the boat then?"

"Yes, indeed. I hadn't known about that, either."

"So you know now?"

"I've known since last night."

"Whose son was he? Was he the child of a gang member? If so, then at least it wasn't some innocent life."

Huo Sang shook his head. "No, he was the son of the private narcotics dealer Hao Caisheng. His name was Hao Qizhen."

"Was he on the boat because he had been kidnapped?"

Huo Sang nodded. He took out another page, and directed my eyes to a second article:

Hao Qizhen, a student at Guomin School, and the young son of the wealthy businessman Hao Caisheng, disappeared suddenly last evening. The police were notified and searched for him without finding a trace. Mr. Hao is well-known in Shanghai society. In recent years, his commercial enterprises have prospered. For this reason, a number of people have speculated that the child was kidnapped for ransom by people demanding a share of his wealth. This is of course just speculation, and remains to be verified. Mr. Hao left for Shenyang two days ago. Since his son's disappearance, his family has been sending frantic telegrams urging him to return and take charge of the matter.

VIII. Capturing the Whole Lot

This latter article began to clear up some of my questions. "I seem to recall seeing that story before," I said.

"It's old news, from the paper dated the sixteenth of this month," said Huo Sang. "Also, in the story about Yu Huibao's kidnapping, which appeared on the eighteenth, Hao Qizhen's disappearance was mentioned. That surely couldn't have slipped your mind completely."

"Ah, yes," I said. "Now I recall that the news item Yu Shoucheng showed us was headlined 'Another Case of a Missing Child.' The word 'another' should have made it evident that Huibao was not the first child to be kidnapped. At the time, though, my attention was focused on him rather than Hao Qizhen. It never crossed my mind that Hao Qizhen could be on the boat as well."

"No one can fault you for that," said Huo Sang. "I, too, didn't think of it until last night. After tying up the gang members, I heard gunshots from the bow and hurried to the cabin to find you unconscious, next to a dead child. In the corner opposite you was a man, also dead. He held a gun in one hand and was still holding tightly onto Huibao's clothing with the other. Only then did I realize that there were actually two boys on board."

"Did you know right away that the dead boy was Hao Qizhen?" I asked.

"As soon as I saw there were two boys, I thought of the earlier news article about Hao Qizhen. I also remembered that the Hairy Lion had thought my surname was Hao when we first boarded the boat, which indicated that we were not the only people he was expecting. For these reasons, I quickly realized that, while one was the Yu boy, the other must have been the Hao boy."

Another mystery was thus solved for me. At the time the Hairy Lion asked about Hao, I had thought I heard "Huo," and had become alarmed for nothing.

"Did you talk to Yu Huibao?" I also wanted to know.

"Yes, I did," Huo Sang said. "Once I learned it was Huibao who had survived, I knew the one who had been killed must have been Hao Qizhen. Huibao told me the gangster guarding them forbade them at gunpoint to make any noise when he heard the shooting outside. When you went into the cabin calling for Huibao, the man grabbed him while the other boy ran toward you. That was when the man fired twice, hitting both Qizhen and you. You then returned the shot, hitting the man in the heart. But that turned out to have been an extremely close call. Had the shot gone just a slight bit lower, it would have hit Huibao instead."

I was shaken on learning all this. "I fired that last shot without thinking. So what happened wasn't due to human intention so much as to divine providence."

Huo Sang nodded without adding anything.

"What did you do after that?" I went on to ask.

"As I was leading Huibao out," said Huo Sang, "the motorized dinghy from the Hao family arrived. I put you and Huibao on it and, after that, carried Hao Qizhen's body onto it as well. Hao Caisheng had completely agreed to the gang's demands and was ready to pay a fifty-thousand dollar ransom. He was on his way to the boat when—"

I couldn't help interrupting. "So that dinghy was Hao Caisheng's? I unknowingly fired a couple of shots at it."

"They thought those shots had come from the gang. But Hao Caisheng, who had been so concerned about his son that he had hurried back all the way from Tianjin, ordered the dinghy to approach the boat, however hazardous it might be. It was fortunate for us that they did. Otherwise, Huibao and I might not have been able to get ashore."

"Didn't you tell me the river police were ready to assist you?"

"They waited a long time. When it got dark and nothing appeared to be happening, they thought that we hadn't succeeded in going aboard, so they left their posts. After I got back on shore, I called them to tell them to go take over the boat and arrest the incapacitated gang members. Only then did they explain the reason for their absence."

"The entire gang has now been taken into custody?"

"Two were shot by you, and the remaining fourteen have been jailed by the river police. All of them have long criminal records and will probably be unable to escape capital punishment."

"How is it that they number just sixteen? What about the one who went ashore to demand full payment of the ransom? Did you include him in the total?"

"No, he alone was arrested by the regular police. I saw to that beforehand. Remember me saying something to Shi Gui as we were leaving?"

"Of course."

"I told him to call Yu Shoucheng after we left and tell him that, if a messenger showed up at his house, he should think of a way to delay him until I could get there. I wanted to wait until we were on our way before telling Shoucheng to do this, as he was too timid and would have stopped me from going ahead with my plans; he just wanted me to play along with the gangsters. When I got back on shore with everything settled, the messenger was still sitting at the Yus', waiting for the ten thousand dollars."

"So the money was of course not paid out," I said.

"That goes without saying. Even the ten thousand I gave to the Hairy Lion has now become the fee for our services."

I was still uncertain. "Did Yu Shoucheng give that to you? Or did you—"

"You're really funny," Huo Sang said, smiling. "I was in the process of returning the whole twenty thousand to him when he firmly insisted I keep the total amount as payment. I repeatedly refused, and we eventually settled on my taking half the sum and donating the other half to factory workers. He said he still owed me and would settle with me later. How could you even think I would go and keep some of the money?"

I also smiled. "Your attitude yesterday seemed a bit vague. Anyway, Shoucheng's money comes from honest business ventures, and it wouldn't matter if you had accepted more of it. If it had been Hou Caisheng who offered to pay you, *that* money is tainted with the blood of drug addicts, and we shouldn't touch it at all."

Huo Sang nodded his agreement. "That's right. But now that some things are clearer to you, you should get yourself some rest. We'll talk about everything else on another day."

I was indeed tired from the long conversation. But I still had questions that I was unwilling to set aside just yet.

"I don't feel any pain right now," I said with renewed energy. "Moreover, hearing all the details of our success has not only driven away my depression but left me greatly elated. So please stay a while and clear up a couple of questions I still have."

"I know that you'll never change your impatient ways," Huo Sang smiled. "So tell me, what other questions do you have?"

"That South-China Swallow, any more about him? Wasn't he a big concern for us?"

"Yes, that's right," said Huo Sang. "It's just that I never got any real indication of his involvement. All I know is that after we left our house yesterday, somebody went there asking for me, and Shi Gui told him I was unavailable.

The man laughed and went off. I have concluded that he must have been the South-China Swallow."

"Do you think he's connected with the gang or not?"

"That's difficult to say. But from what I can see, he's definitely not a member."

"Why, then, did he want to contact us?"

"Perhaps it was actually out of good intentions."

I pondered that in silence. "I have another, relatively minor, question," I then said. "You just told me that, aside from the two gang members I killed, fourteen were captured in all. So the total number would be sixteen. From what I remember, though, there were nine of them in the middle compartment, two guarding us, and two working in the kitchen. So the number was thirteen. Add to that the one patrolling the ship and the one who shot Qizhen and the total comes to fifteen. Why, then, did you tell me that the count was sixteen?"

"That's a good question," said Huo Sang. "I did take a count as I left the boat and thought there were only fifteen. But the report the river police issued later did state sixteen. It also said that, other than the two on the boat who were dead, the other fourteen had all been tied up."

"That's odd," I said, rather baffled. "Where did the other person come from?"

Huo Sang lowered his head and appeared to be trying hard to come up with some sort of answer. "It's not all that unusual for another to be captured, since surely the gang's members are not limited to those we tangled with. Maybe someone came back from shore. Or maybe that man rowing the sampan returned to the ship. That's possible. But what I found strange was the fact that all fourteen had already been tied up before the police ever got there. Yet nowhere in the whole world has there ever been an outlaw who would tie himself up to await arrest. That is well beyond belief!"

What Huo Sang said brought the man in the sampan to my mind again. "Do you know what happened to the sampan rower?" I asked.

"I don't," said Huo Sang. "But since he didn't come to the aid of his comrades when you had that shoot-out with them, I assume he's probably run off."

"Then where did the extra person—?"

The nurse entered the door at that point, with a glass of milk in her hand. She came over to my bed while telling Huo Sang that there was a phone call for him. Huo Sang left the room to answer it just as she was handing me the milk. I had just finished drinking it when Huo Sang rushed back in.

"Bao Lang," he announced in a loud voice, "your last question has been answered."

"What?"

"There's quite a story behind that extra person."

"How did he get on the boat?"

"The extra person was indeed the oarsman on the sampan. It was the South-China Swallow who tied him up and put him on the boat."

I was flabbergasted. "That's inconceivable to me. Why would he do a thing like that?"

"He told me that he meant well when he warned me to stay away from the case, that he sincerely wanted what was good for me. Because he well knew of the cruel acts of Hairy Lion's gang in the past, and how difficult it would be to deal with them, he called to persuade us not to get involved. When he later learned that we had boarded the boat, he himself went to Poplar Beach, ready to give us a hand. He got on the sampan, and after learning what had happened, ended up tying up the oarsman. After some time, he realized that our operation was going well, and so he remained on the sampan rather than reveal himself. It wasn't until we arrived ashore in the dinghy that he took his prisoner up to the boat. And it's for that reason that the river police found another person when they got there."

"So that's what happened." I felt like I had just awakened from a dream. "Did he tell you all that on the phone just now?"

Huo Sang shook his head. "No, it was Shi Gui who called. The South-China Swallow sent a letter to our house to tell us what had happened. I told Shi Gui to open it and read me the contents."

"Well, then," I said after some thought, "we're indebted to him for his help. If we can find out how to reach him, we ought to send him a thank-you letter, don't you think?"

"That's probably not necessary," Huo Sang smirked. "He's been compensated for his services already."

"Really? Who paid him? Was it Yu Shoucheng?"

"No, it wasn't," said Huo Sang. "He himself has admitted that he got his payment through our indirect assistance, for which he remembered to thank us in his letter."

I was again puzzled. "What do you mean by that? Don't tell me he—"

Huo Sang did not wait for me to finish. "Exactly. He was able to resume his old occupation once he got on the Five Blessings Boat, which had a good amount of extorted money stashed away on board. Given an opportunity like that, I need hardly add that he left there with his pockets bulging."

I couldn't help laughing. "He's really something, isn't he? We risked our lives, and he's the one who has reaped the rewards. And he kept us guessing for quite a while. He's not your average thief at all, is he?"

Huo Sang suddenly grew very serious. "Bao Lang," he said softly, "you shouldn't be so exhilarated. Dr. He has told me just now that it will take your shoulder at least a couple of weeks to heal. You ought to rest quietly this first week. After that, you should be aware there will be much work ahead for us."

I looked up at him, not knowing just what he meant.

Huo Sang went on. "Just think about it. Even though we caught a bunch of big fish this time, there must be quite a few others who slipped the net. Do you think they'll forget what we did to their gang? For this reason, we have to be prepared for them. Get yourself some sleep now. I'll be back to see you soon."

I nodded, not wanting to detain him. My eyes followed him out of the room as I turned his final words over in my mind, sensing their gravity. What I didn't realize then was that they were to come true before very long. My journal has since added a bloodcurdling entry—the one I eventually published as "The Five Blessings Gang."

6 Cat's-Eye

I. The Swallow

One item in the newspaper so staggered me I couldn't quite contain myself. While my eyes remain glued to what I was reading, my mouth was gaping in utter surprise.

"Astonishing! I've never heard of anything quite like it!"

The article dealt with a robbery at the Credit and Trust Company that had been reported the day before, though more as hearsay than fact. Today's report not only corroborated the previous one, but specified that the items taken from safe deposit box A-2 included a pearl butterfly brooch and a diamond bracelet with a total value of over a hundred thousand dollars.

My surprise was due to the fact that this was the first time such a thing had happened in Shanghai. I need hardly mention that the vault in the Credit and Trust was made of steel and was without doubt extremely secure. That something could be stolen from that vault was indisputable evidence of the thief's incredible skills. But it also occurred to me that the whole thing could have been an inside job, that perhaps someone working for the company had been able to access the keys and used them to carry out the deed; there need not have been a break-in by some clever outsider. So my strong reaction might have been the result of my own overactive imagination.

"This isn't a matter of your imagination, Bao Lang. Your earlier reaction was entirely correct."

The comment quite startled me. Looking up, I saw my old friend Huo Sang standing in the doorway of the office. I couldn't help being startled. Since he did not have supernatural powers, how on earth could he have known what was going through my head right at that moment?

"When did you get back, Huo Sang?" I asked. "What made you say such a thing out of the blue?"

"When I came in," responded Huo Sang, "you were so busy sputtering that you didn't notice me. But since you say my comment was out of the blue, let me ask you: Was it far off the mark?" He took off his black woolen overcoat and went over to the coal-burning heater.

"I still don't understand how you arrived at it."

"The article you were just reading tells about what was stolen, but not *how* it was stolen. Your initial astonishment was based on the assumption that someone had broken into the vault to get his hands on the goods, and that such a person would have to be superhuman to be able to do so. For that reason, you couldn't help letting out a cry of surprise. But then something else occurred to you that quickly calmed you down. You even smiled, as if you felt your earlier assumption had been too hasty. That was your thought process, which I deduced from calm observation. Now tell me: Did I get it right?"

I had to smile. "To tell the truth, you absolutely did! Your powers of observation and deduction are sharper than ever, Huo Sang."

Huo Sang sat down next to the heater. "It's not all that difficult," he said matter-of-factly. "You just have to know a bit of psychology and then be willing to think a little. Anyone can do it." He extended his hands to warm them over the fire. "So, Bao Lang, weren't you thinking that there has never been such a case in Shanghai? Well, you're right; there hasn't."

I recoiled in shock. "What? Then has such a robbery actually occurred?"

"It has, indeed. That's why I said that your initial astonishment was not an overreaction."

"Did somebody really break into that vault?"

"Yes. I've already been there to look. The steel door was broken open with an electric torch."

"Incredible!"

"There was also a sketch of a swallow on the wall, drawn in charcoal."

"Oh? A swallow?" My attention was immediately aroused, as I recalled the shadowy man long known to us as the South-China Swallow. "Are you now involved in the case, Huo Sang?"

Huo Sang shook his head. "Not as yet. I have a friend in the Credit and Trust, the assistant manager, He Jiexuan, who let me inside to look around."

"Then you think that sketch is the robber's signature? Or is it someone else's way of misleading us?"

He pondered the question. "From what I can see, whoever did this must be a formidable person, whether or not he's trying to mislead us. That swallow—" He glanced sideways at the desk and his face took on a very solemn expression.

"Bao Lang, who brought in that letter?"

I was startled again. "When did anyone bring in a letter?" Sitting up to look, I saw that there was indeed a small white envelope on the desk, addressed in pencil: "For Mr. Huo Sang." Before I knew it, Huo Sang had picked up the envelope and was tearing it open. He pulled out a sheet of white paper on which the following lines were scribbled in pencil in a vigorous hand:

Mr. Huo Sang:
I have not paid my respects to you for a long time. At this moment, my wanderings have brought me to Shanghai. I will be staying for a few days, and would very much like to take this opportunity to satisfy my long-cherished wish to meet with you. Would you be receptive to the idea?

—South-China Swallow
Morning, 15th February

This brief message caused me to break out in a sweat in spite of the winter weather. Even though we had never met this South-China Swallow face-to-face, we had dealt with him indirectly a number of times. He was prominently involved in several cases I have recounted, among them "The South-China Swallow" and "On the Huangpu." What could have impelled him to ask to meet with us now? Were his intentions friendly or hostile?

"You don't know where this note came from?" Huo Sang asked me.

"No, I don't. After you left, Shi Gui brought in the newspaper. I carried it downstairs with me to the office here and have been sitting in my chair reading it. Until you came in just now, nobody else has been in here."

Huo Sang took a quick look at the window. "Was it you who opened it?" he asked as he got to his feet and walked over to it.

"Yes, it was," I answered.

Huo Sang glanced at the envelope again and nodded. "Mm. It must have been tossed in through the window."

"How is it that I never sensed anything at all?"

"For one thing, you had the newspaper in front of your face, completely blocking your vision. Then, too, you were so absorbed in your reading that you didn't even notice when I came in. So how could you have been aware of a little envelope flying past?" He walked away from the open window and sat down on the chair behind the desk.

"But the window doesn't open right next to the sidewalk, there's a low fence in between. How could the letter land right on the desktop?"

"It's just a little skill the man has, no need to be troubled about that. You know, after all, the kind of operator the South-China Swallow is."

"Oh? So you think it was the real South-China Swallow?"

Huo Sang bit his lip. "How could it not be?" he said calmly. "I believe that the Credit and Trust Company case was more than likely his doing."

I was not quick to agree. "I think there's a problem with the note."

"What problem?"

"Neither of us has ever met him face-to-face. But he starts the note with the set expression 'I have not paid my respects to you for a long time.' Isn't that contrary to the truth?"

"Hmm. I'm a bit embarrassed about that. Not to speak of many other cases, you must surely remember the case of 'The Finger-Choppers,' when we were locked up in a Buddhist temple and escaped only through the assistance of the South-China Swallow. Even though we have never seen him, he has surely seen us. So he must have intended to convey a bit of sarcastic humor in using that formulaic opening."

"Then, in your opinion, did he come here this time to do good or evil?" I asked, after pondering the matter quietly.

Huo Sang took a pen and swivelled it in the inkwell before jotting a few words down on the back of the stationery. He then folded it up and stuck it in between the pages of his journal before answering me. "How can he be here to do good? Consider the difference between what we do and what he does."

"We are of course diametrically opposed to him. But then, in the 'South-China Swallow' case with the Sun family in Suzhou we did cover his tracks for him one time. He seems to look upon us with a fair bit of goodwill."

"But he has already paid us back for what we did on at least two occasions. Now that we may be headed toward serious conflict, do you think he will continue to retain that goodwill?"

"If you put it that way, we're going to have to be prepared."

Huo Sang nodded. "Right. I imagine he might be a bit resentful of my inflated reputation in Shanghai. Now that he's committed a crime here, he might very well want to drag me into the case to see once and for all which of us is superior. If I lose to him, I might as well close up shop and disappear, and he will then be able to carry on as he wishes."

"So you think the robbery at the Credit and Trust is his challenge to you?"

"Perhaps so."

"Do you think you can solve the case if you take it on?"

"That's hard to say. This man is not your ordinary burglar. Not only is he brilliant at what he does, but he has recruited a lot of help as well. It definitely won't be easy dealing with him."

"How do you know he has a lot of help?"

"I don't need to point to anything else—just the current case. Up to now, the watchman at the Credit and Trust has not been located."

"The watchman was his henchman?"

"Whether or not he really was, there is a distinct possibility that they cooperated in some way. Otherwise, without wings and without any means of becoming invisible, how could the Swallow have pulled off the heist?"

Ring, ring, ring! The telephone suddenly came alive.

I was startled. "That's probably the Credit and Trust calling," I said.

Without saying a word, Huo Sang stood up and rushed into the other room to answer the phone. After some time, he came back and sat down in his chair.

"Who was that?" I asked him.

"It wasn't the Credit and Trust," he shook his head as he answered. "It was some man named Xu, who lives at 99 Heping Road."

"What does the man want?"

"He didn't really say. He just told me that there's an important matter that calls for our immediate attention."

"What did you say to him?"

"I think we should get ourselves over there to see what the matter is."

II. Empty Box

Mr. Xu's given name was Shoucai. For one term, he had been an assistant to the chief of the Bureau of Liquor and Tobacco. Judging from his spacious Western-style residence with attached garden, as well as his large number of servants, we could see that he had profited greatly from his stint in the government bureaucracy. When we got there, contrary to our expectations, we saw the domestic help going about their jobs as usual, showing nary a trace of alarm. Xu Shoucai was approaching sixty, a man with narrow eyes that did not seem to go well with his full, round face. He had on a dark fox-fur robe, with white silk socks and satin shoes. Welcoming us repeatedly when he saw us, he led us into a finely furnished library. We took our seats and exchanged a few words of casual introduction before he came right to the point: "Mr. Huo, Mr. Bao, you have surely heard of the South-China Swallow, haven't you?"

He cut right to the chase, and the directness rather startled us. So this matter was connected in some way to the Swallow case.

"We have," answered Huo Sang. "We've been aware of him for quite some time."

"So then you must be well aware of what happened at the Credit and Trust Company on the evening of the twelfth."

"We are aware of it," said Huo Sang. "Are you involved in this case?"

"No, that's my cousin Wu Bochang's problem. What was stolen was jewelry belonging to his beloved concubine. He had ignored a threatening letter from the Swallow asking to 'borrow' the jewelry he kept at home. It was only after the loss of a couple of diamond rings that he became worried and put the rest of his valuables into the vault at Credit and Trust. He didn't realize the move wouldn't keep them out of the man's clutches. It didn't take long for those jewels to be taken as well. The man's a real threat, wouldn't you say?"

"He is. He's not your everyday thief for sure. But what is your purpose in asking us to come here?"

Only then did Xu Shoucai solemnly take a letter out of his coat pocket. "I brought up my cousin's problem as a preliminary to my own. This letter is something that concerns me directly."

Huo Sang took the letter in his hands, opened it up, and began to read it in silence. I leaned over to look at it for myself. The letter read:

> Xu Shoucai:
> I hear you acquired a cat's-eye stone during your recent trip to Pei-ping.[1] Since you've been able to enjoy it for a few days now, that's sufficient as far as I'm concerned. Right now the funding to support public education in our city is going through very difficult times, and I'm asking you to donate that cat's-eye to the cause. That would help make up for some of your past misdeeds. I will be coming to get it per-sonally within three days. So be prepared.
> —South-China Swallow
> 14th February

After reading the letter, Huo Sang stared a while at the fireplace before turning his eyes to Xu Shoucai.

"What has happened?" he asked. "Has the cat's-eye already been stolen?"

Xu Shoucai shook his head. "No, not yet. The letter just came last night from the post office. I didn't dare dally once I received it, so I immediately took the jewel out of my safe to hold onto it myself. It's with me here right now." He undid a button on his robe and took out a small brocade-covered box from an inner pocket. When the lid was flipped open, we saw a little yellow satin bag inside, fastened with a red silk string. When he at last opened up the bag, I saw the round, glossy, crystalline cat's-eye, which seemed to

---

1. Peiping was the name given to China's northern capital city during the Republican era (1912–1949), when the national capital of the Qing dynasty was moved to Nanjing (Nanking) in the south. The northern city is now once more called Beijing, having become the national capital of the People's Republic.

emit flashes of light. It was indeed a rare treasure, something I had never encountered before.

Huo Sang looked at it for a while before sighing in admiration. "It's really a rare object! How much did you spend to acquire it?"

"During the Qing dynasty, it was kept as an imperial treasure in the Forbidden City. I had to pay seventy-two thousand dollars for it, but I was told that was only about half of its actual value."

"Even though such treasures don't ever have a set price, seventy-two thousand is surely not too much to pay. Did you really buy it in Peiping?"

"Yes, I did. Think of it. Isn't it frightening that he already has this information?" He returned the cat's-eye to the bag, which he then put back into the box.

"That's because he has informers everywhere. What do you plan to do about this?"

Xu Shoucai's eyes narrowed even further as he shook his head. "Because of this I wasn't able to sleep a wink last night. I've thought everything over, and just could not come up with an effective course of action. Because of what happened with Bochang, I naturally don't want to entrust anything else to the protection of the vault. It would of course be worse to leave the gem at home. I'm also reluctant to go to the police. I don't know if they could really help me, but I do know that doing so would make him my enemy, and my very life would probably be in jeopardy. Therefore I decided to rely on your well-known ability to keep this precious gem safe for me. I will not be ungenerous in compensating you."

Huo Sang kept his head lowered and his line of sight on the flames in the fireplace, pondering his options. His host stared at him with wide-open eyes, evidently hoping for an affirmative response. I also felt, however, that it was not at all easy to respond to this offer.

Huo Sang took his time before answering. "How can you expect us to do what amounts to guard duty?" he asked slowly.

"I am completely sincere in my request, Mr. Huo," Xu Shoucai said with some anxiety. "I do hope you will agree to help me."

"Our job has always been to solve crimes. We don't know how to prevent crimes."

"I'm not asking you to stand guard here. My intention is to hand the gem over to you, to keep it safe for me for three days. If he fails to get his hands on it by that time, I assume he will not dare stay around. In which case, I'm prepared to compensate you well."

Huo Sang frowned. "Mr. Xu, we do not do our work for monetary gain, so please don't mention compensation to us again. I just feel that the responsibility is too heavy. Just think: For someone who could break into a steel vault, would breaking into the little metal safe I have at home be anything more than child's play?"

Xu Shoucai put his hands together, almost as if he were praying. "Don't be overly concerned, Mr. Huo. This person is a veteran thief, not a violent robber. He would never resort to force to get what he wants. Moreover, is there anybody who doesn't know of your sterling reputation? Once he hears that you are involved, he won't dare do anything wild. This is why I am relying on you. Please, Mr. Huo, you must do this for me!" There was an extremely insistent tone to his voice, even as he repeatedly lifted his hands in supplication.

Huo Sang's eyebrows remained knitted as he hesitated once more. "I would say that his aim appears to be altruistic—he doesn't necessarily want your precious jewel. If you really want to keep it, why don't you just follow his suggestion and donate thirty or fifty thousand to the public education commission? That way, the matter could be resolved rather peaceably."

The idea gave Xu Shoucai pause. "There's no reason that can't be done. But I have no way of letting him know. What if, even after I make the donation, he still goes ahead and steals from me? Wouldn't I then be suffering a double loss?"

Huo Sang thought that over. "Why don't you go ahead and donate the money. We will take responsibility for guarding the cat's-eye for three days. Should something go amiss during that time, I will personally pay you back the sum you've expended. What do you say to that?"

Xu Shoucai was quite taken aback. "If that's what you propose, I'll send thirty thousand to the commission. Now please take good care of this gem. I hope that three days from now you'll be returning it safely to me."

He presented the brocade-covered box to Huo Sang with both hands. Huo Sang put it into his pocket after receiving it and immediately stood up to take his leave. I followed him out of the cozy library.

Then a thought struck me.

"I have something to say to you, Mr. Xu," I said. "It's imperative that you keep strictly confidential what we're doing for you. If the Swallow doesn't know about our arrangement, he will of course be less prepared for it. If he does come to carry out his threat, you won't be in danger of losing your precious gem, and we shall be better able to deal with him. Don't you agree?"

Xu Shoucai assented enthusiastically. "That's fine, that's fine. I'll of course follow your advice on that." He escorted us out his front door with great deference.

We talked about what we should do after getting back to our place on Aiwen Road. On the surface, our responsibility would not exceed the thirty thousand dollars. But in actuality, if we failed to carry out our charge Huo Sang's reputation as a professional detective would suffer a fatal blow. The need to succeed in this job was therefore more crucial than it might seem. In my opinion it seemed best to go beyond passive guardianship and actively seek to capture the South-China Swallow. Huo Sang evidently felt the same way.

"How do you propose to capture him?" he asked me.

"I think that if the news of our involvement can be kept secret, he will of course still go to the Xu residence. If we set up some kind of ambush for him there beforehand, it shouldn't be difficult to catch him."

Huo Sang thought the idea over quickly. "The ambush you're suggesting, should it be inside the Xus' house?"

"No. Considering the situation, the place is more than likely filled with spies. If we made a big fuss there, our efforts would go for naught. It'd be better to hide ourselves near the house to catch him unaware."

"Hmm. Not bad. But if we were to wait around there, where would we keep the cat's-eye?"

After some discussion, we agreed that the safest place to keep the jewel would be on our persons. On the other hand, however, were we to become engaged in some kind of physical struggle, we would surely risk losing it. In the end, we decided to split up: I was to guard the safe at home and Huo Sang would hide outside the Xu residence by himself. Even though the responsibility on me was heavier that way, I had no choice but to accept it under the circumstances. On the plus side, we had a telephone in our house, and I had a gun for protection; I wasn't concerned about my ability to respond to a direct attack. After we settled on our course of action, Huo Sang opened the brocade box and examined the gem once more before personally locking it away in our safe.

"Bao Lang," he said, smiling encouragingly, "you've got to be extra careful the next couple of days. Even though this safe is a product of the well-known Göster Company and has held a number of valuables without ever being broken into, the South-China Swallow is not your average burglar. This safe will be nothing unusual in his eyes."

I smiled back. "If he gets his hands on it, the safe will probably become useless. But if he were not allowed to come into direct contact with it, I don't think he'd be able to crack it through psychic force alone."

On the night of the fifteenth, we began our special preparations. Huo Sang instructed Shi Gui to maintain strict watch at the front entrance. No messengers or delivery personnel were to be allowed entry; all unexpected visitors would have to be carefully questioned. After dinner, Huo Sang put on a gray padded cotton jacket and pants, a dark woolen scarf around his neck, and an old gray felt hat with the brim pulled down over his forehead. He also smeared dark makeup on his face to complete the picture of a day laborer from the north side. After some brief words to Shi Gui and me, he was quickly gone. I loaded my handgun before putting it into my jacket pocket and went into the office to keep silent watch over the safe and its precious content.

The weather was quite chilly; foot traffic outside was sparse. A general silence had settled over the whole area, broken only by the wind whistling past the window and the soft crackling of the coals in the heater. I remained on guard half the night without detecting the slightest disturbance. I began to think that, even though the South-China Swallow was an unusual opponent, he had to be somewhat wary of us. Even if he learned that the gem was in our hands, it would surely be risky for him to carry out his earlier threat to come for it personally. Would he then take the easy way out and wait a few days before going to steal it from Xu Shoucai?

Well after midnight—close to 1:00 a.m.—Huo Sang came back, giving no indication of anything having happened on his watch. He told Shi Gui to carefully secure all the windows and doors, and to sleep in the office. Then we went to our separate rooms upstairs.

The following day, the sixteenth, we remained on guard, but nothing unusual occurred. After dinner, Huo Sang left, dressed again as a laborer. As before, I kept watch in the house. As I smoked one cigarette after another, I began to ponder the situation. It was already the sixteenth, the final night of the threat. If nothing else happened, we would be able to say in the morning that we had fulfilled our obligation.

The little porcelain clock continued to tick and tock, rhythmically measuring out each passing second. The wind seemed to have quieted down. Suddenly, the faint sound of footsteps seemed to be drawing closer and closer to the window. As I listened with rapt attention, my right hand automatically went into the pocket of my jacket. But no. The sounds moved past our house and slowly faded into the distance. It was probably just a passerby.

At 11:30, I was startled by the doorbell. Right after that, I saw Huo Sang in his northside laborer's costume—the gray outfit, black scarf, and felt hat—rush in, all in a dither. He came up and whispered in my ear, "It's bad, Bao Lang. His henchmen have our house surrounded!"

"What should we do?" I cried.

"Not so loud!" Huo Sang cut me off. "Get upstairs right now and put on something black to look like a laborer. Bring your gun along and follow me outside."

"What do you intend to do?"

"Don't ask. Go change your clothes! I'll wait for you here."

I couldn't very well ask any more questions. So I rushed upstairs to get a black cotton outfit out of my trunk, and put it on. I also took off my leather boots and put on black cloth shoes. After perhaps fifteen minutes, I came downstairs in a rush and went back into the office, but Huo Sang was not there. So then I headed right away to the front door to ask Shi Gui.

"Mr. Huo just left," he said. "How could you not know that?"

"I was upstairs changing," I said. "Did he say anything?"

"He just told me to keep the door shut tight," said Shi Gui. "Nothing else."

The doorbell rang again. I looked out and saw a rickshaw puller with his vehicle parked right at the front entrance. I couldn't help being a bit taken aback.

"Bao Lang, open up! It's me!" the man said in a loud voice.

"Huo Sang?" I was rather startled to hear his voice.

Shi Gui was quick to open the door. It was indeed Huo Sang. As soon as he stepped inside, he gave instructions to Shi Gui in a low voice: "Please give the Quick Stop Rickshaw Company a phone call and ask them to send someone here to pick up the rickshaw."

"How did you manage to change your disguise so quickly?" I asked Huo Sang.

His eyes widened. "What do you mean? I made the change over two hours ago."

I was astounded. "What? Didn't you just come in here dressed as a laborer ten minutes ago?"

Huo Sang's eyes flashed. "What on earth are you talking about? Hey! Let's get in there right now and see what's happened."

He turned and rushed into the office, with me right behind him. It was only then that I realized something was amiss, that I had been duped. The person who had come in a short time ago had to have been that devious South-China Swallow!

Huo Sang went over to the corner of the room and immediately shouted: "Oh no! He's gotten his hands on the safe!"

When I took a close look, the door of the safe had a hole in it large enough to fit a small box through. "Oh, we're ruined!" I couldn't help blurting out.

Huo Sang maintained his composure. "Wait a minute," he waved his hand at me. "He did burn a hole through, but he didn't have the time to open the lock."

"Hmm, that's right. I remember you put the brocade box on the inside corner. Maybe he never got to it in time." In my desperation, I clung to a ray of hope. Quickly I unlocked the door to look inside in the lamplight—and saw that the box was still there! Again, I couldn't contain myself from shouting for joy, "Ha! Ha!"

"Calm down," Huo Sang said gravely. "Just open the box."

When I opened the box, there was another surprise, which dashed what little bit of hope I still had. The box was there, but it was empty. The yellow satin bag inside had vanished!

III. A Worthy Opponent

All at once, my heart flooded with feelings of shock, consternation, and disappointment. I was utterly benumbed. By the time I looked around for him, Huo Sang was already on his way upstairs. Very quickly, he came down again with some clothes in his arms. He sat down in front of the desk, and slowly changed into them. He also bent down to remove the grass sandals on his feet, seemingly even more at ease than he had been earlier on.

"Bao Lang," he finally said, "what has happened should at least teach you a bit of a lesson."

What was that for? I knew I had been hoodwinked, but why, at a time like this, was he reprimanding me like a stern teacher?

"Say no more," I told him with some resentment. "I'll just pay the thirty thousand myself."

Huo Sang smiled without responding. He picked up the clothes and sandals he had taken off and took them out of the office. Then he produced a couple of Golden Dragon cigarettes, lit one up for himself, and passed me the other.

"Just sit down, my old friend," he said, "and stop getting upset with me. You surely know that defeat is nothing to be ashamed of. It's only when we don't learn anything from losing that it becomes shameful. Your misstep this time occurred because you were unable to remain calm under stress. How else could you have become so rattled you were not even able to distinguish my real voice and appearance?"

Seated across from him, I held on to my lit cigarette in great discomfort, feeling a series of hot flushes on my cheeks. Yes, his words were completely reasonable. I recalled that, even though the person had cleverly stood at an angle to me so I had no direct line of vision to his face, I had thought his voice sounded strange when he whispered in my ear. Still, how could I not have see through all that? Moreover, the man had given me no reason why I needed to go upstairs to change into that black outfit; that was only to buy time for himself. Everything was clear now; but because my excitement had gotten the better of me, I had noticed nothing at the time. My inability to keep my wits about me was indefensible.

"I need only mention one thing," Huo Sang continued. "That man is half an inch shorter than I am. Had you kept your composure, you would surely have noticed it. Furthermore, his felt hat is somewhat darker than mine, with a broader brim—"

"What?" I interrupted in a loud voice. "From what you're saying, you must have seen him yourself!"

Huo Sang released a large puff of smoke and took his time responding. "You're right. I did see him just now."

"Aha!" I couldn't help crying out. "No wonder you're so calm and collected! I suppose you have already arrested the South-China Swallow and turned him over to the police!"

Huo Sang shook his head. "No, I haven't. Even though I did see him enter and exit our door, and even though I got a good look at his face under the streetlights, I never exchanged a word with him. Moreover, I never had any intention of detaining him."

That surprised me once again. "Oh? Why? After finally seeing his face, why did you just let him go like that?"

"He's never done anything to us. Why should I arrest him?"

"What do you mean he's never done anything to us?"

"Well, he *did* just wreck our safe."

"And that precious cat's-eye—"

Huo Sang was quick to cut me off. "He didn't get that after all."

"He didn't get it?" I stared at Huo Sang, befuddled, but he didn't look like he was joking.

"That's right. So you needn't be so upset."

"Where is it, then? Do you have it on your person?"

Huo Sang shook his head once more. "No. That would be too dangerous." He leaned forward slightly, put his fingers into the inkwell on the desk, and fished out the cat's-eye, dripping with ink!

"I told you early on that our safe would be no challenge at all to the South-China Swallow," he said. "I'd be the dumbest person in the world if I kept this gem in there. That's why I moved it into the inkwell, replacing it with a fake stone inside the safe. I figured that if he actually tried to come here to rob us, the safe would be the first object to catch his eye, and in his haste he would not be able to discover my secret hiding place. This is what the military strategist Sunzi's *Art of War* calls 'intermingling illusion with reality.'"

I still felt somewhat resentful. "Why didn't you tell me earlier you'd done that?"

"You have to forgive me for that," Huo Sang smiled. "Had you known the actual hiding place, your every move might very well have betrayed it to the South-China Swallow. Then we would have been unable to prevent illusion from becoming reality."

I was slightly taken aback. "At least when you came in here just now, you should have told me the truth," I said. "You shouldn't have kept me in suspense and led me on as you did."

Huo Sang dismissed my words with a wave of his hand. "You surely know, Bao Lang, that everyone has to pay a price for any gain in knowledge and wisdom," he said with a smile. "You should be no exception to the rule as you learn this lesson."

I had to smile back. "You've been too devious a teacher for my taste."

The room fell silent, filling up with tobacco smoke rather than sound. I thought to myself that, although we had not been defeated, the South-China Swallow would never accept having been foiled. Looking ahead, I saw no reason to be optimistic. I could not but remain disturbed that Huo Sang had just let him off.

"Huo Sang, how did you happen to run into the South-China Swallow?" I then asked.

"Your earlier idea was really good—to have Xu Shoucai keep our involvement strictly confidential so I could go there to stand guard and wait for the South-China Swallow to fall into our trap. But Xu Shoucai had asked us to take care of the cat's-eye precisely because he was afraid the South-China Swallow would come to his house to seek him out. So it's obvious why he would never have heeded your admonition to keep quiet about our involvement. The Swallow, moreover, has extremely sharp ears and eyes. Even if Xu Shoucai had been willing to keep everything confidential, the news would have leaked out anyway. The South-China Swallow never seems to have trouble finding out about such things.

"Therefore I expected him to come looking for me here rather than go to

Xu Shoucai's. For that reason, when I went to the Xu residence last night and found nothing unusual, I came back to keep watch over my own place. When I headed out again this evening, I thought I saw somebody lurking around behind a tree. I felt then that my first disguise had probably been seen through, so I quickly changed my plan. I went over to the Quick Stop Rickshaw Company to rent a vehicle and borrow an entirely different set of clothes. I also got a good taste of what it's like to be a rickshaw puller.

"I waited a while at our street corner, then went around the block a couple of times. At first, I saw two of his henchman hiding across the street. After that, I saw someone dressed like I had been, coming in here. I knew then that the person had to be the South-China Swallow."

Huo Sang's ability to adapt to changing situations was indeed outstanding. Too bad I had been kept in the dark about the whole situation up to that point.

"You saw him come in here but never bothered to arrest him or even get in his way. That was taking too much of a risk." My resentment was surfacing again.

"How was that risky? I didn't arrest him because I wanted to treat him gently; nor was there any reason to block him. My hiding place for the gem might have been right in front of his eyes, but there was no way he would discover it in the limited time he had. Even if he had managed to search carefully, he couldn't possibly have thought of looking in the inkwell. I felt absolutely confident about this."

"Had he taken another tack, tied me up and put a blindfold on me before really looking around, everything would have been ruined."

"No need to fret about that. Had he taken more than a few minutes in here, I would of course have come in and invited him to sit down and have a chat."

"Nevertheless, in my opinion, it was wrong of you to have just let him go. Yes, he didn't succeed in getting the cat's-eye. But the Credit and Trust case is a major one. Had you apprehended him, why—"

Huo Sang turned serious to put a stop to my ranting. "Bao Lang, how can you just abandon the idea of doing what's right? Have you forgotten either the case of "The Finger-Choppers" or "The Black Dungeon"? Even though this man functions outside the straight-and-narrow path of the law, he has never strayed beyond the bounds of honor and propriety. Those he thwarts are all the rich oppressors of society, people who know luxury but not labor. To tell the truth, he is in no way our deadly enemy, someone we would want to destroy. I have no responsibility whatsoever for the pending case at the Credit and Trust. As for the matter of the cat's-eye, I have both completely fulfilled my end of the bargain and now also seen what he looks like. We've also gotten the better of him with my little ruse. So other than suffering a bit of damage to our safe, we can say that we have won a complete victory. Why are you still dissatisfied?"

At this point, Huo Sang suddenly stopped, threw down the rest of his cigarette, and inclined his head to listen to something in silence. Shi Gui came in shortly after that, holding several pieces of cotton clothing, a dark scarf, and felt hat in his right hand, as well as a small paper package in his left.

"Sir," he said, "the rickshaw company has already sent someone by. I explained the situation to him, and he took the vehicle and clothing back. Uh . . . these other articles of clothing also came from him." He put the scarf, the cotton jacket and pants, and the gray felt hat on a chair before handing the paper package to Huo Sang. "This package was delivered by someone else just now, who said it's for you. The person was rather tall, wearing a black silk gown. He left right after the instructions—"

Huo Sang didn't wait for him to finish, but hurriedly took the package and tore it open. It was wrapped in layers of manila paper and contained a letter, a small yellow satin bag tied with a red string, and a small roll of paper currency. Before I realized what he was doing, Huo Sang had unfolded the letter. On it was the same strong, flowing script, rendered in pencil.

Mr. Huo Sang,
I have just learned that the Commission for Public Education has already received a $30,000 donation from Xu Shoucai. That must be due to your suggestion. I am very grateful for your sympathetic help in fulfilling one of my wishes. Since the cat's-eye had been placed in your care, I originally did not want to interfere. But then I thought that if I did not show you what I could do, I would not be able to retain your

esteem. Now I am returning the original article, without so much as opening the container, to prove my true intentions. I've also taken the liberty of including a bit of cash, to pay for the cost of repairing your safe and to proffer my heartfelt apologies. I hope you will convey them to your friend Bao Lang as well.

We will have occasion to interact again; we might then plan to meet face-to-face.

—*The South-China Swallow*
1:00 a.m., 17th February

After reading the letter, we looked at each other in silence, neither of us uttering a word. Shi Gui also left the room, looking rather astounded. The only sounds at that moment were the gentle howling of the wind and the crackle from inside the heater.

Huo Sang stood up after a while and yawned. He put his hands behind his back, keeping his eyes on the carpet while continually nodding his head, as if he were an art critic contemplating an intricate masterpiece.

"Bao Lang," he said firmly, "that South-China Swallow is a good man! Today we have finally met up with a worthy opponent." He paced around a little. "Why don't you make a call to Xu Shoucai early tomorrow and tell him to send another twenty thousand to the Commission? He can use their receipt to reclaim his cat's-eye."

"What do you mean?" I asked. "You want him to put in another twenty thousand?"

"Right. That's what I want. When I asked him to put in thirty or fifty thousand the other day, he chose the lesser sum. Even though I don't know the man's background, I would wager that his coffers aren't filled with unsullied dollars. I didn't take this case for his sake. It was never my intention to do him a favor."

7 At the Ball

I

Xu Zhenyang's brow was furrowed in a deep frown. His large dark eyes, glowering with outrage and resentment, were fixed on the face of Qiao Youmin, the visitor seated across from him. It wasn't that he was particularly upset with Qiao; the frown had been on his face since that strange letter came the night before. In fact, Xu had invited Qiao Youmin there to consult with him on the matter. Although he well knew that Qiao always considered every eventuality before expressing any opinion, Xu was particularly impatient with him on this occasion.

Xu took the expensive cigar he had smoked only a quarter of the way down and tossed it with vigor into the nearby spittoon. He played with the triangular goatee on his chin as he rose from his executive chair of carved citrus wood.

"Youmin," he said to his visitor, "why haven't you said a word? Has the letter intimidated you as well? You've worked as a detective for over ten years. Are you going to say something like 'We can't do anything about it' now?" Qiao Youmin, a tall, slender man, was dressed in a dark leather overcoat. His thick dark eyebrows framed sharp, intense eyes. A single glance told you that he was a daring and capable person. Add to that his quiet and dignified manner, and he looked exactly the part of head of detectives at the main police department.

He maintained his unflappable manner. "Please forgive me, Mr. Xu," he said in a gentle voice. "How could I not do everything in my power to carry out your wishes? But this matter is truly of great importance, and I cannot help being cautious. I imagine, Mr. Xu, that you have heard of the name 'South-China Swallow.' A few years back, he was stirring up all kinds of trouble in Shanghai. He even got the better of the private detective Huo Sang on one occasion."

These words elicited an even angrier response from Xu Zhenyang. "Are you seriously saying, then, that nothing can be done? Do you think I should just present my daughter's emerald necklace to him with both hands? Or would you have me cancel the ball that's supposed to take place this evening?"

Already endowed with broad features, Xu Zhenyang's face had grown even fuller and his girth increased noticeably in the eight months since he had been made chief of the Bureau of Charitable Donations. Because traditional robes no longer suited his fancy, he had recently made the change to Western attire. At the moment, his well-filled-out cheeks were turning scarlet, and dark veins started to throb faintly in his temples.

But Qiao Youmin remained composed. "Please don't be angry, Mr. Xu," he responded pleasantly. "Tonight you're celebrating your daughter's eighteenth birthday. The invitations have already been sent out. Of course you can't very well just cancel the whole affair. But if you think I'd suggest you simply hand the necklace over to the South-China Swallow, you underestimate me. You should know that, for years now, I've been longing day and night for the chance to catch this scoundrel who has done so much to disturb the peace and harmony of our society. Arresting him would add one more glorious page to the record book of my achievements. So tonight's ball could very well present me with the opportunity I've been wishing for so ardently."

These words calmed Xu Zhenyang down considerably. "Then you've been wanting all along to capture this South-China Swallow?"

"Absolutely. It's just that, regretfully, there has never been an opportunity for me to do so. If he shows up this evening, I won't just let him slip away."

"You figure he'll come tonight for sure? His letter merely said that he wanted to borrow that necklace for a bit of fun. It said nothing about doing it tonight."

Qiao Youmin's eyes were riveted on the floorboards. "I think he'll definitely be there tonight," he said slowly, but with conviction. "He has long desired to get his hands on this precious piece of jewelry. Ordinarily, though, since it's locked away in an inaccessible place, it's been well out of his reach. So tonight's gala, with a variety of guests coming together, amounts to a rare opportunity for him. I know that your invitations went out to every bureau and department, so you won't possibly be able to recognize each and every guest.

And there's one more thing. His letter was calculated to be delivered last night, a clear indication that he plans to make his move tonight. For these reasons, I am all but certain he will be coming."

Xu Zhenyang nodded repeatedly. "Not bad, not bad. I was also thinking that it would be really difficult to guard against anything he might attempt tonight. Are you certain you can handle him?"

"I believe I'll be up to it," said Qiao Youmin cautiously.

To Xu Zhenyang, Qiao Youmin did not sound as crisply confident as he would have liked. "Do you really know what you're doing?" he pressed. "If not, we might perhaps think of a less direct way of stopping him."

"What less direct way?" Qiao Youmin asked.

"Simply not have my daughter wear the necklace this evening."

Qiao Youmin gave Xu Zhenyang a quick sideways glance. "Mr. Xu," he said with a smile, "you can't be serious. I know this necklace was crafted from antique materials found in the Qing emperor's palace. Many have admired it. When your daughter was at the home of Cabinet Minister Song for his birthday celebration last week, the necklace created a sensation. The ball tonight is clearly intended to give her admirers an eyeful. So how could she not wear it? If my answers seem hesitant to you, it's because I've been thinking about what he might do, and how we could head him off."

Xu Zhenyang's eyes flashed. His expression changed once more, from desperation to hopefulness.

"So you've already decided how to handle him?" he asked.

Qiao Youmin nodded. "I'm confident I know what to do. I imagine the most important step he would take would be to turn off the lights so that he could do his business in the dark. Therefore, we'll have a number of competent people guarding the light switches to stop him from that. Other than this, I can assign my dependable assistant, Yang Nanshan, dressed as a ballroom page, to watch the entryway. We'll also have someone guarding each of the windows on the outside, so he can neither get away himself nor pass anything to a henchman. If he doesn't come, that's fine. But if he does, with all these preparations, he won't be able to escape our grasp unless he can sprout wings."

Xu Zhenyang's spirits lifted even higher. "Terrific!" he said approvingly.

"Your preparations are carefully plotted out indeed. But you're going to be there yourself, aren't you?"

"Naturally. I'll pretend to be a guest and direct the whole operation. You have to promise me one thing, though. Other than you and me, no one must know what I've just told you. Otherwise, the guests might become alarmed, which would then create opportunities for our intruder."

"Right, right. I'll certainly follow your instructions on that. Do you foresee any kind of danger, though?"

"Just relax, sir. I have to be prepared, of course, for the possibility of violence. From what I foresee, however, there is almost no chance of that. If it does occur, on the other hand, I believe I'll be ready to handle it."

After Qiao Youmin had said his piece, he stood, picked up his fedora and heavy walking stick, and bowed to Xu Zhenyang. "Mr. Xu," he said with a smile, "please don't worry. The ball tonight is in celebration of your daughter's birthday; but I think that, in a few more days, we shall be thanking you for inviting us to her engagement party."

II

It was past nine o'clock that same evening, and the ballroom Xu Zhenyang had reserved in the Great China Hotel was already filling up with a good number of men and women. Some of the guests were still arriving, so the greeters at the door were kept busy receiving calling cards. Xu Zhenyang, the host, in his new black tuxedo and white shirt, was mingling with the guests along with Yufeng, his only daughter. Even though it was a chilly February, the room felt as warm as late spring or early summer thanks to the radiators on each of the four walls. For this reason, the dazzling attire of the women was light and airy. Yufeng's outfit was especially eye-catching: the knee-length Western-style dress of light-blue silk showed off her powdered, jade-like neck and soft bosom. Her necklace of water-green emeralds complemented her charming figure perfectly. Her gold dancing shoes, each topped with a five-carat diamond, would have been attractive enough, but because of that necklace, attention was not easily drawn to her footwear.

"Ooh, the green of those emeralds is simply gorgeous!"

"They're so pure and clear, not the slightest blemish!"

"The workmanship's amazing too. Subtlety and assertiveness so harmoniously blended!"

"What a rare treasure!"

Remarks like these, too many to recount, came mostly from the richly bejeweled women there. Besides bringing a wave of elation to Xu Yufeng, the praise washed over her escort, Tang Dongmei, as well.

Tang was a stylish young man who, at the young age of twenty-three or twenty-four, had already lived abroad. His father was an assistant chief-of-mission in the diplomatic service, so the talent for socializing welcomed by so many of the fair sex came naturally to him. Dongmei had known Yufeng for only three weeks, but their affection for each other had already grown to the point where they were as close as two peas in a pod.

Guests were flooding in by this time. Among them were numerous Very Important People—bank presidents, chiefs in the military, heads of various government bureaus. Soon the music started up, and, two by two, they began to dance.

Hand-in-hand, Xu Yufeng and Tang Dongmei joined the others on the dance floor. They appeared much more accomplished than the other dancers, their deft movements drawing the focused attention of everyone seated around.

There were three people among the onlookers who seemed particularly mesmerized by Yufeng and Dongmei's skills. One was a big fellow in Western garb; his serious expression and erect carriage showed he had held important positions in the military. As he kept his eyes on Yufeng, his large, thick lips opened quite involuntarily. Next to him was a thin man in his thirties dressed in traditional garb and sporting a short, Chaplin-like mustache. His legs were crossed as he leaned back in his chair, fixing his eyes on the whirling Yufeng on the dance floor. Off in one corner was a young woman in a stylish white silk sheath, who kept her eyes on the young couple as well. Although her lips betrayed a hint of a smile from time to time, she did not appear as utterly mesmerized as the male guests.

After a while, the band stopped playing, and the dancing also ceased.

Tang Dongmei walked Yufeng to the chairs at the edge of the dance floor, where they both sat down to rest. It happened that Yufeng found herself sitting right next to the thin man with the mustache.

The young couple exchanged casual banter for a while. "Your father really makes it hard on a person," Dongmei said to her with a smile. "With a necklace like you have, where would I find anything better when we get engaged?"

Yufeng seemed delighted and responded with a pretty pout. "Don't joke with me. Don't tell me that things like this are never seen at your house—"

Tang Dongmei abruptly cut her off. "Hey, the clasp of your necklace is coming loose. I'll reattach it for you." He stood up as he spoke and put his hands behind her powdered neck to refasten the strand. The clasp seemed to be very loose and difficult to rehook. Tang Dongmei fumbled with it and lost his grip, causing the necklace to fall onto Yufeng's lap.

"Oh, that was a clever move," said Yufeng.

Tang Dongmei quickly retrieved the necklace and secured it around her neck.

"Don't blame me," he said with a smile. "The clasp was really loose. Now that I've fixed it, you ought to show me some gratitude."

Yufeng gave no answer aside from a reproachful look. Just then her father, Xu Zhenyang, walked past.

"The band is striking up again," he said to Dongmei. "Why don't you two dance a bit more?"

So the eye-catching twosome started showing off their skills once again.

The band played on for perhaps another two minutes. Just as the dancing couples had become thoroughly caught up in the flow of the music, without warning a pair of shots rang out—*bang, bang!* The frightening explosions immediately turned the carefree spirit of the crowd into panic.

"Shots! Gunshots!"

"Oh, no! Robbers! And—"

The dance floor was in sudden chaos. Screams, hysteria, tables falling over, dishes crashing—distressful sounds everywhere.

"Youmin! Youmin! Where are you?" Xu Zhenyang was screaming at the top of his lungs.

"I'm here!" QiaoYoumin shouted from among the crowd. "Don't panic, everyone! That wasn't gunfire! Just a couple of firecrackers! Miss Xu, please hold on to your emerald—"

Xu Yufeng's quavering wail suddenly rose above the din. "Oh, no! My necklace is gone!"

III

Qiao Youmin had made his loud announcement to calm the crowd. It probably would have worked had Xu Yufeng's shrill, distressful cry not cancelled out whatever effect it might have had. Men and women were again thrown into a state of shock, and their uproar restarted immediately. Qiao Youmin did have an unusual ability to handle the unexpected. He was able to remain in control in what was rapidly becoming a tumultuous situation.

"Nanshan, guard the door!" he ordered in a loud voice. "Don't let anyone get out! Have your weapons ready, brothers! Make sure all the windows are locked! Ladies and gentlemen, please settle down and be quiet." As he was speaking, he took a black handgun from his coat pocket, in readiness for any eventuality.

"Mr. Xu, where are you?" he shouted out again. "The troublemaker can't possibly get away now! We're going to find him by searching everyone!"

Once the guests saw that Qiao Youmin was in control of the situation, their confused tumult gradually subsided. But when they heard that everyone there might be searched, they began once again to buzz among themselves.

Qiao Youmin was able to locate Xu Zhenyang and his daughter in the crowd. He saw that Xu Zhenyang was leaning against a carved marble column, so beside himself with anxiety that he was speechless, staring into space as if his soul had already taken leave of his body. Yufeng was at her father's side, pale and breathing rapidly, even though she was in much better control of herself. Tang Dongmei was still holding onto her arm, his apprehensive eyes fixed on her face, seemingly expecting her to faint away at any moment. His concern was unnecessary, however, as she was nowhere near to losing consciousness. The men and women around them, on the other hand, were evidently in shock, gazing at each other in silence.

"Get ahold of yourself, Mr. Xu," Qiao Youmin said to him. "I truly believe the necklace is still on the premises at this moment. If we search for it quickly, we'll be able to retrieve it for you."

Qiao's words seemed to calm Xu Zhenyang down somewhat. He blinked when he heard the word "search." "How are you going to search for it?" he asked.

"We'll have to frisk each and every person here, before anyone can be permitted to leave," said Qiao Youmin.

"*Everyone* will have to be frisked?" Yufeng asked in astonishment.

Tang Dongmei also seemed unhappy at the prospect. "Don't tell me you plan to pat down the women as well!" he chimed in.

Xu Zhenyang kept shaking his head. "That won't do. Just won't do. If you do have to frisk people, just pick out a few likely suspects." At this point, he shot a quick glance at Tang Dongmei standing next to him, meeting the latter's eyes quite by chance. Dongmei's face reddened perceptibly, and Yufeng was startled to notice it.

Just then, the large fellow with the military bearing pushed and shoved his way through the crowd, anger on his face, to voice *his* objections to Xu Zhenyang. "Are you going to be searching people? Am *I* going to be frisked as well? That's outrageous!"

Other guests were quick to join the protest. "Outrageous! Just outrageous! What an unbearable insult to us all!"

Xu Zhenyang could only sigh apologetically. "Please don't misunderstand, ladies and gentlemen. I wasn't in favor of the idea myself. Please don't misunderstand. Don't misunderstand."

Given the situation, Qiao Youmin acted pragmatically. He knew there was no way to carry out his intention, so he went ahead with what was feasible: He went along with what Xu, his superior, had suggested. "That's right," he said, "we'll just pick out a few of the most likely suspects to search. Let me ask you, Miss Xu. When those firecrackers went off, were you aware of anyone standing near you?"

Xu Yufeng hesitated. "I can't quite recall—I was dancing, and when I heard the *bang* I stopped in my tracks. And then it seemed as if—I can't really say." She inadvertently cast another glance at Dongmei.

Qiao Youmin became impatient. "Please go on. 'It seemed as if' what?"

"It seemed like there was a person behind me."

"Who?"

"I don't know."

"Was it a man or a woman?"

"I think it was someone wearing white—but I'm not sure. I really can't remember. Daddy, why don't we just forget it. There's no need to search—"

By this time Xu Zhenyang felt drops of sweat rolling down his brow and reached his hand into his vest pocket for a handkerchief. As he did so, his fingers came in contact with something hard and cold. He groped further, only to discover it was a necklace! He couldn't help crying out in surprise, cutting his daughter off in mid-sentence.

Everyone's eyes turned to Zhenyang, not knowing the cause of his sudden outcry. In an instant, Zhenyang seemed to regain control, repeatedly nodding his head as if he now knew what must have happened. "Oh, I'm so sorry, so sorry," he called out loudly. "Everyone, please go home now. Our problem has been solved. Youmin, open the doors. Everything's fine now. Everything's all right now."

IV

Five minutes later, nearly all the guests had filed out in small groups, leaving only Xu Zhenyang, his daughter, Tang Dongmei, and a few others. Qiao Youmin could neither stop them nor tell which among the many men and women was the culprit who had stolen the necklace, as he had no idea what the South-China Swallow looked like. All he could do was return his gun to his pocket and sit dejectedly off to one side as Xu Zhenyang approached him with a broad smile on his face.

"Mr. Xu," Youmin could hardly keep resentment out of his voice, "your final decision couldn't be helped, I suppose, given your desire to protect the dignity and retain the goodwill of your guests. So I can overlook that. But by sacrificing that necklace, you have also sacrificed my hopes and dreams."

Xu Zhenyang tried to appease him. "I know," he said in an apologetic tone. "You were planning to use this opportunity to capture the South-China Swallow, an opportunity that has now been lost. But my necklace has not been sacrificed. Take a look. It's right here!"

As he spoke, he reached into his pocket with his right hand and took out the emerald necklace, which he then displayed on his palm.

Qiao Youmin shot up from his chair. He stared at the necklace, his great surprise rendering him momentarily speechless.

"Don't you see?" Xu Zhenyang said with a smile. "You're usually so clever, but this one has you stumped. Whoever the thief was, once he heard that everyone would be searched, he figured he wouldn't be able to get away. So he slipped the stolen goods into my pocket so he wouldn't be caught. Isn't it crystal clear to you now?"

"Ha! So the little sneak had cold feet," Xu Yufeng said delightedly. She took the necklace as she spoke, glancing over at Tang Dongmei once again.

Tang let out a breath. "Wow, that was fortunate!" he said. "I was just having trouble tightening the clasp a short while ago and was nearly considered a suspect because of it. Now everything's fine."

"Oh, no!" Yufeng's startled exclamation brought renewed tension to the short-lived moment of calm. "This isn't the one I had! This necklace is a fake!" Xu Zhenyang immediately grabbed the strand back from his daughter. His eyes grew larger and larger on examining it, and his growing panic and confusion were simultaneously reflected on Tang Dongmei's face.

Qiao Youmin, though, was not surprised. "I anticipated that," he said coldly. "Once he had the goods in his hands, he would never give them up that easily."

"That's awful, just awful!" Xu Zhenyang was back to his agitated state. "We've fallen for his trick. What are we to do now?"

Qiao Youmin gazed far beyond the ballroom's exit. He walked over quickly and found that his assistants were still waiting outside for his orders.

"Where's Yang Nanshan?" he asked them.

"We don't know," said one of them. "He probably went off with one of the guests."

Qiao Youmin looked all around before the trace of a smile appeared on his face, as if to indicate that perhaps there was still hope.

Just then, the phone outside the ballroom rang and Qiao Youmin ran over to answer it. A half-minute later, he hung up and, still panting, returned to the ballroom to report to Xu Zhenyang.

"At this moment the South-China Swallow is at the Great West Hotel, Room 29. He's under the surveillance of one of my subordinates. He came to the ball dressed as a woman. But because of his prominent adam's apple, Yang Nanshan saw through the disguise. I'm going over there right now. Wait here. You'll be hearing from me."

Just ten minutes later Xu Zhenyang received a call from Qiao Youmin. "I was a step late, unfortunately," Qiao said. "When we broke down the door and entered his room, he had already escaped through the window. The white silk sheath he had worn was left in the room, with the emerald necklace in its pocket. Was this carelessness on his part? Or was it because he didn't want us to hunt him down and so left it intentionally? I can't really say right now. I'll be back soon, and we'll talk later."

The good news lasted perhaps another ten minutes before suddenly changing once more. The necklace Qiao Youmin brought back was also a fake!

At noon the following day, Xu Zhenyang received a thank-you letter as he was about to have lunch. After reading it over, he completely lost his appetite. The letter read:

Mr. Xu Zhenyang:
I especially want to thank you for the emerald necklace, which you have kindly allowed me to acquire. I have already turned it into cash, which I will distribute for the relief of refugees in the northwest. This should help you make up for past wrongs and accumulate some good karma, which I think you should find agreeable. You acquired the necklace, after all, by exploiting the blood and sweat of the common people; for me to use it for their benefit now should surely meet with your approval, if you have any conscience at all. At the very least, you and your kind should take a lesson from what has happened. You must be aware that ordinary people like them find it difficult even to come by enough wild roots or tree bark to feed themselves. You who style yourselves public servants should at least have some qualms of conscience when you pursue your utterly decadent ways of life.

In conclusion, please pass on my regards to those detectives who made such meticulous preparations and saw through my disguise. They are surely destined for future success, and have my utmost respect.

> *Till we meet again,*
> *South-China Swallow*

8 One Summer Night

I

The way in which country folk pass the time during the summer has always been very simple. A few may spend their lives drinking and gambling, but most people gather together under a shady shelter, such as a vine-covered arbor, to listen to ghost stories from the past. Sometimes, when the stories are sufficiently stimulating, participants even exercise their vocal cords and belt out a field song or two. While this custom would hardly interest urban dwellers, those who participate evidently derive great pleasure from it.

One evening, Big Mao's family in Red Tree Village was having just such an event. As the host, Big Mao had been scurrying around the open area in front of his house, happily doing one thing or another in preparation. Right after dinner, he lined up a few wooden benches, as well as a high-backed bamboo chair, under the locust tree there. Soon enough, Old Man Wang was sitting in the chair, while the Shen sisters, Xinfeng and Xinzhu, from next door were settling themselves on one of the benches.

Old Man Wang, from the Wang family house nearby, was past fifty. When he was young, he had spent a number of years away from home, learning written characters and reading books. What he was known for, however, was storytelling. Everyone from all the nearby villages agreed that Uncle Wang's drumlike belly was chock-full of tales about ghosts and goblins, past and present. Each year during the summer and fall, he would become as busy as an errand boy in order to meet the constant demand for his invariably enthusiastic presence at gatherings where he narrated his ghostly tales. He never refused an invitation from any village within walking distance.

On this particular evening, Wang had hurried to Big Mao's place right after dinner, with his long-stemmed pipe that doubled as a walking stick.

When he got there, however, his earlier anticipation couldn't help but be dampened when he saw that Big Mao's aged mother and the Shen sisters were to be his only audience. The fact was that, although Big Mao's mother, seated on a wooden chair up against a tree, was ready for a story, her eyelids were even then losing their ability to remain open. Her head seemed be stuck in greeting mode, bobbing continuously up and down to her chest, and it was evident that, even before Wang could begin his narration, she would already have drifted off to slumberland. Shen Xinfeng, on the other hand, was just seventeen; she liked to doll herself up and was considered one of the beauties of Red Tree Village. At that moment, though, it could not be determined whether she was there to listen to stories or whether she had some other purpose in mind. It seemed even less likely that her sister Xinzhu was there to listen rather than play. She would run to the bench and sit a while, then romp about the open area. She was only fourteen, after all, and the sight of her hopping and skipping about made it apparent she had yet to leave her childhood behind.

So it was easy to see why, after he had settled himself in the bamboo chair, Old Man Wang was covertly knitting his eyebrows together as he filled his long pipe. Grasping the situation, Big Mao hurriedly poured a cup of cold tea from a large clay teapot and went over to Wang deferentially.

"Uncle Wang, please have some tea. It's so good of you to come. My wife went to her mother's yesterday, but my brother Little Mao, Xinfeng's older brother Mugen, as well as Li Junior, the young owner of the bean-curd shop, have all gone into town. They've all promised, however, that they'll be back right after dark to listen to you. They'll probably be here very soon. I know you've had to walk quite a way through the fields to get here. Why don't you rest up right now. We'll be able to get going in just a little while."

Old Man Wang took the cup and gulped down a mouthful. "It's uncertain whether there'll be enough moonlight tonight," he said. "I may have to leave early."

"No problem with that," Big Mao quickly replied. "We can always escort you back."

"That won't be necessary," Wang said, sticking out his lower lip in a pout. "I've walked through cemeteries by myself, even in the dead of night. I don't need you young fellows to accompany me anywhere. It's just that it's a bit boring to have to sit around like this."

Big Mao was well aware of what he must be thinking. Wang was in effect a star performer who was quite upset at finding himself with no real audience. The three who had said they would be there had not come, making it difficult for Big Mao to know what to do. Just as he was thinking of what else he could say to the old man, the strains of a song wafted across the fields. Big Mao was overjoyed.

"Hey, they're back! That's Li Junior's voice. If he's in such a happy mood, they must have been boozing it up. My little brother, though, has always been weak and sickly. I've told him time and time again to quit his drinking, but he just won't listen to me. There's nothing I can really do about it."

It is uncertain whether these last words were really meant for his mother, in the hope that she would say something to his younger sibling. At any rate, by this time the old lady had broken down the gates to slumberland and was about to step inside; she couldn't have heard a thing. Xinfeng, though, quietly stuck out her lower lip, clearly mocking Mao's attempt to play big brother. Because Old Man Wang's attention was taken up right then by Xinzhu, who was grabbing at his pipe, he didn't hear what Big Mao was saying either.

Fortunately, in a short while Little Mao, Li Junior, and Xinfeng's older brother Mugen arrived, walking one behind the other along with a fourth person, the bean-curd maker from Li's shop. As they drew near, the smell of alcohol was evident every time one of them exhaled. Li Junior went right under the umbrella-like foliage of the locust tree to strike up a conversation with Xinfeng. "So you're here as well, Miss Xinfeng," he said. "When I told you the other day I wanted to tell you some stories, you said you didn't like listening to such things. So why are you here now? Could it be that you've come to see—"

"Don't bother her with your gibberish, Junior," Big Mao was quick to cut him off. "Uncle Wang's here. Why don't you say hello to him?"

Xinfeng, in turn, glared angrily at Li Junior. "There you go again with your nonsense," she rebuked him. "Uncle Wang has been waiting here for quite a while. Just be quiet, sit down, and listen."

Li smiled apologetically at Wang. "I'm sorry, Uncle," he said. "But I came tonight because I truly want to hear your stories. I've even brought along

Tusen, the bean-curd maker from my shop. Please pick an amusing story for us, so we can enjoy a good laugh or two."

Old Man Wang blew out a cloud of smoke. "Take a seat now, all of you," he said. "I've got a story about a ghost who had committed suicide by hanging herself. I don't know if you're brave enough to listen to it, though."

"Excellent!" Big Mao was the first to voice approval. "Ghost stories are my absolute favorites. I've hardly forgotten a word of the zombie story you told in the teashop last time."

Li Junior and Tusen also chimed in. "Great! That sounds great," they said. "We're not frightened of anything. Go ahead and tell us the story."

The girl Xinfeng seemed a little hesitant, but she did not say anything. She just moved slightly closer to her brother, as if to bolster her courage.

Soon enough, Old Man Wang, having gulped down a full cup of tea and coughed once to clear his throat, launched into his story about the ghost of a woman who had hanged herself. Once he got started, everyone fell silent. Big Mao and Little Mao's mother was the quietest of all; she even stopped bobbing her head. Xinzhu alone seemed unwilling to sit still, occasionally tugging at Little Mao's clothing or pulling Li Junior's hair.

Old Man Wang was completely focused on his story, which he began as follows:

A long time ago, a young scholar on his way to take the civil service examinations took shelter for the night inside a dilapidated temple. He had fallen asleep there when he was awakened around midnight by a series of strange sounds—*shoo, shoo, shoo.* Startled, he jumped up from his bed and opened the curtains. Pale moonlight poured in through the window, but within the four walls of the room all was deathly quiet. When the young man looked out the window, nothing was moving other than the leaves of the trees, which were rustling in the wind. He went back to bed to try to get to sleep again, but found that he couldn't keep his eyes shut.

Soon after, he sensed the presence of a shadowy figure outside his bed curtains. Greatly shaken, he was about to cry out when he noticed the figure was moving closer and closer, stopping right at the opening of the curtains. He was thrown into a state of utter terror. Something seemed to be plugging up his throat so that he could not utter a sound. His hands and feet felt as if they had been tied up, and he could not move them at all. But he could still see clearly that the figure outside the curtains was that of a woman with an unruly mop of such loose and disheveled hair that it appeared it had never been touched by a comb. At that very moment, a cold wind blew in from the window, making all his hair stand on end. The wind also blew open the curtains, allowing him to see a woman in white lit up by the eerie rays of the moon. Her ashen face was truly terrifying. Her gleaming dark eyes, topped by two thick eyebrows, were staring straight at the scholar in his bed. Her mouth was open wide, revealing a row of shockingly white teeth on top. Her lower teeth were concealed behind a blood-red tongue, the tip of which stuck out more than an inch and a half. This sight would frighten anyone out of his wits. The young man let out a horrified screech as he tried to push himself up with his arms in an attempt to get away. But he couldn't quite do it, because his head started spinning and he fainted dead away.

At this point Old Man Wang paused to refill his pipe and take a short break. As if by prearrangement, a cold wind howled overhead, setting the leaves and branches of the locust tree into wild motion. The whistling of the wind through the branches, combined with the far-off barking of dogs, was strangely unsettling. The crescent moon, intermittently visible then invisible, shone through the open spaces of the tree, its light unceasingly fluctuating with the movement of the leafy branches, shimmering on and off the listeners, making it seem that the ghostly figure Wang had just described was right there in their midst.

Just then, Xinfeng grabbed her brother's arm. "Let's go home," she whispered to him. "It's a bit chilly."

Little Mao seemed to agree. "In that case, let's just continue the story tomorrow," he said.

His brother, however, was the first to object. "Don't you cut him off like this," he said. "We want to hear the rest of the story. How is it going to end?"

Young Xinzhu also wanted the session to continue. "Yes," she joined in. "Uncle Wang, just go on. What will that shadowy figure turn out to be? What's going to happen to the young scholar?"

Tusen, the bean-curd man, was also impatient to learn the ending. "Tell us more, Uncle Wang. I want to hear about what finally happened to the scholar."

"Undoubtedly, the woman was somebody who had hanged herself," Shen Mugen mumbled to himself. "I would think that the scholar would be frightened to death by her."

"If I were the young man," Li Junior added, "I would jump right up, grab hold of that ghost, pull out her tongue, and slam her to the floor."

"The more you people talk, the more frightened I become," Xinfeng said loudly as she held on to her brother. "I don't want to listen to any more of this."

Her brother Mugen was actually getting to his feet to take her home when Little Mao also rose from his place on the bench. "It *is* getting chilly now," he said. "We should all go to bed. Let Uncle Wang continue his story tomorrow."

Since two of the eight listeners wanted the narration to end, even Mugen and Xinzhu began to leave their seats. By that time, the Maos' mother was snoring loudly, which left just three—Big Mao, Junior, and Tusen—who wanted to keep going. Old Man Wang, however, had lost interest in continuing. So the gathering, which had started with enthusiasm, came to a premature end.

II

In the morning the next day, an important piece of news came from Red Tree Village: Little Mao, for reasons unknown, had been found dead in his room. The circumstances of his death were extremely peculiar, leading to feverish conversation all over the village. His room was located on the left side of the house, with a wood-framed window facing the open area in front. His body had been found lying on the floor beneath the window. He was naked from the waist up, wearing only a pair of beltless shorts. The expression on his face was ghastly indeed. His eyes and mouth were wide open, though his tongue was not sticking out. There was no trace of a wound anywhere on his body, only a sickening pale-yellow tint to his skin from head to toe. His brother Big Mao had found him. At first sight, he thought that the house must be haunted, and that a vile ghost had killed his brother.

By 10 a.m., the police station in Willow River Township had sent a captain and patrolman to investigate. The captain was Zhang Desheng, who had been to the police academy for six months of special training and was therefore thoroughly confident of his expertise in police work and criminal investigation. As soon as he arrived at the house, he went straight to the room to look things over. He saw that the bed on the dirt floor was placed next to the wall, with a mosquito net dangling down over it. Zhang Desheng lifted up the net for a look. "The bedding is rumpled," he mumbled to himself. "That means the victim slept here last night." He then examined the victim's remains for some time before coming to his conclusion. "There are no wounds or bruises anywhere on the body; the only thing abnormal is the yellow color of his skin. There's no doubt he's been poisoned."

He summoned the victim's brother and mother to question them in detail about the circumstances of the case. Big Mao and his mother told him that after the storytelling session, the family had come into the house to retire for the night. Because the weather had cooled down and they were tired, they had slept straight through to morning. When Little Mao had failed to emerge from his room at breakfast time, Big Mao had gone to knock on his door and call out his name. Even though he'd thought that something might be wrong after getting no response, Big Mao had not been able to enter because the door was locked from the inside. Finally, he'd had to go through the little door from the attached dining area. Once inside, he had found his brother lying, stiff, face-up, on the floor near the window. Leaning over and touching him, he found that the body had already become completely cold. He still had no idea, though, how the death had occurred.

At this, Zhang Desheng scribbled something in a dirty old notebook. "Did either of you hear a noise last night?" he asked.

Big Mao's mother beat him to the answer. "No. Both our bedrooms are located to the right of the living room. Neither of us could have heard anything in Little Mao's room."

"If he had had a violent stomachache and shouted out for help," said Zhang Desheng, "surely you would have heard him."

"Of course," said Big Mao. "But we were fast asleep last night and didn't hear anything at all."

"Was there anything out of the ordinary as he was going to bed?" Zhang Desheng asked.

"After he came into the house, he drank two cups of tea and headed right for his room. There was nothing unusual at all," said Big Mao.

Zhang Desheng lowered his head, seemingly lost in thought. "You two brothers usually get along?" he suddenly wanted to know.

Quite taken aback by the question, Big Mao was unable to respond right away.

"We got along quite well," he finally said.

Zhang Desheng looked as if he had stumbled onto something.

"*Quite* well?" he smirked.

"That's the truth," the old woman was quick to say. "My second son was not in good health, and his brother was always concerned for him, telling him to stop his drinking. There were times when the younger one just ignored the advice, or even argued about it. Other than that, the two of them were rather fond of each other."

"But did they ever have a real squabble?" Zhang Desheng persisted. "You must tell me the truth."

The old woman hesitated. "This past spring, my second son was impatient for me to arrange a marriage for him, as his brother had found a wife the winter before. The older one thought that, since his brother hadn't yet recovered from his heart problems, he should wait a year or two before doing anything like marrying. This made the younger one upset enough to have a fight with the older one. But the matter has since blown over, and you shouldn't read anything into it."

Zhang Desheng nodded quietly, indicating that he had come to a conclusion. He went into the living room to look around. Heading almost immediately to the square table there, he picked up the teacup resting on it. "You said that your brother had some tea last night before going into his room. Is this the cup he used?"

Big Mao's eyes grew large. "Yes, it is," he said softly.

Zhang Desheng smiled triumphantly as he wrapped the cup in paper and put it into his pocket. Seeing this, Big Mao seemed suddenly perturbed. "Sir, are you . . . are you suspecting *me*?" he asked haltingly. "That's all wrong. My brother might have been killed by . . . by . . ."

"Killed by whom?" Zhang Desheng asked.

"By a ghost," said Big Mao.

"Hogwash!" said Zhang Desheng. "He clearly died from poisoning. Don't even *think* you can bamboozle people with that!"

"Was it really from poisoning?" said Big Mao. "Then I think that Li Junior would be the prime suspect. Do you want to hear why?"

Zhang Desheng wasn't sure he wanted to bite. "I don't know. Why should we suspect him?"

"Three of them went drinking with my brother in the village market last evening," said Big Mao. "Couldn't any one of the three have slipped something into his liquor?"

This information gave Captain Zhang pause. "Who went drinking with him?" he asked.

"One was Li Junior, the young owner of the bean-curd shop. Another was Tusen, Li's bean-curd maker. Then there was the older brother of the Shen sisters next door, Shen Mugen," Big Mao told him.

"If all these people were drinking together, why are you pointing your finger only at Li Junior as a suspect?"

"There's a good reason for that," Big Mao explained. "My brother had feelings for Shen Xinfeng next door, but Li Junior was taken with her as well. So some jealousy between them was unavoidable. Maybe it's because of this—"

Zhang Desheng was quick to cut him off. "Don't go about making wild speculations. We'll determine eventually whether there's anything to the triangular relationship. Frankly, you are one of the suspects, so you should stay quietly at home and await the results of our thorough investigation. If you have any idea of running away, just know that you would be making more trouble for yourself."

III

That afternoon, after officials from the county had come to the village and investigated, they too said it was a poisoning. Toward evening, Big Mao was arrested by police from Willow River Township, which set his mother to weeping and wailing, utterly helpless as she was. Meanwhile, she had to set aside her grief to tend to funeral arrangements for Little Mao. It was fortunate that Xinfeng was such a warm and considerate soul, coming over herself to provide help and comfort. Big Mao's wife, who had hurried home after hearing the bad news, learned that her husband had been arrested on suspicion of murdering her brother-in-law and had been taken to the county jail. So she put together a few necessities and a bit of cash and planned to implore someone to take her into town to see what could be done about clearing him. There was already much buzzing about the case there. Some were saying that Big Mao was a good, honest fellow who would never harm a member of his own family. Others, though, thought that the brothers might have been in conflict over their inheritance, and that this had led Big Mao to commit the murder.

On the following day, Li Junior, the young owner of the bean-curd shop, was also arrested and taken to the county seat. This, in turn, brought a sudden shift in the gossip among the rural folk. Everyone recognized that Li Junior had not always been a straitlaced young man, having eyed and flirted with quite a few of the young women in the village. But to say that he would murder Little Mao out of jealousy seemed beyond the bounds of credibility. There was no evidence of what poison he had used or when he had given it to him. Moreover, how could it be that the others drinking with them—Mugen and Tusen—were unharmed? Until these questions could be satisfactorily answered, he couldn't possibly be considered guilty.

As the case unfolded, Old Man Wang kept himself quite busy. He helped with the arrangements for Little Mao's burial. He also went to Xinfeng's house to investigate, though no one knew what he was investigating. Later, when he got the news that Big Mao and then Li Junior had been taken into custody, he seemed to be unconvinced of their guilt, though he did not say much of anything.

Another development occurred on the third day, when Xinfeng and Xinzhu's older brother, Shen Mugen, was also arrested by the authorities. The arrest was based on Li Junior's testimony that on the day they had gone out drinking, Shen Mugen had emptied a little bag of brown medicinal powder into his own wine, which he had then drunk down. The bean-curd man Tusen had asked him what sort of medicine it was, and Mugen had told him it was for backache. Even though the medicine had been for himself alone, he could have slipped some other drug into Little Mao's drink, using the "backache powder" as a decoy. Had he been caught, he could have claimed that the drug was merely medicine and therefore harmless. Shen Mugen, moreover, had recently been to Shanghai, a place where all sorts of exotic poisons were available; he could very well have purchased some there. As for motive, it could simply be that he had been upset over Little Mao's interest in his sister Xinfeng. This seemed so convincing that Shen Mugen was now the prime suspect among the three who were in custody.

IV

A week later, just about the time the official disposition of the murder case was to be handed down, Old Man Wang, the one with so many stories to tell, rushed to the county seat, impassioned to provide further testimony. "Little Mao was not poisoned," he boldly announced to the county magistrate. "All three of those arrested are innocent. Please, Your Honor, I beg you to let them all go. You should know, sir, that Big Mao's mother is about to go mad, her younger son having died so tragically and her older one having been detained as his murderer."

The magistrate was greatly surprised. "Then how did Little Mao die? Do you have any idea?"

"He died from fright," said Old Man Wang. "He must have been so terrified that his gall bladder ruptured, diffusing yellow bile all through his body, eventually killing him.[1] He was already quite shaken by the story he had heard that night. But immediately after that, someone played a trick on him outside his window, frightening him mightily. Who could have known that scaring him again right then would cost him his life? The fact is that his heart was already weak from illness, but the person who scared him did so with no intention of doing him any harm."

"Is this what actually happened?" the magistrate was clearly surprised. "Who is the person who scared him? Was it you?"

"No, it wasn't," said Old Man Wang. "It was Shen Xinzhu, the young girl who lived next door to him. She has always been a spirited, mischievous child. That night, she had come up with the idea of smearing her face with powder

---

1. Traditional Chinese believed the gall bladder to be the physical organ directly affected by fear. In extreme cases, the gall bladder would burst, releasing bile throughout the body and imbuing the skin with a yellow tint.

and putting rouge on her cheeks and chin before stealthily going outside Little Mao's bedroom to play her trick on him. She could never have imagined that when he got up from his bed to go over to his window on hearing some noise she'd made, he would keel over and die from fright. The girl was horrified, of course, but she didn't say anything to anyone. It was only after her brother was arrested that she didn't dare to keep silent any longer and told me everything. There was no way she could have foreseen what happened. Furthermore, she's still a child. So, please, Your Honor, do not punish her. If you want to assign culpability, then assign it to me, whose bones are old enough to accept punishment. That this tragedy occurred at all was because of the story I told them. Please be just, and allow me to take the blame for what happened."

Thus it came about that all three suspects were released after the testimony of righteous Old Man Wang. Neither Shen Xinzhu nor the old man ever received an official reprimand. But from then on, on clear, moonlit nights, when Old Man Wang was invited to spin his tales, he would tell exclusively of the deeds of chivalrous gallants and other righteous individuals, and never again of the ghosts of people who had hanged themselves.

About Cheng Xiaoqing

CHENG XIAOQING's life spanned the era of the most drastic cultural and political changes in China's long history that resulted from the large-scale influx of foreign ideas and values at the turn of the twentieth century. Most affected were the large urban areas, particularly Shanghai, where Cheng spent his formative years and where he participated so prominently in the new popular culture created by modern media. As well known as he became, particularly for his stories of crime and detection, his name, like the names of others who also wrote for entertainment publications, is not to be found in most histories of modern Chinese literature today, even though his works have been reedited and reprinted in a number of collections in Shanghai, Beijing, and Nanjing since the mid-1980s.

Born on August 2, 1893, in the Old City or Nanshi area of Shanghai, Cheng Xiaoqing was the eldest son of a former peasant family that, a couple of generations earlier, had moved there from Anhui Province as a result of the disastrous civil war known as the Taiping Rebellion (1850–1864). He had a poverty-stricken childhood, particularly after the textile store in which his father worked had to close down. His father then sold newspapers to feed his family, but died in 1903, when Cheng was just ten years old and a promising student in a private elementary school. He had to leave school five years later because of the family's straitened circumstances and eventually, at sixteen, became an apprentice in Hope Brothers and Company, a very prominent clockmaker's shop in Shanghai. A fellow apprentice loaned him books, which he devoured in his free time and which, according to one biographer, stimulated him to write creatively. The first short stories Cheng submitted for publication were mostly rejected, but the one or two that were accepted provided him with a welcome bit of extra cash. In the same year, he started taking English classes at the Shanghai YMCA.

Before long Cheng was submitting manuscripts to a number of fiction magazines in Shanghai, including the very prominent *Xiaoshuo yuebao (The Short Story Magazine)*, whose editor, Yun Tieqiao (1878–1935), despite having rejected Cheng's first submission, recognized his talent. Yun arranged to meet with the young Cheng and advised him to resume his studies and to continue his avocation. They corresponded regularly, and Yun became an important influence on Cheng's subsequent development as a fiction writer. It was at about this time that Cheng Xiaoqing published his first piece of detective fiction, which he entitled "The Shadow in the Lamplight"(Dengguang renying). He entered the piece in a contest conducted by the literary supplement of a Shanghai newspaper and won. Moreover, the published story was well received by its readership. But perhaps because of a typesetting error, his hero's name was changed from Huo *Sen* to Huo *Sang*—which remained the name of his detective character ever after.

In the spring of 1915, Cheng accepted a position to teach the Wu, or Shanghainese, dialect to foreign teachers and moved his family, including his new bride, to Suzhou, a highly cultured city a short distance away from Shanghai. There, he became friends with an American teacher of English at the high school attached to Soochow University, exchanging language lessons with him. Cheng's grasp of English improved to the point where he could confidently begin reading it on his own for the immediate purpose of translation. This he began to do between 1915 and 1916, when he collaborated with the writer Zhou Shoujuan (1894–1968) and others in rendering Sir Arthur Conan Doyle's stories of Sherlock Holmes into classical Chinese. Published in twelve volumes, the translated work featured a preface by the popular author Bao Tianxiao (1876–1973) and was reprinted over twenty times in the next two decades.

Without doubt, Cheng's translation work gave added incentive as well as direction to his own creative writing, which he at first wrote in the terse and elliptical classical Chinese language rather than the more exhaustive and particularized vernacular. In 1919, he published the relatively long *Jiangnan yan* (The South-China Swallow) in classical Chinese, in which the central character Huo Sang was first portrayed in detail. The work became immensely popular and was made into a movie. Thereafter, Cheng began producing story after story featuring Huo Sang as a Chinese Sherlock Holmes, a coura-geous and high-minded private detective who solved crimes mostly through intellectual prowess. (The stories were now rendered in the vernacular.) Cheng both competed with and cooperated with his friend and contempo-rary Sun Liaohong (1897–1958) who, like him, Sinicized a European original by writing his own stories of the master thief Lu Ping, modeled upon the character Arsène Lupin of the French writer Maurice Leblanc. It is highly likely that the South-China Swallow portrayed in Cheng's stories here was also heavily influenced by Leblanc's universally known character.

Cheng Xiaoqing's popularity reached its zenith from the mid-1920s through the early 1940s, when his fictional adventures of Huo Sang and his partner, Bao Lang, appeared regularly in various popular periodicals in Shanghai. It was also during this period that he cooperated with Yan Duhe (1889–1968) and others in producing and writing for *The Detective World (Zhengtan shijie)*, a magazine devoted entirely to detective fiction. He also be-came a screenwriter, authoring over thirty screenplays. He even wrote at least one successful popular song. His translations of detective fiction eventually extended well beyond the works of Conan Doyle to include, according to his friend Liu Ts'un-yan, the works of Maurice Leblanc, Earl Derr Biggers, Leslie Charteris, and S. S. Van Dine (Willard Huntington Wright). Cheng was also very active in various literary societies formed by the popular writers of his day. In March 1930, he accepted the editorship of the World Book Company's project to retranslate all of the Sherlock Holmes stories into vernacular Chi-nese, with modern punctuation and illustrations, which is still the standard Chinese version of Conan Doyle's work.

For these translations alone Cheng Xiaoqing would have deserved the title of "Grand Master of China's Detective Fiction," conferred on him by Fan Boqun, a scholar of Chinese popular fiction. No one else did nearly as much to introduce and promote the genre to Chinese readers. But, aside from his translations of the Sherlock Holmes stories, Fan was clearly referring to the stories that feature Huo Sang and his partner, Bao Lang, for which Cheng will ultimately be remembered. Even during the early years of World War II, when Cheng briefly used a variety of pen names in order to avoid having to write for pro-Japanese publications, he continued to turn out stories and screenplays and to translate —all the while teaching high school. Between 1941 and 1945 he had had to move his family to Shaanxi, and then to Huaihai, but continued his writing despite these dislocations. Even before the Japanese surrender in August 1945, he assumed the editorship of *Xin zhentan* (New detective), another detective fiction magazine from the World Book Company in Shanghai. Most important, during the same year the company published a "pocketbook" edition of the Huo Sang stories in thirty volumes, the major source of the many collections of Cheng's detective fiction reprinted in the 1980s. Cheng returned to Suzhou with his family after the war to resume teaching language and literature in the high school attached to the newly reopened Soochow University. But his most productive years as a writer and translator seemed to be over.

In the two and a half decades that followed the establishment of the People's Republic of China in 1949, modern Chinese and most foreign crime fiction, as well as other kinds of fiction characterized as foreign or feudalistic, were all banned, with minor exceptions during periods of political "thaw." Certain Sherlock Holmes stories were circulated underground, but Cheng Xiaoqing's theretofore highly productive writing career essentially came to an end. He published just three sensational adventure stories in 1957, a year after he retired from teaching high school. From then until his death on October 12, 1976, he wrote mostly poems in the traditional style, while living in the Suzhou house he called "Cocoon Cottage." These were later gathered together and published in New York in 1982 by his daughter Cheng Yuzhen, who has been living in the United States since 1948.

For someone who never left Chinese soil, Cheng Xiaoqing was indeed remarkable for his firm grasp of a truly foreign genre of fiction and his ability to adapt it so naturally to a Chinese environment that readers in Shanghai, a place that did not even have private detectives, were both entertained and educated by what he wrote. Perhaps more than any other writer in his time, he demonstrated that, in fiction, what entertains and what educates can be— and often are— inseparable.

Publicon Notes

*Because Cheng Xiaoqing's work never received the editorial or scholarly attention de-
voted to writers of what was considered truly "serious" fiction in his time, his stories were
not only not dated in most recent collections, but were sometimes altered between their
initial publication in magazines and later collection reprints. Of the eight included in
this collection, only four can be easily traced to their original publications—and hence
dated. The dates of the other four are simply not readily available. The translations in
this collection were done principally from the sources first cited, except for "The Other
Photograph," where the punctuated later reprint was used as the primary text.*

1. The Shoe *(Yizhi xie)*
Reprinted in a number of collections, including Wu Shaochang and Wu Cheng-
hui, eds., *Yuanyang hudie pai yanjiu ciliao* (Research materials for the Mandarin
Ducks and Butterflies School) (Shanghai: Wenyi chuban she, 1984), 2:1159–1200.
Originally published in the magazine *Kuaihuo (Happiness)*, no. 8, in 1923.

2. The Other Photograph *(Di'erzhang zhao)*
First appeared in 1927 in the magazine *Hong meigui (Red Roses)*, published by
the World Book Company in Shanghai. Subsequently reedited and reprinted in various collections of Cheng Xiaoqing's works, including vol. 4 of *Cheng Xiaoqing wenji:
Huo Sang tan'an xuan* (Collected writings of Cheng Xiaoqing: Selections of cases investigated by Huo Sang), edited by the Jiangsu branch of the Zhongguo zuojia xiehui
(Chinese Writers' Association) (Beijing: Zhongguo wenlian chuban gongsi in De-
cember 1986), pp. 44–95.

3. The Odd Tenant *(Guai fangke)*
Reprinted in *Huo Sang tan'anji* (Collection of cases investigated by Huo Sang)
(Beijing: Qunzhong chuban she, 1987), 6:233–253.

4. The Examination Paper *(Shijuan)*
Reprinted in *Huqiu nu* (The woman in fox furs), another collection of Huo
Sang stories, ed. Zhang Rong with an important postscript by Fan Boqun (Beijing:
Qunzhong chuban she, 1997), pp. 412–420.

5. On the Huangpu *(Huangpu jiang zhong)*

Collected in the no. 2 "xiuzhen" or "pocket" edition, under the general title *Huo Sang tan'an* (Cases investigated by Huo Sang) by the World Book Company (Shijie shuju) of Shanghai in 1942. Reprinted in *Cheng Xiaoqing wenji: Huo Sang tan'an xuan,* 2:1–46. See 2 above.

6. At the Ball *(Wuchang zhong)*

Published in the magazine *Hong meigui,* vol. 6, no. 1 (1930), 1–16. See 2 above.

7. Cat's-Eye *(Mao'er yan)*

Reprinted in *Huqiu nu,* pp. 89–104. See 4 above.

8. One Summer Night *(Xiayede canju)*

Published in *Hong meigui,* vol. 3, no. 7 (August 6, 1927), 1–13. See 2 above.

Works Consult

Cheng Xiaoqing. "Tan Zhengtan xiaoshuo" [Discussing detective fiction]. 1929. Rpt. in Rui Heshi et al., eds., *Yuanyang hudie pai wenxue ziliao* [Literary materials on the Mandarin Ducks and Butterfly School], vol. 1, pp. 61–67. Fuzhou: Fujian Renmin chuban she, 1984.

——. "Zhentan xiaoshuode duofangmian" [The many directions of detective fiction]. 1933. Rpt. in Rui Heshi et al., eds., *Yuanyang hudie pai wenxue ziliao*, vol. 1, pp. 68–76.

——. "Zhentan xiaoshuo yu '?'" [Detective fiction and '?']. 1933. Rpt. in Yuan Jin, ed., *Yihai tan you* [Seeking the profound in the ocean of art], volume of the *Yuanyang hudie pai sanwen daxi* [Collection of essays from the Mandarin Ducks and Butterflies School], pp. 221–223. Shanghai: Dongfang chuban zhongxin, 1997.

Fan Boqun, ed. *Zhongguo zhentan zongjiang, Cheng Xiaoqing* [The grandmaster of Chinese detective fiction, Cheng Xiaoqing). Nanjing: Nanjing chuban she, 1994.

Kinkley, Jeffrey C. *Chinese Justice, the Fiction: Law and Literature in Modern China*, pp. 170–240. Stanford, CA: Stanford University Press, 2000.

Lee, Leo Ou-fan. *Shanghai Modern: The Flowering of a New Urban Culture in China, 1930–1945*. Cambridge, MA: Harvard University Press, 1999.

Liang Qichao. "On the Relationship between Fiction and the Government of the People." Trans. Gek Nai Cheng. In Kirk A. Denton, ed., *Modern Chinese Literary Thought: Writings on Literature, 1893–1945*, pp. 74–81. Stanford, CA: Stanford University Press, 1996.

Link, Perry. *Mandarin Ducks and Butterflies: Popular Fiction in Early Twentieth-Century Chinese Cities*. Berkeley: University of California Press, 1981.

Liu, Ts'un-yan. "Introduction: 'Middlebrow' in Perspective." *Renditions*, nos. 17 and 18 (Spring and Autumn 1982), pp. 1–40.

Lu Runxiang. *Shenbide zhentan shijie—Cheng Xiaoqing Sun Liaohong yishu tan* [The mysterious world of crime detection—discussions on the art of Cheng Xiaoqing and Sun Liaohong]. Shanghai: Xuelin chuban she, 1996.

Pollard, David, ed. *Translation and Creation: Reading of Western Literature in Early Modern China, 1840–1918.* Amsterdam/Philadelphia: John Benjamins Publishing Company, 1998.

King-fai, Tam. "Cultural Ambiguities of Modern Chinese Fiction." In Ed Christian, ed., *The Post Colonial Detective*, pp. 112–139. Basingstoke, Eng.: Macmillan/Palgrave, 2001.

———. "The Detective Fiction of Ch'eng Hsiao-ch'ing." *Asia Major*, 3rd ser., 5.1 (1992): 113–132.

Wei Shaochang, ed. *Yuanyang hudie pai yanjiu ziliao* [Research materials on the Mandarin Ducks and Butterflies School], Vol. 1. Shanghai: Wenyi chuban she, 1984.

Wong, Timothy C., trans. *Stories for Saturday: Twentieth-Century Chinese Popular Fiction.* Honolulu: University of Hawai'i Press, 2003.

 **About the Translator**

Timothy C. Wong is professor of Chinese at Arizona State University, where he teaches Chinese fiction and directs the graduate program in Asian languages and civilizations in the Department of Languages and Literatures. A former grantee at the East-West Center in Honolulu, he received his M.A. in Asian Studies from the University of Hawai'i, Manoa, in 1968, and his Ph.D. in Chinese from Stanford University in 1975. His previous publications include a book on the eighteenth-century Chinese satirist Wu Jingzi (1978) and *Stories for Saturday: Twentieth-Century Chinese Popular Fiction* (2003). He has also published a number of studies on China's tradition of fiction-making both before and after the influx of modern and foreign influences.

Production Notes for Wong / *Sherlock in Shanghai*

Cover design by April Higgins

Interior design by University of Hawai'i Press production staff with display type in Italia and text in Minion

Composition by inari information services

Printing and binding by the Maple-Vail Book Manufacturing Group

Printed on 55# Maple Antique, 360 ppi

CPSIA information can be obtained
at www.ICGtesting.com
Printed in the USA
LVHW091918160621
690286LV00013B/341